THE THIRD LAW OF MOTION

MEG FILES

ANAPHORA LITERARY PRESS

COCHRAN, GEORGIA

ANAPHORA LITERARY PRESS
163 Lucas Rd., Apt. I-2
Cochran, GA 31014
www.anaphoraliterary.wordpress.com

Book design by Anna Faktorovich, Ph.D.

Cover Design and Illustration: Denice Hart.

Published in 2011 by Anaphora Literary Press

The Third Law of Motion
Meg Files—1st edition.

ISBN-13: 978-1-937536-15-2
ISBN-10: 1-937536-15-7

Library of Congress Control Number: 2011945711

THE THIRD LAW OF MOTION

———————

MEG FILES

For Anast,
with appreciation for your
fresh, wild story,
    Meg

ALSO BY MEG FILES

Meridian 144

Home Is the Hunter

Write From Life

The Love Hunter

Galapagos Triptych (with Sally Cullen and Susan Reimer)

Lasting: Poems on Aging (Editor)

For Steve

and for Jim

CHAPTER 1

I met Lonnie at dancing class. I never really learned to dance.

My friend Annie Halverson convinced me that we'd get asked out if we knew how to do the twist and the jerk. "How's any guy supposed to know?" I said. "You gonna get a big tattoo? 'This chick can do the funky chicken?'" Really, I thought, Annie was guilty of the post hoc fallacy—she believed we didn't have dates because we couldn't dance—when both were just symptoms of our invisibility. Besides, bodies couldn't be *taught* to twitch and beat the way Annie and I had seen them at the armory dance. When my mother caught me trying it before the full-length mirror, she said, "Don't grind. That's nasty." Annie said the girls who put out were the tamest dancers. Wild or subdued, they all moved in an oily repetition that I knew couldn't be learned.

Still, I went with Annie to the studio downtown and lined up with the other rejects where for six Saturday mornings we shuffled around under fluorescent lights to rock-and-roll played softly.

On the final Saturday, when Lonnie Saxbe was paired with me, he said he was a junior at Battlebush, ran track, and wanted to take me out.

"I'm a senior," I said. "At Central." I didn't know if I was saying yes or no.

He said he'd pick me up next Friday if I'd tell him where I lived.

When I told Annie on the bus, she said, "For a track star, you'd think he'd be able to dance. He dances like he's made out of cardboard."

"And I'm so great," I said.

"But he is cool-looking," she said sadly. "Well, now you'll be with him and I still can't dance."

"He's clean-cut. A very good-looking young man," my mother said sadly. Lonnie made everybody sad, as if his presence fixed my future. "But he isn't so great in the brains department, is he?"

"I'm not going to marry him, Mom. But it's nice to do something on Saturday night besides watch Gunsmoke with Dad."

"You don't want to live your life with a man who's your intellectual inferior," she said. "Whatever else, at least your father's got a sizeable brain."

By January I'd been accepted to the small private college I'd chosen for its reputation for scholarship and its junior-year-abroad program. Nobody would force me to marry Lonnie Saxbe. We went to movies and ate pizza and made out in the back seat of his maroon Tempest. We didn't mention his junior or my senior prom.

My parents were merely parents. My father paid my extravagant tuition and set up a checking account for me, no questions asked. My mother wanted to help me plan a college wardrobe. I didn't think about what they were to each other.

In the summer, Lonnie worked at a Shell station, pumping gas, checking oil, and cleaning windshields. His father had some disability and no job. Lonnie took me once to their trailer. His broad-faced mother wore man's pants and served macaroni, hot dogs, and beans for supper.

"The musical fruit," his father said, and Lonnie turned red.

The father was small and gray. The mother's head seemed too large even for her sturdy body: megacephalic was the word, I thought, though it might just have been the thick bouffant hair.

"Your old man does what?" Lonnie's father said.

The hot dogs were terrible, boiled instead of grilled, reminding me they were made of animal parts like lips and glands. Lonnie sometimes called himself my old man. I chewed and chewed the rubbery meat and worked at the question: Did he want to know what Lonnie did to me in the back seat?

"He does something with drugs," Lonnie answered for me.

"Drugs?" Mrs. Saxbe made the word two shocked syllables.

"Oh, my father," I said. "He does research. Pharmaceuticals."

"What I said," Lonnie said.

After dessert of red Jell-O with Cool Whip, Lonnie's father turned on the black and white television and his mother ran a sinkful of soapy water in the tiny kitchen.

"I'm taking my girl down to the lake," Lonnie said.

His mother looked at me over her shoulder, her hands in the dishwater, looked at my white rolled-up-sleeve blouse and my pink-checked Bermudas and my sandals and then back up to my face. His *girl*. My head felt too small for my body.

"Thank you for dinner," I said. "It was awfully nice to meet you." It came out sounding like Hayley Mills.

"That boat don't go out in the dark," his father said. "You hear me?"

At the lake, we took turns changing behind the boathouse. Everything was dark and marshy-smelling. On Saturday afternoons we'd raced the boat around the lake, and I'd learned to rise in the heavy water and ski it. But this night we drove slowly and in the middle of the lake Lonnie cut the outboard motor. We lowered ourselves into the dark water and swam, splashing gracelessly through the glass bubbles the boat's headlights made, and we hung on the side of the boat and kissed, shivering.

In the boat he wrapped me in a towel and drove to a lagoon

overgrown with lily pads and killed the lights. We kissed and kissed in our wet bathing suits. I didn't lift his hand away from my breast. Behind the boathouse I'd crossed my arms and tested the feel of my breasts, and so I knew all he felt was stiff cotton and wire. I let him unhook the top of my blue and white dotted bathing suit. I let his dark hands feel my shriveled and clammy breasts. I thought they must feel like meat straight from the refrigerator.

In July he wanted to take me out for dinner. "Fancy," he said. He said the word slowly, the way he said my name, Dulcie. "It's our nine-month anniversary."

Annie and I had laughed secretly at Whitman's "Ninth-month midnight." *Nine months* were giggly words, scary words. Nine months meant shame swollen under loose dresses. Nine months meant someone in trouble, sent to a sister in California or somewhere to miss the rest of senior year, exiled from parents and hometown to live the rest of her life blooded with whispers: *in trouble, gave the baby up.* Nine months meant the mystery of bodies joined, as on the dirty cards Annie's brother had, tiny smudged bodies standing front to back with a rope of flesh joining them. I shivered. I'd kissed Lonnie with my mouth open and I'd put my hand on the front of his white Levis. Everything was so secret. In nine months Lonnie and I could have made a baby, I thought. *Made a baby.* It was an impossibility, as if touching flesh could create flesh. It was as random and mysterious as chemistry experiments, dipping a glass rod from beaker to beaker until a liquid smoked or sizzled or reeked.

Getting dressed up for the anniversary dinner, I put my palms on my bare stomach. My skin and my insides felt dulcet, my secret name-word which meant soft and smooth, tender for my secret impossible baby. My skin twitched under my hands, and I was abruptly terrified of ropes of flesh like boiled hot dogs, of composite shapes—lips and saliva and tongues and glands and bellies snipped up and molded into an embryo.

Lonnie's idea of fancy was Bill Knapp's. I ordered the ham croquettes, as I always did when my parents and I ate there after church. Though it was Saturday night, the restaurant's light was just as frank and guileless as on Sunday afternoon.

"This is for you," Lonnie said and pushed a little box across the table. He'd wrapped it in yellow paper with too much Scotch tape.

A pair of waiters stepped toward us with a cake and lit candles. Not nine candles in this public place, I thought. They set the cake in the midst of the family next to us and sang: "Happy birthday dear Julie, happy birthday to you."

In the box, clenched in blue velvet, was an engagement ring.

"The wedding band has diamond chips, too." He leaned across the table to look at the ring. He laughed. "Probably still be paying on it when we have our sixth kid."

"Lonnie—you're still in high school." What had I done to make him think I'd marry him?

"Well, yeah, I know," he said. He looked uncertain, then laughed. "I go for older women."

"But you know I'm going to college. Next month." I had a picture of my assigned roommate in my purse, a sweet-faced girl with dark hair in a flip just like mine. Her name was Katie Leeview. I thought of her in Minnesota staring at my senior picture, laughing at my blonde flip. Would she understand that the angle of my head was the photographer's pose, that my lifted nose gave me a false face, that I wasn't really stuck up but scared?

"Yeah, I know," Lonnie said. "I thought you'd stay here, though. We could get married now. Stay with my parents at first. Or I can just get a job and we can find an apartment. What do I need another year of shop or stupid English for, anyway?"

"You're crazy. You have to finish high school." I wasn't going to argue with him about my beloved English classes. I wouldn't marry Lonnie Saxbe if my life depended on it.

"You better not say I'm crazy," he said, low. "You just better not, Dulcie. I admit, another year of track wouldn't kill me. But I'd give it up if you said."

I closed the ring box. "Here, you keep this. You'll find the right woman sometime." It was odd to say woman not girl. I imagined Katie Leeview watching my gentleness. I spoke the grand lines softly. "You know I care about you, Lonnie. But I'm not the right one for you."

I thought he was going to cry. "But—I *love* you. I've been saying I love you."

That was true. In the Tempest's back seat, steaming up the windows, putting his hands under my blouse and on my thighs, he'd been saying he loved me, the words coming out wet against my neck, *I luff you.*

At the next table, the mother reached across and tapped the birthday girl's shoulder. "Don't stare, Julie sweetheart," she said.

"Let's talk about this outside," I said. "People are looking."

"Well, goddamnit, Dulcie, let them look."

"Take this." I stood and set the ring box beside his plate. He hadn't finished his Salisbury steak. He grabbed my wrist. "I said I love you. I'm going to marry you. I'm going to."

I tried to pull away. He held on. "What do you say?" he asked the staring family at the next table. "Don't I have the right to marry my girl?

Huh? Don't I?" The armpits of his yellow oxford cloth shirt were wet. His face was wet and blank, as if disbelief and outrage canceled each other out.

"Let me go." I jerked my arm free and strode past all the ordinary people eating their croquettes, their pork chops, their little pots of au gratin potatoes, out into the humid night. I wore my true face. I was full of powers—to cause Lonnie's love, to stash him in my past.

The sweet-faced girl sat on one of the little dorm room's beds, with the fat pink bonnet of a hair dryer on her head. She looked up at me and ripped it off. My parents stepped back into the hall to let us confront each other alone, as if we were dogs strange to each other or lovers after a separation.

We made shy arrangements: her bed, my bed, her desk and mine, her record player, mine sent back with my parents, her French dictionary, my Thesaurus, her Tchaikovsky, my Beethoven, her Brontes, my Tolstoy.

The first night we lay on our narrow beds in the little room and to Swan Lake in the sanctified darkness confessed our lives. Katie had said goodbye-forever to a boy in Minnesota, and we compared endings. I told her about the scene in Lonnie's bedroom last Sunday when I told him to forget me.

"You did it in his bedroom?"

"It was Sunday afternoon. I figured his parents would be there but they weren't."

His single bed had a brown plaid bedspread and no headboard. On the wall above a small pressed-wood desk hung a crucifix. That surprised me. We hadn't talked about what we believed. We talked about movies and track and his car. With Annie Halvorson it was *Anna Karenina* and my piano lessons with Bernard Fink over at the university and her brother's dirty cards and our parents' conformity and the nature of God. Lonnie was my date. I liked going out with him, I liked feeling his hand on my elbow as we walked, I liked saying my boyfriend. He looked cool, dressed cool, wore a letter sweater, and went to a different high school so nobody knew he was in shop while I was in college-bound English. He was a walking, talking boyfriend.

"I did it in Alex's car," Katie said. "I wish I'd thought of the bedroom."

"Private. Intimate. But it didn't turn out so hot."

He'd come to see me at college, Lonnie said. It was only a hundred miles away. He'd tool up on the weekends.

"When I said no, forget it, he ripped the crucifix off the wall," I told Katie. "He yelled, 'A hell of a lot of good you are,' and threw it on the floor."

"What a scene," she said. "Weren't you scared? Alex just started crying."

I thought of how the picture hook flew out, how chips of the wall fell away, showing the cardboard under the plaster, how he hurled Christ to the linoleum floor.

"They'll remember us for the rest of their lives," Katie said. "They'll have jobs and get married and have kids, but they'll always remember us."

On Saturday we walked together into town and bought blue and green plaid bedspreads, matching curtains, a shaggy rug, and two prints—a Renoir of two dappled girls, a blonde and a brunette, on a river bank; and a Picasso, the head and torso of a woman we named Old Virgin Face. We readied our cell where for nine months we filled in each other's words, watched rain fall to Rachmaninoff, located ourselves in each other.

"Why did the three old ladies dig up Tom Dooley?" Glenna said. Her room was next to ours, and she didn't like her roommate.

"Why?" Katie said.

"They wanted to see how he was hung."

We were silent. Shouldn't it be hanged? Why three old ladies? What was the joke?

"You dummies," Glenna said. "They wanted to see how he was hung. Get it? How he was hung?"

"We don't get it," Katie said.

Glenna had been to boarding school, and we invited her into our room whenever we needed an interpretation of some guy's possibly suggestive comment or something we'd read in a novel or the psych text. She always knew the carnal meaning but her explanations, once she'd quit laughing at us, were metaphorical and vague. An Oedipus complex was like this older brother of this girl she'd known in boarding school who still needed his mother to tuck him in. Tom Dooley's being hung was something like horses.

She knew all the answers, we knew, because she'd signed out to stay with a townie and then spent the entire night at a motel with Rick, the senior she was going out with. And she showed us how to dance. She brought over her records and did the jerk. *She's got a ticket to ri-hide.* She got Katie and me to go over to the mixers at the state university, where we had more anonymity, more choice, too, than at our prim private school. The three of us, in knee socks and kilts, would walk over in the dusk, and I felt like a lit wick, in the center of guttering fall, in the center of the shadows, the yellow leaves, all the molten world. Glenna would find us guys—no, they were men, not guys, she said—and we'd dance fast and we'd dance slow beneath strobe lights, and they'd walk us back to our dorm.

There the kissing couples were assembled by the front step and in the lobby. Nobody wanted to risk getting in late after the doors were locked. Mrs. T, the housemother, supervised. If a couple strayed out of bounds, she said, "Ah ah, you mustn't do it on the rug, only on the tile."

When Lonnie called, I talked to him on the hall phone, politely telling him about my classes and politely listening to his pleas. "My blood feels like sand," he said one time, and I kept thinking of that, blood like sand, blood slick like quicksand sliding through him.

On Friday nights, Katie and I went to the university mixers with Glenna, and on Saturdays we went to football games, more to be outside in the bright Michigan fall, with the sweet crowd and the smell of hot dust around us, than to see the game, for we thought football was stupid. Saturday nights we went out together with a pair of sophomores, roommates also, Josh and Bruce.

But when Lonnie showed up during the week, I'd go riding with him if I didn't have a test the next day. I liked being among the girls with a leftover boyfriend. We were women with a past. The others could show off their letters, but my old boyfriend was in the flesh. "The man's obsessed," Glenna said one night in the bathroom, and the other girls, putting their hair in rollers, looked away from the mirrors at me, a good-looking guy's obsession.

Before finals, Katie and I began pulling all-nighters with the rest of the floor. Coffee tasted nasty, and we tried Glenna's No-Doz. "That could be dangerous," my mom said when I told her how we stayed awake to cram. "I don't like the idea of that." Katie and I quizzed each other on fetal pig parts and French vocabulary and B. F. Skinner, everything magnified in our wide-awake eyes. Our room was next to the bathroom, and every time a toilet flushed we jumped. I told her about my discovery that everything was connected, that all the subjects, chemistry and French and plane geometry and orchestra and social studies and even P.E., were part of each other, that crystals and proofs and counterpoint and grammar and bodies were all connected. And she nodded, no explanation needed or possible. We sat face to face at our desks, wrapped together in diaphanous continuum.

Now and then we'd stretch and walk down the hall to the lounge where others were dozing or trying to study or eating soup in the middle of the night.

"What, are you two roomies joined at the hip?" Glenna's roommate, Andrea, said. "I have to get away from my roomie's snoring to concentrate." We knew they didn't really like each other. We knew Glenna wasn't going to make it through her freshman year.

"We're not roomies," Katie said. "We're chambries."

I knew immediately that she'd transformed *chambre* and made us a dulcet name. "That's right," I said. "We aren't like the rest of you roommates. We're chambries."

In our room we talked about operant conditioning and God. By dawn we were silly with fatigue. We laughed at Old Virgin Face on the wall. We identified the different sound of each flush on the other side of our wall and named the toilets—the plasher, the singing serpent, the screamer, the barbaric yawper, the crepitator, and the next-to-the-last one at the far end that nobody used, the virgin.

Before we left for our separate homes, where we would still be children, we gave each other Christmas presents. I gave her *Sonnets from the Portuguese* and Beethoven's Emperor Concerto. She gave me *The Collected Poems of W. B. Yeats* and Tchaikovsky's Violin Concerto.

We wrote to each other every other day during the break. I imagined our letters flying between Minnesota and Michigan, riding currents, crossing each other in the air, leaving contrails that wove together high above the blue snow. *Dear Chambrie*, she wrote, *I can't wait to return to our little room, to the crepitator on the other side of the wall, to more all-night study (talk) sessions, to Josh and Bruce and doing it on the tile, to Old Virgin Face, and to the only one who's ever understood me.*

On Christmas morning, I slept until nine, and Mom finally woke me. "Hey," she said, "don't you know Santa's been here?"

"Mom, I'm almost nineteen years old."

"Well, maybe you could play along for our sake. Did you ever think about how this is for us, our only child gone?"

I brushed my hair, which I was letting grow long, and tied a pink ribbon around my head, Alice in Wonderland style. I could be their little girl for the morning. For a moment, I wondered what I had been to them: to them as a married couple.

My mother had mothered me in the ordinary way, I supposed, and commiserated with me when Dad said no to something until we learned to stop asking him, and Dad had been there in my background, eating my mother's meals, automatically saying no if I asked permission to spend the night at Annie's or to ride the bus downtown on Saturday, paying for my piano lessons, going to work where he made money doing I didn't know what exactly and hadn't really asked. They were just the parents, the grown-ups, and I'd been the one who'd counted.

I was glad I'd bought them thoughtful presents last week and wrapped them carefully, like an out-of-town guest.

It was strange to think of them meeting at a dance at Michigan State and falling in love—had that been something swooning, something that would happen to me sometime? and would that make my life like their boxed-in go-to-work make-the-beds what-will-the-neighbors-think life?—strange to think of them in bed making a baby, making me, and Dad falling asleep and burning a hole in the green MSU blanket we still had, while Mom lay in pain waiting for me to come out of her.

After we'd opened all the presents from relatives and each other, Dad brought out two small boxes, store wrapped in silver paper. "For my women," he said. He rarely bought us presents, just paid for what we picked out for each other in his name.

I held my box, panicked for a moment, not one of his women like Mom, nobody's woman, remembering Lonnie at Bill Knapp's sliding the ring box across the table.

Mom's was a diamond. All these years she'd worn the plain wedding band he'd bought as a student.

Mine was a garnet, my birthstone. I couldn't look at him. "Oh Walter, oh Walter," my mother kept saying, "oh Walter I can't believe it." I didn't want them to see me ready to cry. My mother and I had relegated the man to background. Why was I anything at all to him? I saw myself as if through gauze: a typical teenager, as my mother said, words I relished because I'd been such a reject in high school, but also words that infuriated me—terrible twos, typical teen—flattening me and dropping me into a slot. I saw myself in my blue mohair sweater and pleated skirt and in an x-ray flash I saw my body walking through his house in the lightly padded bra and garter belt and nylons under the clothes. What was I to him? I used to climb onto his shoulders in Lake Michigan and dive from him into the waves. Through the gauze, I saw my graceless self that was nothing to anybody but Katie Leeview, and in a welter of guilt at my secret loyalty and at my neglect and at the secret light that shined on my parents between the sheets without me, I put the ring on, and uttered breathlessly, "Thank you, Dad," and ran upstairs to cry in the bathroom.

After dinner, I was modeling my new clothes for Mom and Dad, strutting through the wrappings on the living room floor, when the phone rang and I knew Lonnie's deep voice wanted me.

He was wearing a yellow button-down collar shirt under a brown V-neck sweater, and brown corduroy pants. I hadn't seen him for at least a month. He'd let his hair grow longer. He shook hands with my father and presented a box of chocolates to my mother.

"I have something for Dulcie out in my car," he told them. He winked at Mom. "Would it be all right with you if I took her for a ride?"

I hadn't bought him anything. I imagined telling Katie about the scene, the poor guy trying so hard.

Still parked in front of the house, he handed over a large white box with a pink ribbon around it. Inside were a short yellow skirt and a pale yellow angora sweater.

"It's to match your yellow hair," he said. "I made your mother tell me what size."

"Lonnie, Lonnie," I said, "you'll never learn, will you?" I shook my head, feeling my mouth warp into a sort of smile. If Katie's old boyfriend gave her a Christmas present, we'd compare scenes.

I watched the Tempest pull away, as if my bucket seat were in a movie theater. In the old black-and-white film the car slid around the curves of the lake road, the sepia cottages and snowy banks and sanded road blurring. I watched the car stop silently on a driveway beside a small brownish-gray boathouse. The boy in the brown sweater climbed over the seat. Through the thick pale clumps of falling snow, I saw him stretch out his arm to the girl. She took off her heavy raccoon-collared coat and let the boy pull her into the back seat. I watched the two move together in a grainy embrace.

But then I was seeing Lonnie's hand move under her sweater from behind the girl's eyes, and the sweater was blue and his shirt was yellow and the big flakes of snow falling past the steamed windows were blue-tinged. Lonnie lifted my sweater over my head and unfastened the back hooks of my bra with one hand, and the air in the car was warm on my thin nakedness. He put his mouth on my breasts.

His hand went to the crotch of my blue-checked stretch pants, and then he pulled them and my pink underpants off. He took off his sweater and shirt and pants and white underwear, and laid them neatly with mine over the front seats. My hands were pale on the dark hair of his body. We fell back on the seat.

Here with all the colors sharp, here with the arousal of being naked outside, in winter yet, here the violin concerto was supposed to be overlaid on the scene like a sheet. But when his penis touched me I was numb. While he rocked on me, my whole body went to sleep, like a limb left in one position too long, and I wasn't sure it could be rubbed past pins and needles to life again.

At home I found the surprise of blood in my underpants. I had forgotten about that. In junior English, when we'd read about the beautiful Hymen with his torch, Douglas Deakins behind me whispered, "What's a torch but a hot, hard stick for breaking hymens?" and Freddy Leon, trying to laugh silently, sounded like a dog about to throw up. That night Annie and I checked the dictionary on hymen and read about a fold of mucous membrane. "Sounds like nostrils," I said.

The next morning Annie was all excited on the way to school. "I figured it out in the middle of the night. Hymen means cherry. When someone loses her cherry, it means someone got his thing under that fold."

After that, when we wondered how far some couple had gone, we said, "Do you think he's picked her nose yet?"

I scrubbed the underpants and hung them in the back of my closet to dry where Mom wouldn't see. So Lonnie had broken my membrane. I wondered if there was blood on him. I hoped he wouldn't let his mother find my blood on his white underwear. I didn't love Lonnie but he had torched me and caused blood.

"If you neck too much," Mom started saying after I'd been out with Lonnie twice, "you won't be able to stop. You'll go too far. It'll be like Becky Mead. Now the Meads can't face anybody. They don't even go to church. You'd ruin our lives."

I could have stopped. I had stopped time after time. I could have stopped, but tonight I just hadn't.

Under my blue quilt in my old bedroom, I thought of Gary Puckett and the Union Gap singing about how she cried a single tear and how she is woman now. I put Heifetz playing the Tchaikovsky Violin Concerto on my record player and got back in bed. Emily Dickinson must have been torched, too. I've finished that, that other state, I'm woman now. The music only made me want Katie under her blue and green bedspread across our narrow room from me under my blue and green bedspread.

In the morning I hadn't changed, hadn't modulated into any other state. I was just Dulcie White eating my mother's pancakes and being told to sort the old clothes in my dresser and closet before putting the new ones away. I wore a new garnet ring and on a hook in my closet was a pair of stiff pink underpants. That was all.

"Cheer up," Mom said. "It's the day after Christmas, you've got all that new stuff, you still have another whole week of vacation. Your parents love you, you're smart and pretty, you have your whole life in front of you. So don't look like you've just lost your best friend."

After all our passionate letters, Katie and I were a little shy, together again. We had to shake off the fact that we were our parents' children.

"Well, what's new?" she said.

"What's a snoo?"

"Thanks. I was really hoping you'd turn into Emily Simperson over the break."

"Anyway," I said, "nothing much that I didn't already write you. Except that I got my nose picked."

"You got your nose picked? What's that supposed to mean?"

Katie pushed her empty suitcase under her bed. Her dark hair was as long as mine. She wore a sweater we'd bought together. My mother had been angry for some reason when I told her we shared clothes. Suddenly I couldn't tell Katie. If I told her, we would both be changed.

"Nothing. I'm just talking silly," I said. "Let's see what you got for Christmas."

"It isn't nothing, Dulcie. I know you."

"Look at all these new clothes my mom got me." I dumped the pile on my bed desperately.

"Be that way," Katie said and lay down with her face to the wall.

We went separately to dinner. I took my tray to a table by myself. Josh and Bruce sat down with me. "Where's your evil twin?" Josh said.

"I wouldn't know," I said.

We all saw her at the other end of the dining hall sitting with Glenna.

"Uh oh," Bruce said. "Lovers' quarrel."

"Go sit somewhere else," I said. "I'd rather be alone."

"Misery loves—" Bruce said.

I started to rise. "I mean it, you guys."

"All right already," Josh said. They picked up their trays. "On the rag," I heard him mutter.

I sat at my desk all evening without any studying to do since classes hadn't started yet. I tried a letter. *Dear Chambrie. Guess what. I cried that single tear. I'm woman now.* How phony could you get. I couldn't write the truth—*Dear Chambrie, I betrayed you.* I worked myself into tears. I needed my dark-haired double. I didn't even know why I'd let Lonnie do it to me.

I was in bed when she returned. She undressed in the dark and got into her bed. I heard the bedspread snap as she jerked it up.

In a few minutes I went into the bathroom. I took the rarely used stall and flushed the Virgin. When I got back in bed, we stayed silent. Then her bed began thumping the wall rhythmically.

Finally I said, "Are you laughing or crying?"

"I know what happened. You got flushed, didn't you?"

Next door somebody flushed the screamer and we started laughing. "At least it wasn't like that," I said over the plumbing's high-pitched howling. We couldn't stop laughing. Our beds beat against the walls with our shaking. I laughed wetly until I had to get up for Kleenex. "I'm blowing nose bubbles," I said.

"That's what happens when you let somebody up your nose."

"My mother told me once it wasn't any big thrill," I said. "It isn't. But it is, too." I kept rewinding it, like my father's reel-to-reel tape recorder, the details blurring and then snapping to a stop with the wheels on rewind. Then I'd run it slowly again, stretching and distorting the ride to the boathouse when I knew without actually deciding that I would let him, slowly slowly removing each piece of clothing, crystallizing the cold until it hurt my skin, separating the shivers into slow shudders.

The next afternoon, after our first classes, we walked downtown and ate at the ten-cent store's lunch counter. The store was high ceilinged and dim and smelled just the same as the Woolworth's at home, like sawdust and cheap cloth and hamsters. After our grilled cheese sandwiches and cherry Cokes, we looked for something to buy. Katie needed a new hairbrush. I got a black velvet hair ribbon. In the pet section, gerbils huddled in the corners of their glass cages, though they could have run in the treadmills, and parakeets picked under their wings. We bought a fishbowl, colored stones, and a pair of goldfish.

In our room we transferred the fish from the Chinese take-out container to the bowl and set them on the windowsill. We named them Andante and Vivace, Andy and Viv for short.

Every day, two hours before dinner, we walked through the snow to the music building where we found two unoccupied practice rooms. We wheeled the piano from one room into the other, closed the glass door, and set up our music. We worked on the Tchaikovsky first piano concerto, Katie playing the piano part and I an arrangement of the orchestral score. By graduation, we figured, we'd be perfect. We decided we would play it on two grand pianos in Stinton Chapel for the entire school. In the meanwhile we had the immensity of two pianos and Tchaikovsky closed up in the little room with us.

Dr. Harris used thirty whole minutes of the fifty-minute period to read my paper to the class. He'd written on my title page: "This is the best paper I have ever received in Engl. 103. You cannot imagine the pleasure I have had reading it."

I'd titled it "A Study of Dehumanization." I'd shown how the characters in *Heart of Darkness* and *Steppenwolf* and *Notes from Underground* and Ellison's *Invisible Man* each denied facets of his mind and/or body and thereby lessened his membership qualifications for the genus Homo.

"What is Miss White saying here?" Dr. Harris asked. "Who can paraphrase? And take it to the next level. What is this saying about society? About events such as the March on Washington? Or—what is it saying about you?"

I'd thought my paper was about the particular men. I'd thought it was about doing to oneself, not about being done to. It hadn't been about civil rights. It hadn't been about me, either. It was just a good paper with good words, such as phantasmagoria, about characters. Maybe the men were representative, but not of anyone I knew. Suddenly I saw universality as a nimbus around certain people—such as Dr. Martin Luther King, Jr., such as our president, now that he was dead—and I wondered how it would be to walk in your own shining cloud. Would you need to kick through it now and then or stick your arms out, so people could see your skinny ankles or your rough knuckles? Or would you be your hard self inside the cloud and everybody else, seen through it, insubstantial and bland?

When I showed the paper to Katie, we saw that Dr. Harris had written "image" instead of "imagine."

"Well, we know what he means," Katie said. "Still, it's a shame to have your brilliance marred by his carelessness."

"You hear that, Old VF?" I said to the Picasso print. "She said I'm brilliant."

"Too brilliant for Lonnie Saxbe," she said. "So what if he's a doll. He's not good enough for you."

"So what if he loves me."

"I grant you, adoration is appealing. But you aren't in love with him. It doesn't matter if he loves you. We've got all this—" She spread her arms to take in our room and our life.

"Yes, Mom. I have my whole life ahead of me."

She laughed. "I know. But, you know, my parents and everybody act like this is all preparation. Like we're getting ready for real life. When the truth is, this is our life."

It wasn't as if all our books and music, all the literature and psychology and philosophy lectures, all the dancing and the boys who kissed us, all Katie's and my intimate life together steaming in our little room weren't enough. It was all too much. Lonnie worked for contrast, maybe. Lonnie siphoned off enough of the intensity to keep me from exploding. Lonnie was my other life.

"You're right. I know you're right," I said. "But it's not like I chose him."

"So you're just suffering your fate? What, just because he chose you, you think you have to go along with it?"

Maybe, I thought. Or—I heard Dr. Harris's classroom voice—*what is it saying about you?* Maybe it wasn't about doing to yourself but only about having things done to you. Katie and I believed in free will, but that was philosophy. Free will was in a nimbus too and it had nothing to do with me and Lonnie making out in the back seat.

On Sunday afternoon Bruce borrowed a car from an upperclassman who charged him twenty dollars and we drove over to Lake Michigan and walked along the beach. The shoreline was scattered with driftwood that storms had tossed out of the water. I carried a piece along with me, smoothing the wood with my thumb, imagining how it must have entered the water somehow last fall, just an old hunk of tree, and spent the winter underwater, the sand scrubbing off its bark, ice rubbing down its knolls, the cold water turning it over and over.

That's what I'd be with Lonnie, I thought. I would spend my life in cold water, worn down by forces I'd have no say in. I would become faceless and smooth as an egg.

Bruce and I sat on the beach and ate sandwiches. The wind off the lake was cold and he moved his arm around me. We kissed for a while, and I carefully blocked his hand when it moved toward my breasts. He had to try, of course, and I had to resist. I was a good girl, he'd been Grosse Pointe raised to be a gentleman, and we were more shadows of Katie and Josh than a real couple. Between kisses, the wind blew sand onto our wet lips and we had to wipe our mouths before we could put them together again.

Wednesday after dinner, Emily at her switchboard paged me on the hall phone. "He is here," she said and gave a big sigh.

"What's that for?" I said.

"Oh nothing," she said. I figured Lonnie was standing right there. I could never tell if her emphatic announcement of him was sarcastic or admiring.

"Anyway, I'm glad he's here. Tell him to keep his pants on. I'll be right out." My mother's expression at any impatience—just keep your pants on—had popped out. I hoped poor homely Emily Simpson, a work-study student stuck at the dorm switchboard every night, hadn't immediately pictured Lonnie Saxbe with his pants off. I was glad he'd shown up, though. I was going to tell him to keep his pants on.

As soon as we were in the car, he said, "I'm starving. Baby, I am starving in every way." He kissed me. I kept my lips together, but he pushed his tongue between them. I'd let him do it twice since Christmas. There was no real reason to refuse. "You're giving me an extraction," he whispered.

"A what?" I buckled my seat belt across my lap.

"You know," he whispered.

I didn't know. "Listen, you're hungry. Let's go get a pizza." If I told him in public, he couldn't carry on too dramatically.

At Bimbo's we sat at our regular table. "Where's Charmaine?" Lonnie asked the waitress.

"She's off tonight," the woman said. She was large, her flesh so tightly packed in the red checked uniform it was hard to say if she was flabby or solid. "Her kid has chicken pox."

"We'll have the super," he said. "And bring me a beer. Dulcie, you want a Coke, right?"

"Nice try," the waitress said. "But I'll need to see your ID."

"Look, damnit, I'm old enough. Just get me the beer." Lonnie's face looked purple in the dim reddish light. He looked like an angry six-year-old ready to cry.

"You cuss at me again, I'll haul you back there to the ladies' and wash your mouth out," the waitress said and walked away.

Lonnie held onto the edge of the table. "Hey, take it easy," I said. I thought he might heave the table over. His fingers were white but the nails looked purple. "It's not a big deal."

"That bitch isn't getting a tip out of me," he said, low. He was pitiful, I thought, my chest hot with shame.

"I don't think she needed to embarrass you like that," I said.

"I am not embarrassed, Dulcie," he said.

I picked up the menu and read about the original Bimbo's owner and the restaurant's guarantee of satisfaction. Lonnie *should* be embarrassed, I thought, like some thirteen-year-old acting too big for his britches who's reminded he's still a child. *I can't get no satisfaction*, I thought. The song was supposed to have secret dirty lyrics if you played it backwards. Or was that *Louie, Louie*? We'd tried it with Glenna's records but heard only hoarse devilish warnings we couldn't fathom. How did you actually play a record backwards anyway? Glenna said the one was dirty enough forwards. "It's about this guy who can't do it." "Why not?" Katie wanted to know. "Is this something about horses again?" I said.

"It's funny," I said, trying to raise Lonnie from his angry embarrassment. How could I break up with him in this mood? "When she wanted to see your ID, I pictured it in writing, in lower case—she wanted to see your id."

"Ha ha," he said. "Why's that funny?"

"You know, Freud. Id, ego, superego. She wanted to see your id."

"You saying I'm conceited, Dulcie? That what you think?"

"No—it was supposed to be a joke. Never mind. It's too complicated to explain."

"And I'm too dumb for your fancy college humor."

"No, Lonnie." I slapped the table and looked around. "Geez, is that pizza ever going to get here?"

"Oh screw it all," Lonnie said, rising. "I'm gonna make a pit stop."

When we parked, I felt light-headed, as if I'd had a beer with the pizza. I'd never had a beer in my life, or anything else. In tenth grade once, Annie and I had dropped aspirin into our Cokes, but nothing happened. My parents had a cocktail every night before dinner, and I knew that I would never drink like that.

Lonnie was moving a finger all over my back. "Guess what I'm writing."

"You're writing, Goodbye Dulcie, I'm running away with Charmaine."

"Wrongo, baby. Wrong-o. But I never thought she'd have a kid. Be married."

"You thought she was waiting tables until you came along and swept her away to a better life?" I was getting angry, though I didn't know why. Maybe I didn't want anybody else to have him. Maybe I was in love with the picture of Lonnie at forty, living at home still, missing me forever, trying to drown his love every night in some bar. Maybe I despised his self-delusion: that he was such hot stuff Charmaine or Emily Simpson or I or anybody was just breathless.

"Write it again," I said. "I'll pay attention." Maybe I wanted his hand on my skin. Of course he was spelling out I love you, and maybe I wanted to hear it one last time.

"God, baby, I love you," he said. "I don't know how much longer I can wait."

I let him kiss me. *I can't get no-o sat-is-faction.* I didn't know what satisfaction might be available. I let him pull my sweater off and unsnap my bra. But when he started sucking on me, I pushed him back up to my face.

"Lonnie. I have to tell you. This is our last time together. I mean it this time. Really. I do care about you. But we both need to get on with our lives now."

He pulled his hand away from my bare shoulder and held it out. For an instant I thought he meant to slap me, but he just stared at his hand.

"I don't want you to come over here any more," I went on. "Don't call, don't come over. All right? I mean, you agree it's not going to work. Don't you really? So—" I clapped my palm on his thigh, everything all settled. "Let's just say a nice goodbye."

His hands fell to the seat and he fell forward. His forehead hit the steering wheel. "Please, Dulcie," he said. "Please. I won't come over so much. I won't be so serious. I won't bug you about getting married. I'll wait as long as you make me. Just..." The skin of his face was stretched tight over his forehead down to his blue-tinged jaw.

"No," I said, "no. There's no point to it."

He lifted his head and dropped it, hitting his forehead on the top of the steering wheel again, and lifted his head and let it fall again and again.

"Quit that," I said. "Now you just quit that." I sounded like somebody's mother. I thought of the waitress's threat to take him back to the ladies' and wash his mouth out. I knew she meant the restroom, but I pictured a half dozen ladies in red-checked uniforms back in a storage room waiting to scold or spank or do some magic.

His shoulders heaved and he cried out loud: hoo, hoo, hoo. The cries rose in the middle and broke.

"Quit that. Don't cry." I put my hand on his back and let it ride up and down. "It'll be all right. You'll get over this. Hush now."

He grabbed onto me, tight, as if I'd given in, and held on, shuddering. He took a huge breath. He dropped his head to my bare chest and sucked. His face was wet and hot. I could feel his slick mouth and his whiskers. I was hot with shame for us both. We opened separate doors of the car, took our pants off outside in the dusk, and got into the back seat. I saw his penis and its ground of dense, dark hair as he held it and slid the rubber on. He had that springy hair, too. I wanted to see his hands, how would that be, to have yourself in your hands. I lay under him for one last time, with one knee jutting up and the other foot on the floor. My skin felt steamed and abraded. He rocked and then went heavy on me.

At the dorm I went into the bathroom before going in to Katie. I sat spread-legged on the toilet. My muscles pushed downward, and I pushed my fists against my stomach.

Finally I combed my hair and went to our room. Glenna and Katie were doing the monkey. I told them I'd broken up with Lonnie for good. I sat on my bed and watched them dance. Emily called and said the pizza they'd ordered was here.

"Help yourself," Katie said. "You must be hungry. Breaking up is hard work."

"Breaking up is hard to do," Glenna sang.

I picked up a slice, but the thick pale mozzarella smelled like vomit and I couldn't eat it. "I've already been pizza-ed tonight," I said. I knew Glenna would laugh. "Since you're here, oh worldly one," I said then, "I have a question." Katie's and my innocence had become a joke. "And don't say a thing about horses. But what's an extraction?"

"Extraction? You mean like a tooth?"

"No, he said I gave him an extraction."

Glenna fell over sideways on the floor, hooting her wild laugh. "An extraction," she gasped. "Oh God but you're an innocent... You give him an erection."

"I thought he said extraction."

"I hate to say it," Katie said, "but what exactly is an erection?"

Glenna sat up and hugged herself in pain. "You've seen how a horse kind of extends his thing? Until it's hanging way down?"

"No horses," Katie said. We all rocked hysterically.

Finally I said, "I didn't know it could change."

"You know what you say when that happens?" Katie said. "You say neigh."

CHAPTER 2

He'd come to know that she'd go with him if he just took her. It made him feel cheap, that she wouldn't say yes if he asked, and he disliked her for that: to her he was worthless and unacknowledged. Saturday nights he parked a block off campus where she might see his car if she was looking and he staked himself out among the trees on the dark slope in front of the old brick building where she'd return by eleven o'clock. He carried a Battle Boosters' cushion and sat on it, leaned up against a big old pine, or he'd get his ass wet waiting for her. There was always a wet pine smell and something else, a dead mouse or something. For the Letterman Club initiation he'd been made to carry a raw hamburger patty in his underwear all day at school and then fry it and eat it, and that was the smell of the darkness where he waited for her. She'd taken to coming back with the same guy. This pansy who needed a haircut. Who wore glasses that had dark frames. One time he wore this dinner jacket and that was the time he stepped her into the trees and Lonnie saw how he leaned forward from the waist and puckered his mouth and that was how he kissed her. Lonnie had a blackjack in his glove box. He chugged the rest of his beer and left the bottle upright against his tree where she could see it in the morning on her way out to church if she was looking.

The old man had eased up on him or given up on him. He still made it to school most days. His mom left him a plate in the oven and he ate sometimes at two in the a.m. when he got back from watching her or parking with her or just sitting in the boat and drinking a six-pack.

The dog at the switchboard was Emily who always looked at him like she had a grasp on the situation. Like she gave a damn how Dulcie treated him like pond muck. One of these days, he told her, I am going to dump her and take you. Both of them knowing the true facts: she was a dog, he would never want to touch her, he was going to marry Dulcie White. Emily paged her, *He* is out here for you, and just shook her head at him.

One time Emily said, without calling, she isn't here, Lonnie. All soft. You better just forget it this time, she said, but her eyes cut for a flash to the lounge. There Dulcie sat at the piano they had in there and some fruit was beside her on the piano bench and all those hands were playing and her leg rubbed his when she worked the pedal. La de da. He just stepped onto the carpet right up to the piano and the hands collapsed on the keyboard. You leaving, he said to the fruit, or am I kicking your ass?

Lonnie, don't, she said.

Neanderthal, the fruit said.

He slammed the fruit's hands down on the piano keys and the noise got an old lady charging over. You young men are taking your young butts out of here, she said. Now.

He waited in his car that he called the Witch and in ten minutes she got in and he peeled away. He parked in their spot in the boonies. Nobody said a thing. He got out and believed he was going to puke. She just got in the back seat and waited and he stomped around on old broken corn stalks in the cold. Then he got in with her. You're acting crazy, she said. This is it, Lonnie. We're done. It's over.

He grabbed onto her. She didn't know he was getting her fur collar wet. Maybe I am going crazy, he said. I can't stop myself.

You and Lou Christie, she said. Lightning striking.

He was nothing to her. The sky was dark yellow the color of the tomcat piss crusted on the side of the trailer. He needed a beer. His mother had been crazy when he was a kid. She was supposed to have been in a TB sanitarium but he had figured out it was a nuthouse. His blood felt like sand scraping under his skin and behind his closed eyes his brain was dark piss yellow. He drew her hand to his pecker. She pressed on him. He cried onto the thick fur of her coat's collar and got his hand under her sweater.

He had figured out at Christmas she'd let him do it if he didn't ask and just took charge. Afterwards at her front door she wouldn't kiss him. He tried to lip-read what she said through the storm glass. Goodbye, was probably all. He didn't think her lips had moved enough for I love you. But it had been fine, he thought. He wished he'd taken his socks off. But he'd done the bra good.

His niece Mitzi left her big doll over at the trailer a while back. His sisters had never cared for dolls but now they bought them by the crate for their kids. We didn't need no dolls, Marie said. We had the baby. And he was the baby. He got one of his mother's big cotton brassieres from her top drawer and put it on the doll. To get the tension right in back he had to fold it over in front. He stapled it together. He practiced with his eyes closed. He held the doll in different positions and practiced unsnapping the brassiere's hooks. Pretty soon he could pop it easy with either hand. What an athlete, he said, what a star. If his mother ever noticed the little holes where he'd taken out the staples she never said a thing.

The elastic had snapped on Dulcie's skin with the exact same sound as on the vinyl doll.

She had said not one single word afterwards. She put her clothes back on and brushed her hair. At her door she said something through the storm glass. She had a private look like he hadn't had any part of what they had done beside the boathouse.

He let the Witch hit sixty-five on the highway back toward the lake. Big wads of snow hit the windshield and the wheels kept losing traction. I love you too, he said. He accelerated and turned the Witch into the tire slides.

He ended up back at the boathouse. He got out and the snow smacked on his forehead and his chest. He left his varsity jacket in the car. He crouched and dug proper toeholds in the snow like it was cinders and sank his fingers in tripod position into the snow. Get set, he heard called out and he raised up a bit and his triceps took the forward weight. At go he dived forward. His arm was out and up and he ran a little forward and sprinted with his breath held and he kept his eyes not on the tape but ten yards ahead in the gray snow.

The first Friday she was back at that college he took a chance and showed up. Hey, what's new, gorgeous, he said to Emily at the switchboard. I don't know, she said, what's a snoo?

Dulcie was actually there. She had stayed in to write this big paper for her intro to fiction class, she said. Her roommate was out with this guy named Josh. She smiled at him. I was starting to feel sorry for myself, she told him, all by my lonesome here on Friday night. Can't even watch Gunsmoke with Dad.

He took her to Bimbo's. They ate a pizza and he downed a couple beers. He winked at the waitress, Charmaine. He knew she would serve him without checking ID. He knew which tables were hers.

He drove the Witch out to their old cornfield. He kissed her and did the bra pop with his left hand.

Stop, she said then. Listen, Lonnie, I don't want to get pregnant.

Rough blood gorged his hands and sudden nausea rolled in his gut. He smelled dead meat.

I meant to tell you this anyway, he said. I was going to tell you before we got married. The bad news is we aren't going to be able to have kids of our own.

He held the nausea still. He told her how he'd had the mumps back when he was thirteen. He had swollen up and missed the last five days of seventh grade. That was no big deal, he said, but it spread and inflamed my—uh, you know—my balls. The doctor told my mother I would be—you know, sterile.

She frowned. He kissed the two frown creases between her eyes. Listen, he told her, if we really want to have kids someday —

To heck with someday, she said. She stuck her chest out and reached both arms back and fastened the bra. I never heard that about the mumps, she said. I just don't want to get pregnant. It would wreck my life.

The nausea boiled in his gut. She did not believe him. Having his baby would wreck her life. He leaned over the seat and got the little package out of the glove box. He took the rubber out and he threw it at her and he left her there.

He ran trying to keep the liquid in his stomach level and out of her sight he leaned over and puked onto the old corn stalks in the shallow snow.

He buried the puke and chewed snow and sloshed the water back and forth. The dead meat smell was gone but the rough blood rasped in his veins. In the back seat they undressed themselves and he unrolled the rubber over his pecker.

It's good of you to grace us with your presence, your highness, his mother said Saturday noon when he got up.

Ease off, Bernie, his dad said. He'll get over it. Every boy's got to have that first love. Which is never the last.

Let's hope the sweet thang don't catch something she can't get over, she said. I'm the one does the laundry around here, don't forget.

Late afternoon he stopped at the Texaco where his buddy Mark worked. Fill 'er up, Marcus, he said. I'm gonna make a pit stop.

The bathroom stank and wet toilet paper hung from the blackened sink. He dropped quarters into the dispenser and pocketed the rubbers and washed his hands. There were no towels.

Outside Mark thumped him on the butt. Don't do nothin' I wouldn't do, he said. Given half a chance.

He tooled the hundred miles to Dulcie and parked in front of her building. Dormitory. It sounded like someplace for secret medical experiments. Cutting girls open and removing parts and closing them back up to see what happened. He saw Dulcie and her roommate Katie leave and walk across the campus. She had on a blue parka and the blue and white stretch pants he'd removed. She bent over and made a snowball and chased Katie. Then they were beyond the hill and he settled down behind the wheel to wait.

He took the six white matchbook packets of rubbers from his pocket and lined them up on Dulcie's seat.

Forty-five minutes later Dulcie and Katie and some other girl came laughing down the slope and went inside the dormitory. Nobody spotted him. He waited. He watched guys go through the doorway alone and come out with their arms around girls in heavy coats. Here was some pansy in a ski sweater. No jacket. He was giving her an hour. Then he would go in and get her. He gripped the steering wheel to keep his hand off his pecker.

When he was a sophomore his dad bought him this white orlon ski sweater. For no reason at all. His dad just chucked it to him after supper one night. Catch, sport. It had a big black and red horse head on the back. He wore it to school the next day. The horse's nostrils flared below his shoulder blades. All morning everybody mocked him. *Giddy-up.* They neighed and blew through loose lips. *Saddle that boy up.* In English Mrs. Sanderson said, Sharp sweater there, Lonnie. That had done it. He had gone home at noon. He told his dad it was too heavy for school, he'd sweated all morning.

Since the sweater he wore only the shirts his mother starched and ironed, with dark pants or white Levis and his plain brown belt. He could not stand to be dirty. He almost punched Jerry Angus one time when he said, Hey, what you scratching, Saxbe? You got cooties?

He gripped the steering wheel hard. Dulcie and Katie were coming down the walk side by side with a guy beside each of them. She wore her dark green coat unbuttoned and he could see the yellow skirt and sweater under it. They walked right past his car and he thought she saw him. But in that yellow skirt and sweater he had given her she looked up at the faggot and laughed and he put his arm around her waist under her coat.

Ah God ah God ah God, he said. He needed a gun. He needed to kill the faggot who was putting his hands on her body where her own husband had touched her. Lonnie might as well be her husband. He would be her husband. Ah God. The faggot would be feeling her up. Weaseling his hands under the yellow sweater. Kissing her with his old lady puckered lips. Ah God ah God. Screwing her. He opened the six white packets and took out the six oily rubbers. He found a safety pin in the glove box and bent it open. He put his left index finger in the rubbers' tips, one by one, and pricked the pin into each one until he saw a dot of blood on his finger.

After school they did wind sprints and then on his way home he stopped at Walgreen's and bought a green tube of Duco cement. All day he'd kept thinking of the broken crucifix. For no reason. The pieces were wrapped in a plaid handkerchief of his father's. He could feel the rough broken edges scraping his skin. In the middle of civics he saw those pieces. They were in the second drawer down. His socks, that his mother rolled into pairs, were in the top drawer. Then his underwear that she bleached and washed at the laundrymat and folded into fourths. In English they were reading some play out of a magazine. The college prep class got a different magazine. Lonnie's class got this magazine every month and Mrs. Bundy had to collect them back for the next dumbhead class. There were hardly ever any stories about white kids. Just Negroes or Spics who always lived in some projects. He was thinking about the busted crucifix and lost his place in the play and got chewed out. He was supposed to be this new guy at school who was scared of this gang. He at least got to be the white guy this time. The first time they did a play Joey Willis refused to read. I'm no nigger, he said, and Mrs. Bundy got tight lips and Joey was in detention for a week. Now everybody just read and Mrs. Bundy didn't notice how they let these little accents creep in.

In shop he worked on his bookcase. He thought he could glue the crucifix back into one piece and hang it up again. Maybe hang it over his bed this time. He sanded the bookcase. Everybody knew he was building it for his girl. She had all these books. Freddy Greathouse needed to build a dozen headboards for his hog, the word was, the way the top of her head banged them up. But his girl had all these books.

He shut the door to his room and took out the handkerchief and laid the pieces out like a puzzle on his desk. One of the feet was missing and some chips. He laid it out on his notebook and just poured glue over the mess.

He didn't think she was going to get pregnant now, not by him anyway. It was like the trial spelling tests back in sixth grade. If you got all the words right on Tuesday, you didn't have to take the test on Friday. But if you did lousy, it didn't matter, it was the test on Friday that counted. Making cramped love to her in the Witch didn't really count. Nothing would happen until they were married and slept together all night in a double bed.

He took to keeping the ring he'd bought last summer in the glove box.

Everything ticked along. His feet were on the track. He would be done with school soon. Graduating was no big sweat when you were vocational. Foompa, foompa. His feet hit the dirt track. She wouldn't be allowed to break up with him. He'd get a job in June. Foompa, foompa. Every step he took was to her. He had the power.

Sunday his sister Marie was over with his brother-in-law Davis and his niece Mitzi. His mother had a giant tuna casserole. Mitzi kicked up a fuss and Marie made a bologna sandwich and brought it to the table for her. Davis said, You baby her. She'll eat what she's served, she gets hungry enough.

His kid would get whatever he wanted. His and Dulcie's kid would be spoiled rotten.

His dad had spoiled him, his mother said when she got out of the hospital. His sisters weren't really his dad's kids. They'd finished high school in Portage at Aunt Rose's when their mother went into the sanitarium and Lonnie had stayed in the trailer with his dad. He hadn't seen his sisters the whole time she was in the nuthouse and that had been the end of something. Now Marie and Suzie came around every week or so with Mitzi and Suzie's kids Patsy and Sissy and griped to Mom about their rotten husbands. They came over so Mom could chew them out and tell them to shape up and feed their girls and get them all to laughing.

In the afternoon him and his dad went down to the lake to work on the boat. As soon as the snow was gone every year or sometimes when there was still some rotten black ice at the roadsides, they got the boat ready for the water.

Your mother wants me to have a little talk with you, his dad said. She's worried.

Tell her to get off my back, he said.

Hey, buddy boy. Let's have a little respect for your mother. She ain't had it easy. She works hard. And she don't need grief from you.

He looked down so his dad wouldn't see how his eyes smarted like they did when he ran into the wind. Yeah, he said. I know.

You using protection? his dad said. With that girl?

I had the mumps. Remember? I can't make babies.

Mumps schmumps. You using protection?

He looked down again. He nodded. His face felt hot even in the cold wind off the lake. He was ashamed and he was proud.

He hated her that she made him cry. Still, he hadn't had to cry. Not really. He made himself do it so she would have to know how he loved her. She couldn't just shove him away, out of her life. He was in her life like a ball thrown from second into a mitt. She had to see that. It was funny. Acting like a pussy gave him power over her.

The crucifix stuck to his loose-leaf notebook and he worked it off. It stayed in one piece with blue threads stuck to the back. The missing chips were filled in with glue and the whole mess was coated with dried yellow glue. Jesus shellacked Christ, he thought. It looked like he had just been born and was covered with membrane, like in the health book. Or it looked like he was inside a big rubber full of dried stuff. He had bought the crucifix at this junior high fair at St. Mary's once. He and some guys had gone over to check out the parochial school chicks. This one in a plaid skirt just like everybody else's was selling beads and crosses and stuff out of a booth and he just went up and bought the crucifix. For no reason. He liked the way she looked. He didn't know Dulcie then. His parents didn't go to any church. They weren't any of them Catholic. Bless me Father for I have sinned, was what those Catholics said. He kept running his fingers over the thing now. The bumps of the nails. The diaper about to fall off.

The broken beard. That face, especially that face. If it hadn't been dark in the car, Dulcie would have seen that look, that sad and proud look of somebody who knew the real story.

She couldn't stop him from seeing her. In town he always drove by her parents' house. She wasn't there now, he knew that, but he saw the swingset in the yard where he had pushed her until the frame shook and she laughed and yelled how he was going to send her all the way over. He saw her face behind the storm door after their first time. Then her dad put up the screen door and he saw her face through the mesh like a picture in a newspaper. He saw her as she was before he knew her. This little girl with long straight hair. He saw her wearing little shiny black shoes and white ruffled socks like his sisters put on his nieces. He saw her running around in just her little flowered panties. At night sometimes he parked across the street and when her parents turned out the lights he let his pecker out and watched Dulcie run in the yard and sit on the swing and pump hard and fly over and around and again and again. If he didn't blink he could see her. Up pause around and down, pump hard, up pause around and down. If he didn't blink she stayed in the yard like a ghost and he could see the white house and the swing's chains right through her. Then he had to blink and she went inside and walked up the stairs to her room and took her panties off and climbed onto her bed and stretched out so white and thin he could see the blue quilt through her.

She couldn't stop him from seeing her. If she wasn't in, he shot the breeze with Emily. After dark he sat down against his tree. Sometimes he watched her come back just before eleven but he hadn't seen her leave and he figured she was sneaking out a back door. At school the girls by their lockers said *my honey* when they talked about their boyfriends. He didn't think Dulcie said *my honey* about him, with that know-it-all tone they had. He had yellow roses delivered to her and he signed the card Love, Your Honey. She was never in any more when he checked with Emily.

One time Emily said, Look, can't you figure it out, she is never going to be in anymore.

He showed her the pair of rings. Sometimes he wore them on his little finger. Can't you help me out here, gorgeous? he said. Can't you tell her how great I am?

One night he followed her and her roommate. They went into some building that turned out to be the library. He found them on the third floor. They were side by side at a table, way at the end. He worked his way up and down the rows of books. Finally he was almost right behind them. He watched them through a bookcase. Their backs were to him. They had papers and books spread out but they kept whispering more than reading. He couldn't make out what they said. The books on the shelf in front of him were about math. Trigonometry and Hyperbolic Functions. Vector Analysis. Statistics and Probability. He didn't want to look at them. He tried to breathe quiet. Nobody else was around. The place was dead. If he sat down across from her, she would pack up and walk away. He needed to touch her hair. He stood behind the bookshelf and rubbed his extraction. He watched her lean close to Katie like she was planning on kissing her. He could see her bra through her white blouse. Katie's too. He could feel her skin under her blouse and he could smell her.

He found out her roommate's last name from Emily. Katie Leeview. He thought he could write her a letter. But he didn't know how to say it so she would understand and explain to Dulcie how she had to see him. He wanted to say it exactly right but he couldn't hardly ask Mrs. Bundy to check it over for him.

He got his dad to give him gas money and he tooled over with WLS on all the way. He called from a pay phone in town. He stood in the dirty booth, not touching anything but the receiver, and watched the cars. It was getting to be convertible time. He liked being held in by the walls and roof of the Witch, though. Katie said she would meet him in the dormitory lounge without telling Dulcie.

She was sitting on this old-lady chair in a white blouse and a gray skirt. Dulcie told him they all had to dress up to go to the dining hall except Saturdays. They had to wade through the snow, even, in their skirts. Katie slammed her book closed when she saw him. She had long dark hair. If he didn't love Dulcie he would think Katie was prettier. She made him nervous, how she looked at him.

I don't know what you want, but—she started in.

Come on, he said, I'll take you for a ride. Get you out of here for a while.

She shook her head and he gave up and sat down on the old-lady chair beside her. I know what you want, she said. You want me to persuade a certain party to go out with you.

No —

But I'm not going to intercede for you. In fact, you have to give up on this fixation. This isn't healthy for either of you.

Now you're making me mad, he said. You two have been reading all that head-shrinker garbage. You think you know so much.

I'm not going to debate —

No, you listen. You can't figure me out. But that's cool. All you have to do is tell her to see me. Please—I'm going... I can't stand it. You have to tell her. I love her.

Doesn't it matter that she doesn't love you, though?

She will, he said, she has to. She will love me.

I'm going to be blunt here, she said. She is one smart girl and her life is going to mean something. She doesn't want to have anything to do with you. I *told* her you wanted to come over here and work on me.

You liar, he said. I can't hardly believe you lied to me.

Can hardly, she said.

You queer. You're queer for her. He knew something was wrong. She hadn't really told Dulcie he was coming. She just wanted her all to herself.

She got up and walked away but turned around halfway out of the lounge and came back. You are sick, she said. He grabbed her arm.

She jerked away. He hoped she'd have a bruise. If you ever come back here, she said, I'm telling Mrs. T and she'll call security. She'll call the police.

He held his hands open in front of him. How had it turned out like this? His breath suddenly snorted out like he was going to cry. You cunt, he said. You're the one that should leave her alone. But she was across the room. She ran her hand along the piano on her way out. Queer, he said. Homo cunt.

He watched her for another couple weeks and then he tried again. He could wait until summer if he had to. He could watch her sitting in the library reading. He could even watch her come back at eleven at night with some fruit. One evening he watched her and a whole pack setting up some kind of carnival. She hammered the same as she threw a softball. From the elbow. In the summer she would be at home and then she would be with him and she would understand what she was doing to him.

Oh give it up, Emily said when he tried again.

I thought you were on my side, he said. After all this, probably even ugly Emily wouldn't go out with him. Just give it a try, he said. Can't hurt.

Well, gloryoski, she said, what do you know. Dulcie says for you to go wait in the lounge.

He thought it might be a set-up. Maybe they were calling the fuzz. But he waited anyway. He wasn't doing a thing. What could they charge him with? Asking a girl to go for a ride? Being in love?

He almost didn't know her when she came down the couple steps into the room. He saw her run her hand along the big fancy piano just like her roommate and he looked again. She had cut her hair. She had on Bermudas and this big shirt like something of her father's. She wasn't a dog like Emily but she wasn't his pride, either. In four weeks she had lost her beauty. His heart was ripping along like he'd just run the 440. Ah God. He loved her. Thanks be to his glued-together Jesus Christ.

She acted like nothing was any different. Blithered on about her classes. About some poem which had this great athlete croaking in his prime. She said it to him but it didn't make sense. The faggot poet was saying it was better to die young if you're somebody than peter out and get old and be a has-been. What did he think of that? she wanted to know. He was a runner, how would he feel when somebody beat his record, would it be better to be dead young while you were still somebody?

Yeah, but I haven't set any records, he said.

But in theory, she said.

He thought of his father. He had been in the war at least. Now he sat in his recliner and watched the games and his wife cleaned other people's houses. I can see it, he said.

You'd stay young forever, she said. Maybe it's not so bad to think about dying now. Before things start to go wrong. You could hold onto your fields where glory does not stay. She was all worked up.

Hey, he said, what are you so mad about? I'm the one that's supposed to be mad, my girl won't see me all this time. But I'm not. I'm happy. You're here and we're just cruising along. I'll show you glory in a field, baby.

But when he parked in their spot in the boonies, she wouldn't get in the back seat. She turned sideways toward him in the bucket seat.

Listen, Lonnie, I'm just going to say it—she started in.

Come over here, he said and patted the console. She shook her head and leaned against the window. She looked like her father. Which she didn't usually. He had kind of buggy eyes and no chin.

I'm going to have a baby, she said.

Just like that. He couldn't say anything. Jesus shellacked Christ. Glory.

Finally he got out, I'll take care of you, baby. I'll marry you. He pulled her over to him and held her tight. I love you, he said and he rocked her back and forth, I love you, I love you.

I don't know what to do, she said into his shoulder.

It's okay, he said. I do. I know what to do.

He got the ring out of the glove box. First you put this on, he said. He slid the engagement ring with its row of diamond chips onto her finger. She held out her left hand. It was shaking. I have never been so happy in my entire long life, he said. He wanted to get out and run around his beautiful baby-making Witch, around and around a hundred times. He wanted to charge out into the field and vault the furrows and run back to her on his fleet foot. Like her poem said. On his fleet foot. He wanted to pull her up on top of the Witch and dance.

Let's celebrate, he said. He had to do something. He slid his hand up under her big shirt. But she gave him the famous elbow-block maneuver. Okay, he whispered, all right, then you touch me. He held her hand and pulled it down to the front of his white Levis. She let it rest there light and he thought he would go crazy if she didn't press if she didn't move and he put his own hand on top of hers to show her. Help me celebrate, he whispered. She pulled her hand out from under his like a kid playing that game of piled-up hands. Do you want to see it? he whispered and started to unzip. Do you want to see the power that makes babies? He took her hand and pulled it down but she resisted and tried to pull it away. Oh baby oh baby, he was saying, touch me oh please oh. He forced her hand down but she wouldn't do anything and he pushed her hand down hard and began moving against it.

Suddenly she yanked back her hand and jerked the door handle up so hard she could have snapped it off and practically fell out of the car.

He let her walk away. She couldn't go anywhere. She would have to come back. They were way out in the boonies. He was sick. He shouldn't have tried to make her. His pecker had shrunk up like it was trying to hide in shame.

He leaned his head back and closed his eyes. Shame. Years ago the Finch twins, Ricky and Jimmy he still remembered, had gone house to house selling these tickets. They made them with one of those stamp printing sets. They were selling them for two cents, for this circus they were putting on. His dad bought one and gave it to him and sent him down to the Finches'. His mother was in the sanitarium that year. His sisters were gone. The twins had some chairs lined up and a bunch of kids sitting on the grass too. He was probably the oldest. They were all just a bunch of little kids. He was nine or ten and he took one of the chairs.

The twins climbed up on their swingset and put their arms out. Ladies and gentlemen, they said together, presenting those daring acrobats the Flying Finches. All the little kids clapped. Ricky and Jimmy hung by their knees and grabbed hands upside down, they stood up on the swings and pumped hard and held an arm out. They bowed after each trick and the kids clapped. He had seen the same look that the twins had, on his sisters' faces once when they put on a magic show for their parents and the baby. Proud and smart aleck. Ain't I cute.

They goofed up the next trick. The kids started clapping anyway. He stood up and yelled boo. All the little kids started yelling at the twins boooo, boooo. They tried another trick but everybody just yelled boo, boo no matter what they did. He stood up on the chair and booed.

Then the twins' mother came out in the yard. He still could see her in her apron. She stood off-kilter with a baby riding on her hip. She looked straight at him and she said, What's the matter with you? You're big enough to act better. Shame on you

That's what his mother had said. You're a dirty boy. Shame.

Ricky and Jimmy gave up and went inside. They never did cry. All the kids went home.

Baby, I'm sorry, he said when Dulcie got back in. You get to me, baby, that's all. I was just so happy. I'll never do anything like that again. I promise you.

Driving the hundred miles back home, he floored it. He kept the radio off. He hated her that she wouldn't even put her hand on him. But her other hand was wearing his ring. That was what mattered. He loved her more than anybody had ever loved any girl. He and the Witch ripped through the night full of power and near town at every crossroad he turned off his lights and cruised with no shame right through all the intersections.

CHAPTER 3

For the past week I'd had a terrible, rancid taste in my mouth. I tried breath mints and Dentyne gum and everybody's mouthwash, I brushed and brushed my teeth, but nothing got rid of the taste. I hadn't even kissed Bruce in the lobby the other night, after we'd studied together and then met Katie and Josh at the snack bar.

I couldn't stand my long hair, and when Katie and I walked to town on Saturday, we went into a beauty shop and had our hair done. She just had her split ends trimmed, but I had mine cut short. It felt like a cap, and I missed the weight, but it had irritated me.

There was a dress I couldn't stand, either. My mother had made it, a burgundy printed shirtwaist, and it used to be one of my favorites. I gave it to Katie for keeps. And there was a pair of shoes, black flats with ties across the insteps. I could not stand those shoes.

I had to quit using Cover Girl make-up. The smell of it made me sick.

It was raining, and we had Swan Lake on low so we heard it through a veil of rain. It was late, and we were nearly asleep when Glenna walked in.

"I can't sleep," she said. "Something's bugging me and I can't just let it alone. I need to have a heart-to-heart with you two."

Katie got out of bed and shut off the music. "What's going on?" She cut a look at me. We figured Glenna was dropping out or flunking out. She was on probation from last semester. She'd probably get married now that Rick was graduating.

"Dulcie. This is about you. Maybe I'm way off. But when was the last time you had your period?"

We were barely awake. We heard the rain ticking on the window.

"I don't know," I said finally. "I never did keep track."

"I thought I was pregnant once," Glenna said. "Back when I was at boarding school."

"She can't be," Katie said. "She just can't be. I don't believe it."

I swallowed my terrible saliva. I knew something was wrong. "What did you do?" I asked Glenna.

Katie grabbed the burgundy print shirtwaist off the hanger in her closet and threw it on the floor. "I don't want your stupid dress," she said. She stomped on it. "I hate your stupid dress, I hate it, I hate it."

"Look, I went to the doctor," Glenna said. "Turned out, I wasn't knocked up after all. Maybe you aren't either."

I opened my desk drawer and took out a pair of scissors. I crouched beside Katie and stabbed the dress on the floor. I gave her the scissors and she stabbed the dress again and again until she broke the point off. We kneeled together, crying, and tore the dress apart.

"What are we going to do?" Katie said. Finals were in three weeks and then we'd have to go to our separate homes for the summer.

It was raining again. We watched the rain past our goldfish on the sill, watched it fall on the hills behind the dorm.

"What if I said," she said carefully, "those hills look like white elephants?"

"You've been doing your reading."

"You wouldn't want to ... ?"

"*And once they take it away*," I said in my reading voice, "*you never get it back*."

"Yeah, well, I knew that."

We knew the truth about my condition, but it was still theoretical, some melodrama happening to somebody on another floor, some book that would make us cry at the end, and we hardly believed it.

"Okay, try this," Katie said. "Suppose we get jobs somewhere for the summer. In New York or someplace far away. Then we tell our parents we're having a great learning experience and we want to stay longer."

"We could work in a ghetto. Or with retarded children. We'd have to be doing something meaningful."

"Then we could come back here. Or even go to school somewhere else."

"We'd still want our junior year abroad. Since we're supposing, we might as well keep France."

"Okay. So we find this lonely old woman. She lives in a big house just a few blocks from here. She's all alone and she's about to lose her house because she can't pay the property tax."

"And the chambries save the day! They rent the upstairs. They keep her company and pay enough so she can hold on to the house."

"Yeah, and she can baby-sit while we're in class."

We hadn't said the word *baby* until then. Still, we went on.

"The chambries buy a second-hand crib," I said. "They paint it yellow. They fix up a nursery, paint it, make curtains. If it's yellow, it'll work for a boy or a girl."

"Of course, we'll know by then."

I counted months on my fingers. Oh, really, nothing had happened inside me. Had it? It was impossible. I wasn't going to grow gigantic, with something live growing inside me.

"But yellow's nice," Katie said. "Yellow's good. It's all right. We like yellow."

"I hate myself."

"The chambries buy little undershirts and diapers. Rubber pants. Sleepers with feet."

"I'm sorry. I am so so sorry."

"Okay," Katie said. "Okay, we'll get them diaper service."

I put my face against my arm to let my sweater sleeve absorb the tears, then looked at my poor poor Katie. "The chambries buy a mobile for the crib," I said. "They buy a goddamned teddy bear."

Glenna made me an appointment and borrowed Rick's car. "Say you're me," she said. "I used my name. I don't care what anybody thinks."

Outside the clinic a nurse stood arguing with an old man leaning on a chrome walker. He picked it up and stamped it soundlessly on the pavement. "Maybe it's not what you think," the woman said.

We sat together in the waiting room for a half hour before Glenna's name was called. Following a nurse toward the horrors in the labyrinth beyond the swinging door, I looked back quickly, one last look, at Glenna and Katie sitting among all the swollen women in their pastel maternity smocks, resting their hands on their bellies. I was leaving them in their girlhood, I thought, and when I came back, I would be different. I almost turned around and went back to sit with them, safe and collegiate, so sorry for myself I was choked up again and the nurse took my elbow and gave me a Kleenex.

I had to take off all my clothes behind a curtain and then lie on a table with a sheet over me. Sweat ran from my armpits and pattered on the paper covering the table. I pulled the sheet over my head. Naked and dead. All I needed was a tag on my toe. I lay there with my eyes open against the blurred white of the sheet, playing dead, until I heard the door open. Anyway, the dead didn't sweat.

The doctor looked at my face and said, "Is your mother here with you? She could come in, if you want."

I only shook my head. Anything that came out would only confirm that I wasn't old enough to be doing this.

His rubber-gloved hands went to work.

"Breasts swollen or painful?" he asked.

"No," I said.

"Nauseated?"

"A little."

"Well, call the lab after three days. But I'll tell you right now it's going to be positive." He handed me an envelope of tiny white pills. "For nausea. You can get dressed now." He shook his head. "And tell your mother," he said.

There was a spring dance the Saturday before finals week. Josh and Bruce had mailed an invitation to us. They'd made the card themselves. On the front were two elegant men in tails, bowing, saying: May we have the honor of escorting you, and the inside said *To the orgy* and was peopled with a dozen little half-naked characters running around with their tongues hanging out and their eyes crossed.

Katie and I shopped for new dresses. Mine was a pink waffled material, scalloped along the bottom.

Twice during the dance I left Bruce to swallow little white pills in the bathroom.

The lights dimmed for the last dance until we were moving slowly in the dark. Bruce held me close. Somewhere in the crowded dark, Josh was holding Katie. I was nearly asleep against Bruce's shoulder. *And once they take it away, you never get it back.* But who were *they*? The only *it* I wanted to keep was this slow darkness, where my college life with Katie would remain. When the lights came back up, all the couples swayed to a stop and stood holding each other. They were blurred, watery, suddenly men and women, male and female, face to face, body to body, penis to opening, and I blinked in the midst of all the coupled life.

The four of us went first to the men's dorm, and Katie and I waited in the commons room while they changed. Then they waited in our lounge while we put on shorts and sandals and knit shirts.

The post-dance party was at a lodge in a woods somewhere. It had one large room with a concrete floor, set up with a stereo and records, and a horse trough filled with ice and bottles. We danced fast. Josh and Bruce drank beer, and Katie and I sipped Cokes.

Later Bruce led me outside, into the woods. He pulled me down against a tree and kissed me. The beer made him taste like grain—like Lonnie.

"Dulcie, doll." His breath was jerky in my ear. "Oh Dulcie, Dulcie."

It didn't matter now. I almost laughed, thinking of puppies in a litter fathered by different dogs. I didn't think it worked that way with humans. And was I going to spend all the rest of my life with Lonnie as my only experience? Bruce's hands cupped my breasts. They went under my shirt and unhooked my bra. His palms rubbed my breasts, gently though his breath was fast, gently and slowly, unlike Lonnie's hard hands. This was my last chance. Now. Now or I would never have anybody else, only Lonnie. I lay back on the ground, and his hands moved softly on me, smoothing me down.

Then I rolled away and sat up. "No," I said. "I can't. I'm sorry. I want to go back in now."

"Why not? Oh doll."

"It isn't you. I can't tell you."

"Oh," he said, disappointed understanding in his voice. "I get it. It's... that time, isn't it?"

I let him think it was my period. It was funny to imagine guys talking about that among themselves, maybe the way we talked about wet dreams: all these secrets hidden under clothes and sheets. I had done it—or had it done to me—I had conceived, but it was still all shivery mystery.

I had conceived. I was knocked up. I had a loaf in the oven. As my dad said. I was in the family way. I was expecting. As my mother said. I was pg, as we used to whisper in high school. I was with child, like Mary. Male and female he created them. Now Lonnie knew Dulcie, and she conceived and bore a son. And thus. It was all wicked and holy.

"I'm sorry," I told Bruce. "I really am." We helped each other up and brushed the pine needles off, and I held him, full of regret. I could almost feel the embryo inside me, curled up, like a shrimp, naked and veined. I couldn't let Bruce touch my child. Nobody must touch him.

CHAPTER 4

On Saturday his mother was doing the Goldbergs' house. Second richest Jews in town, his dad said. On Tuesdays she did the Gerbers'. First richest Jews in town. The Tigers were beating Baltimore and they were working on a six pack together. Boog Powell struck out.

Dulcie and me are getting married, he said.

Look at that McLain, his father said. Ain't seen his like since Dizzy Dean. He drained the Bud. Well, that's fine, he said. She's a pretty girl. A classy girl. But not too classy for the likes of the Saxbes, huh? Is she pregnant, son? His little blue eyes watched for a lie.

It'll be all right now. She wants to marry me now.

His father made a fist and punched his shoulder and he had to catch himself from falling off his kitchen chair. You aren't so dumb, are you? his father said. His eyes looked milky. You son of a gun, he said.

My pappy was a pistol, he said. Dad—I can't hardly just say it—but, just thanks. He couldn't say he always looked for his father at the meets and always found him. Home and away. He couldn't say he loved this thin little man. Benjamin the senior.

His sister Suzie brought Leonard and the girls over for supper. His mother fried hamburgers. He messed around outside with Patsy and Sissy. He galloped around the trailer with one and then the other on his back. Enough, brats, he said at last. You want Uncle Lonnie to lose his lunch?

Inside Suzie was telling their mother how Leonard kept getting calls from his ex-wife. She wants more money, Suzie said.

Blood out of a turnip, Leonard said.

What she really wants, Suzie said, *is* your turnip. She laughed but she was mad.

Later his father drove them back to their own trailer and Lonnie had to tell his mother. He cracked a beer. Guess what, he said.

She was at the sink doing the supper dishes. You drink too much beer, she said. Your dad needs to quit buying it for you.

Yeah, well, he said and chugged half the can and swallowed the beer belch. Guess what. Dulcie and me are getting married.

She didn't even turn away from the skillet she was scouring out. And I'm Queen Elizabeth, she said. That fancy gal isn't going to marry you.

You don't think I'm much of nothing, do you? he said. Marie and Suzie are hot shit on a gold platter. To you I'm just plain shit.

She whipped around and smacked him across the face. Soapy water flew. Keep that filth out of your mouth in my kitchen, she said. He tasted greasy dishwater. Now you tell me this, she said. Have you made her pregnant?

He shook his head. It ever occur to you somebody might just love me? I'm not dirt to everybody?

You liar, she said. You can't lie to me. Her hand went up again and he ducked. Couldn't keep your stiff little prick to yourself, could you. Could you.

You didn't do this way to Marie, he said. Everybody knows Mitzi wasn't no premature birth. Then he was sorry he said it. She dropped down in his father's chair. Where she never sat. She was crying.

Look, you're my son, she said, and I know you. You don't know some things. And Davis treats Marie good. And my grandbaby. But you with that girl—no. She rubbed her face with her apron. Now, I can ask Mrs. Goldberg. He's a doctor. They maybe can get it set up. I'll have to use up my stash. But you—you're going to get yourself a job and you're going to put back every cent. I don't get down on my hands and knees for the likes of all those proud ladies to clean up your messes.

You're saying—? Oh no. We're getting married. We are.

Just what do you think her folks are going to say about that? Come to that, they can pay to get rid of it. They're rolling in it, what I hear. And it isn't like their precious girl didn't spraddle her legs.

He was shaking. He crushed the beer can. He hated her. He wanted to say, Go back to the nuthouse where you belong. She'd disappeared on him and he hated her. He hooked the rest of the last six-pack out of the refrigerator and stepped quietly out of the trailer. His hands shook with need. He got in the Witch and started her up and backed out like he was underwater. Dulcie was his precious girl. He got to the lake and figured he still had enough gas to get back in the morning. He was out of money. His precious girl would keep him out of any nuthouse. His dad and him were always having to cut slimy ropes of water lily off the outboard. He had his knife under the car seat and he would do it in the daylight. He got in the back seat and drank the rest of the beer. The last can was warm but he finished it anyway. The lake smelled rich and deep even with his windows rolled tight. He saw his own body wrapped in ropes of lily upright at the bottom of the black water and he slept.

He found them a Yellow Pages doctor for the blood tests and they went together. Her parents didn't know yet. The doctor sat them down one at a time in a chair in this hallway. He liked the smell of the place. Like the janitor's closet at school. He liked the rubber tube snugged tight on his arm and even the smooth needle. He watched Dulcie's face get white when it was her turn.

He'd made them an appointment at this little Baptist church on the lake road. The minister said they had to come out first. The counseling is standard practice, the man said.

Haven't you got it down yet? he said. That why you need practice?

The man laughed over the phone. They say practice makes perfect. See you at three, Mr. Saxbe. You and your fiancée.

At the empty church the man took them to a room downstairs. The walls were white boards and the floor had the exact same tile as his bedroom. The minister turned a chair backwards and sat across from them with his chin on the chair back. The room must have been a Sunday School classroom. There was a Jesus on the wall standing by this door that didn't have a doorknob. There was this banner over the picture. So faith, hope, love abide, these three; but the greatest of these is love. 1 Corinthians 13.

He held Dulcie's hand. He nodded at the wall. I like that word, he said. Abide. That's a good word.

The minister was this plump man with thick white hair. So you want to get married, he said and squeezed his lips together. He tapped on the back of the chair.

We were hoping in a couple weeks, he said. We were thinking Saturday. The twenty-seventh.

What about your own church?

Oh no, Dulcie blurted out. My parents would die.

The minister checked her over. Ah, he said.

My dad used to bring me here, Lonnie said. To Bible School.

I guess that would be before my time here, the man said. He was watching Dulcie. Why do you want to get married now? he said. I like to urge young people to wait a bit.

We love each other, Lonnie said. He didn't like the way the man said Young People. Like they were in Vacation Bible School. Sitting on those kiddie chairs listening to the stories. The teacher holding up the pictures. Look at Joseph's Coat of Many Colors. What's David holding? That's right, a little lamb.

I'm sure you believe you do, the man said. He put his chin down on the chair back and looked at Dulcie.

It's because I'm pregnant, she said. As I'm sure you've figured out. She pulled her hand away and wiped her eyes with her fists.

Ah children, children, the man said and closed his eyes.

The next morning he picked Dulcie up. She had a bag of beach stuff. I told my mom we were going over to Lake Michigan, she said.

You haven't told them yet, he said. The less time they had to think about it, the better, he thought.

I can't, she said. Maybe I'll just run away.

I got me a job, he said. Over in Waterton. I told you I'm going to take care of you.

My mother hates my hair short like this, she said.

Listen, it'll grow.

Then I'll just have it cut again.

He didn't really like her hair, either. He liked showing her off with her long blonde hair that made her prettier than she was.

I thought we'd go over to Waterton now, he said. Find us an apartment.

I guess we're really going to do it, aren't we? she said. What's the job you found?

Walsh Brothers. I get to sell shoes. I get to fondle ladies' feet all day. Are you jealous?

Waterton was a beach town. It had two hotels and bunches of cottages for the tourists and a block of downtown. A Sears catalog store, a drugstore, Walsh Brothers Shoes, and a cafe on one side. A movie theater, Judy's Girls and Women, which was a clothing store not a whorehouse, a laundrymat, an Ace Hardware, and an empty store with whitewashed windows on the other. The whole town was gritty.

They bought a newspaper in the drugstore and sat up at the counter. Two coffees, gorgeous, he said to the woman.

Don't you gorgeous me, she said. She was grinning away.

They read through the apartment listings in the classifieds and circled the three that were furnished and cheap. They sipped at the coffee. I don't really drink coffee yet, Dulcie whispered. He didn't like the black taste, either.

The first place was in an old house. The front part was a chiropractor's office. The back three rooms had been made into a small apartment. They checked out the other two places. Which both turned out to be filthy. Back at the little apartment he put down a deposit and said they'd move in at the end of the month.

He drove along the old shore road away from town. Half the big old summer houses were boarded up. Years of blowing sand had blasted most of the paint off. He stopped at a pulloff and locked the Witch and led Dulcie over dunes to the beach. The sand was gray in the late afternoon. The beach grass made cuts on her bare legs.

Put the ring on, he said. I want to see you wear the ring. She had worn it to the doctor's and to the church.

I hid it in my room, she said. She took off her sandals and walked down to the hard wet sand. He watched her, in his pants and hard shoes.

She waded into the water to her knees and turned around and looked at him.

Maybe I'll just keep going, she said.

He watched her go. She walked the way people did in water. Dragging their heavy legs through the slow water and turning their shoulders like the air was heavy too. The water hit her Bermudas and she kept going. Lake Michigan was clear and clean and the bottom was nothing but ripples of sand. Not like Chippewa Lake with its mucky bottom and its dark water and the slimy weeds. You hardly ever saw fish in Lake Michigan. Now and then little fish like sparks flying. Dulcie was up to her waist.

Come back here, he called. You get back here. Dul-cie.

She walked straight out up to her chest and up to her shoulders and up to her chin. He took off his cordovans. She ducked her head under and he whipped off his belt and started to unbutton his pants but then ran into the cold water with his clothes on. He hurdled the waves until the water was too deep and then he Spitzed out, blowing and sucking, and when he saw her head right in front of him he grabbed her. She snaked out of his arms and headed out again. He caught her again and they wrestled and he couldn't tell if they were playing or fighting. She spurted out of his hands like a bar of soap.

Suddenly she rose up in the water. Like magic. Like Jesus. She was slick with the water running down her body.

She laughed and held out her arms. The sun was going down behind her. She was standing on a sandbar. She was laughing and shivering halfway out to the horizon.

CHAPTER 5

"Man on floor," girls kept calling out as their fathers and brothers and boyfriends came to carry out their trunks and boxes. I heard Katie's voice, "Man on floor," but then when she didn't open our door, I looked out into the hallway and there was Josh prostrate on the carpet. "Man on Floor," he proclaimed, as if he were a work of art. He was driving Katie home on his way to Colorado.

Bruce had already left for the East. He had a job at a boys' camp. I hadn't seen him after the dance. He'd left a note at the desk for me, with the address of Camp Cayuga and a quick Bye, Doll, Write me? If I were returning in the fall, we'd probably continue to use each other benignly, as acceptable, good dates, as easy doubles for Katie and Josh, liking each other without really talking.

Katie and I ignored the fact that I wasn't coming back. We divided up the clothes and records we'd bought together without acknowledging that we wouldn't share them any more, never take turns with the big blue sweater, never listen to the cello concerto in our dark room. We would write, we would call long-distance when our parents let us, we even planned for me to take the bus to Minnesota to visit.

"Man Hefting Ton of Bricks," Josh said, carrying out a box of Katie's books. He walked out in slow motion. "Male Descending Hall."

When I saw that Katie was going to cry, I grabbed my purse and a book left over from my abnormal psych paper. "Just—don't," I said. "I have to take this back to the library."

"I can't stand to go away," she said.

"You'll be back. We'll see each other. Quit it. It's time to gallop off into the sunset."

"There you go with Glenna's horses."

"It was unbridled passion," I said. "That was my problem. But who ever heard of bridled passion?" I wished it had been passion, something ecstatic in the back seat, instead of my inert body spread like the starfish we'd dissected in Biology 4.

"Write to me. Tomorrow. I mean it."

"I will," I said. "I'm going to the library now. Oh, goodbye." I stepped blindly down the hall and ran into Josh.

"Uh oh," he said. "Woman with Leaking Eyeballs."

"Goodbye, Josh," I said and ran on. Goodbye, goodbye, goodbye cruel world.

I swallowed another little white pill at the Sunday dinner table, not hiding it from them, but they didn't ask. Tomorrow the marriage license would be registered in the paper. People would see it and call in congratulations, wanting to know the real reason Lindsay and Walter White's good, smart-as-a-whip daughter was quitting school and getting married. I had to tell them before the neighbors did. Sitting there with my mother's Sunday dinner of stuffed pork roast and green bean casserole, with the gravy my father made—why did men make the gravy?—sitting there at the solid oak table with the silverware, the silver salt and pepper shakers, the yellow linen napkins, the butter dish, the basket of rolls, the glasses of iced tea, sitting there with my parents in their church clothes, although my mother had changed her heels for slippers, with everything clinking and real, I knew I wouldn't run away with Katie or with Lonnie, and I knew I wouldn't kill myself for shame.

The vapors of the stories—of flight, even of dulcet death—had kept me in a trance even while my body threw up and wrote exams and wore its spring clothes. Eating watermelon in the dining hall, I repeated my father's joke about swallowed seeds growing, and Katie said, "Well, that'd be one way to explain it." We'd laughed because we knew but didn't believe I was going to blow up like the enormous women in the clinic's waiting room, because we were entranced. Now the chandeliered light, the fork handle, the tablecloth, now everything was textured, even them—my father's shaved face and creased knuckles, my mother's teased and sprayed hair, her kid-leather wrinkles, my linsey-woolsey mother. And I had to bring on my own coarseness.

I waited until my father finished his second piece of rhubarb pie. "I have a surprise," I said. I held out my left hand with the ring on it.

"What?" my mother said. "Whose is that?"

"Well, it's mine."

"But who gave that to you? You didn't tell me about anything serious."

"Lonnie and I are getting married."

"Lonnie," she said. "You don't want to marry him."

"Next Saturday," I said, looking away from the slimy pink rhubarb strands, sick. "We're getting married next Saturday. It'll be in the paper tomorrow."

"Oh God, what will everybody think?" she said and paused while she realized what everybody would think. "You aren't pregnant, are you?"

"No," I said.

"Walter?"

He pushed his dessert plate away and wiped his mouth. "Well then, you aren't getting married next Saturday. Keep the ring if you want, and then if you still want to go through with it after you've finished school, we'll see. But you are not getting married now."

"We have an apartment. We had blood tests. We're doing it."

He stood up, banging his legs on the table, and grabbed my arm. "Get upstairs to your room. We'll stop this right now."

My mother was crying. "You are pregnant, aren't you? You might as well tell me now."

I thought about saying: You promised you'd always love me no matter what. But I only nodded.

My father's fingers were tight around my arm. He yanked me into the living room. He sat down hard on the piano bench and pulled me over his lap and spanked me. I could hardly feel his palm cushioned by clothes but then he flipped up my dress and slip. Like a child I tried to get my hands over my bottom. He caught them in one hand and hit me and hit me. As if from above, I saw my blue underpants and garter belt and nylons. I stopped struggling and listened to his hoarse breath, and finally he shoved me off.

My father went across the yard to the garage and stayed there all afternoon. I pictured him in the oily dark. The garage had an attic where I'd raised mice for a biology project in high school, and the musk of straw and rodent had sifted down and mixed with cut grass souring on the lawn mower and oil-soaked sawdust on the concrete floor.

"Little hot pants," my mother said to me when he shut the door.

I walked heavily up the stairs to my room, hot and heavy as if I were enormous already. I lay on top of my blue and white checked bedspread, exhausted and huge, in my blue and white childhood room. I remembered only one other spanking from my father, years ago when I kicked the piano. "I hate that stupid piano," I'd yelled and kicked it. Why had I been so wild? I remembered that my mother was making me practice. If we're going to pay for lessons, you're darned well going to practice, she said. They'd bought me the baby grand piano for my twelfth birthday. Later I thought my mother had just liked the elegance of a baby grand in her living room. But I had loved the piano. I loved my book of études and my Beethoven sonatas. I set the metronome for practicing: presto, allegro, moderato, andante, adagio, larghetto, largo. I loved the words and the steady ticking, safely set under tempo until my fingers knew a piece. When I was alone in the house, I would play without the metronome, setting my own timing, allowing what was called expression into the music. My hands would be infused with feeling the way saliva rushes at hunger.

One day after school, pounding the Rachmaninoff third concerto, I realized I wasn't going to grow up to be a concert pianist. I could play, I was good technically, I performed well in recitals. But that one day I heard my passionless playing and saw my foolish face full of juvenile transport. I continued the lessons, but the day of the spanking I'd been wild with my mediocrity, yelling at my mother who had said to sit down on that piano bench and practice for a half-hour, kicking the beautiful piano until my father spanked me and diverted my fury to him. I was so glad his handprints stayed on my bottom. In my room I'd pulled down my pants again and looked over my shoulder at my red buttocks in the vanity's mirror.

Now lying face up on my bedspread, exhausted by the weight of the shame, I slept, and after I woke, sweaty in my church clothes still, I changed into Bermudas and went downstairs. My mother sat at the kitchen table with the phone book and a notepad. Her face was blotchy but dry. She got right up and hugged me.

"I'm sorry about that hot pants dig," she said. "It's just that I know what it's like. Your father knows, too. Your father—he's a highly sexed man. I tried to warn you."

"What's Dad doing?" I turned him back into a dad.

"He's out in the garage He won't let me in. He's just sitting there in the dark. On that orange crate. I looked through the window and he's just sitting there—crying. He used to get angry. More than you ever knew. But I've never heard him cry before."

"I'm kind of surprised," I said. "I mean, I knew it'd be hard to take." I'd assumed that she'd do the crying for them both, that he'd continue his mild silence while my mother suffered the pain.

"Sit down," she said. "I've been sitting here making a list. We need to be practical here. First of all, are you sure you're pregnant? Lots of things can cause a girl to stop menstruating, you know."

When I told her about the clinic and the test, she said, "Even so. Tomorrow we'll get you in to see someone. Let's be sure before we get to the point of no return."

We went down her list. Call the Saxbes. Arrange the small, family-only wedding. I told her about the Lake Chippewa Baptist church and she added Call Minister to her list. Order flowers. "You can at least have a corsage," she said. "We'll order him a boutonniere."

"It's not the prom, Mom."

"At least it can be nice," she said. "This is your wedding. Now. We'll go through the house. There's enough extra around here that we can set you up in linens and dishes. There are those curtains boxed up in the attic. What size windows does that apartment have?"

I'd turned into someone aloof, apart from her, not just *daughter*, a separate body with secret sex. Her response was to grow brisk—and also intimate. Now I was an unattached outsider who might be told *her* secrets. Now that she knew I had hot pants, I was another woman and Walter White was more her highly sexed husband than my father.

"Mom—I know nothing's going to be the same ever again."

I wondered if Lonnie would have whiskers in the morning, if he'd make the gravy.

"Do you remember the priest when you were in the hospital?" she said. "In second grade, when they thought you had leukemia?"

"I remember a nun. She must have been a nurse. She was trying to make me take a huge pill and I couldn't swallow it. I was crying and gagging and she held my mouth closed. I remember finally a doctor came in and made her stop. He held out his hand and I spit out the slobbery pieces of pill."

"But you don't remember the priest? I didn't want you to. I came to your room once when it wasn't visiting hours, and a priest was in there with you. He was stroking you all over, your hair and your arms and your legs. You were lying propped against pillows, not making a sound, with tears running down your face."

"I don't remember that at all."

"I didn't want you to. I went out and bought you a big stuffed rabbit. And your first watch."

"Dale Evans. I remember that. It had a gun in her hand that went up and down with the seconds. I loved that watch. What ever happened to that watch?"

"I reported the priest to the hospital administration," she said. "They got rid of him. There had been other complaints before. I don't think he ever did anything but touch you."

"What did Dad do?"

"Oh, you were his little girl. How could I tell him? I was... well, I was afraid."

It was funny that it was that nun holding my mouth closed I remembered, that and the time a nurse brought in something covered on a tray and said she was going to give me an enema and I got all excited because I thought she said animal.

"You saved me," I told my mother. "You and Dale."

CHAPTER 6

His parents and his sisters, Suzie and Marie, and their husbands and kids sat in the first two rows on one side. Her parents sat on the other side. He couldn't stand still. He held up his hand and watched the fingers twitch.

The broad playing the piano shut up and Dulcie came out this door at the side. She had on a pink dress not white. The bottom of the dress was wavy. Like Mitzi's birthday dress. He almost expected she'd have on little socks with lace and black shoes like his sisters put on their kids when they wanted to look like somebody. He stepped toward the center to meet her. He touched her hand and she moved sideways away from him.

The minister said his words. Dulcie's father stood up and said, Her mother and I do. Do you, Benjamin Lon Saxbe, Jr., take her to sleep with in your own bed. To have waiting for you closed up safe in your own place. To carry your son. Until death. He had already taken her and that night he would take her again and they would make the baby over again. I now pronounce you.

Afterwards her father handed him an envelope with two hundred dollars in it. Marie butted right in and said, We're going to toast the bride and groom with champagne over at our house. Won't you please join us?

Well, la de da. He was glad, though. He had showed all of them. Suzie and Marie hadn't hurt him none. Probably they didn't remember, even. Ancient history. He wanted to kiss Dulcie smack in front of all of them and show them. See, Mother? See?

The Witch was already loaded. When they got in, she wanted to know if they could stop at that phone booth by the Texaco and she could call Katie. Oh what the hell, he said and got her a pile of change in the station. He sat there behind the wheel and watched her hump-backed and wiping her eyes inside the booth. Then he watched the goldfish in the bowl on the floor. They belonged to her and that damn Katie. They probably wouldn't survive the trip to Waterton.

This couch was already here, Marie was telling Dulcie's parents when they got to her and Davis's. I don't like this green, do you? I'm going to get the landlord to trade it for this white loveseat I saw at this other rental he has. And I'll get one of them plastic covers. I don't believe in keeping your kids off the furniture, do you?

Dulcie's mother looked blanked out. I can't even remember when mine was that age, she said. You might as well let them do what they want. Dulcie had told him the doctor gave them both tranquilizers. She didn't take any but her mother did. Neither of the mothers had cried like women were always supposed to do at a wedding.

Davis popped a champagne bottle and the women shrieked like somebody'd been shot. Go get Benj, Davis said.

Their fathers were outside looking at the Whites' new Super Sport. Their heads were down and they scuffed at the gravel like they were thinking about racing. He'd have given his left nut to hear what they were saying about him.

Inside beside Dulcie on the green couch he put his arm around her for them all to see and Davis brought over glasses of champagne. Even Dulcie took a couple swallows. Patsy and Sissy climbed over and tried to get on her lap. Suzie said, Now leave Aunt Dulcie alone, and then let them climb around her until Dulcie's champagne spilled on her wedding dress.

He pulled her up and announced, We've got a drive ahead of us. Guess we'd better hit the road.

Yeah, Leonard said. And I know you want to get a good night's sleep. He jabbed his elbow at Davis.

Dulcie blushed and everybody shut up.

Well, folks, he said, it's been real. It was his mother's expression.

It was an hour over to Waterton. He turned on WLS and Dulcie closed her eyes. She held the fish bowl between her feet. He touched the stiff blotch on her lap. Hope the brat didn't wreck your dress, he said. You sure looked pretty, baby. The water in the fish bowl vibrated. The fish shook like they were being electrocuted.

He carried her into the apartment. She kicked and said, Don't be corny.

He held her up and kissed her hard.

Let's bring the gear in first, she said.

They carried in her suitcases, his dad's old duffel, the fish bowl, and boxes of dishes, pans, towels, sheets, and junk from her mother. Dulcie lined up the wedding presents on the kitchen table: a set of glasses in three sizes from his sisters, nice plastic dishes for four from his parents, a toaster from some friend of hers named Glenna, and a box of records from that for god's sake Katie. Beethoven Edition, it said on the box, 9 Symphonien.

She must have got a scratch-and-dent discount, he said. Look at that, symphonies isn't spelled right.

She gave him such a pitying look he couldn't let it go. Wiener Philharmoniker, he read. Who wants to listen to a bunch of wieners?

The living room was going to be the bedroom too. He took the cushions off the couch and pulled it open. Dulcie dug around in a box for sheets and made the bed. She tucked and smoothed and took her time. She let her dress ride up when she bent over. He watched her as long as he could stand it. She hadn't let him touch her ever since the night she'd told him and he'd been so full he wanted to jump up on top of the car. Finally he turned her around and unzipped the dress. The *wedding* dress. She held up her arms and he pulled it over her head. She stood beside the bed and let him take off her slip, her bra, and her panties. Everything under the dress was white. The cherry bride, he said. He had never seen her before, not really, just messing around in the back seat in the dark. It's going to be different now, he said. God, I love looking at you. She stood still with her arms down and let him look. He didn't see how there could be any baby in her.

Then she undressed him while he stood as still as he could. He was shaking. He had to help with his underwear. Well what have we here? she said when he straightened back up. She put her hand around it and he twitched like the fish vibrating in the electric water.

You didn't do this with any of those others, did you? he whispered.

She put her arms around his back. You know I didn't.

He laid her down. He kissed her neck and entered her. Like sliding home. He pumped and the bed whoomped like his feet on a dirt track, one stroke two strokes three strokes four, and at six he blew.

Just like that champagne bottle popping, he said when he could breathe. Her breath was hot against his shoulder. Did you come? he said but she didn't answer.

When he rolled off, she got up and went into the bathroom. She came back to bed wearing baby doll pajamas with blue flowers on them. He put on his underwear and pulled the sheet up over them.

She moved close and put her head on his chest. I wanted to buy a sexy nightgown for the occasion, she said. But I could hardly ask my mother for money for a negligee, could I?

I'll buy you one, he said.

She squirmed against him. You know what? she said, like she was surprised. I love you.

He woke before dawn. She was flat on her stomach. Gritty wind hit the window by the bed. He got up to pull the shade.

The goldfish on the windowsill slept near the bottom of the bowl. If fish slept. They looked faded like Katie and Dulcie had kept them out in the sun. He could practically see through them like they had penlight bulbs screwed inside them. The light showed the half-circles of scales on their sides and he could see all the way through the fins. They looked more than half dead. The water had a gray scum on top. These fish weren't much longer for this world. One of them had a dark ropy cord hanging from underneath it.

He carried the bowl into the bathroom and locked the door. Slowly he poured the stagnant water into the toilet bowl. The fish pepped up and started swimming. When the water was gone they flipped around in the colored gravel. He dumped them in the toilet and flushed. They whirled around, dead or alive, he couldn't say.

In the morning he'd comfort Dulcie. For fish, they lived a long time, he'd say. I didn't want you to wake up on our first day and see them belly-up.

CHAPTER 7

After the little wedding, where nobody cried or threw rice, I called Katie. She knew what I was doing, we'd been writing letters fast and furious, as my mom said, but I needed to say farewell and draw a line between the girl I'd been and the wife I'd become.

"What was it like?" she wanted to know. "The ceremony."

"Nothing much. What you'd expect. I wore that pink dress I got for the dance, remember? Can you believe I wore that dress?"

"Well, why not? It's a good dress. Listen, are you going to be all right? I worry about you all the time. I'm a mess. Alex keeps calling but I don't want a thing to do with him. Or any guy, to tell the truth."

"It was the only thing to do. It's the only way to keep my baby. And he really loves me. He'll do anything to make me happy."

"You're crying on your wedding day."

I turned my back to poor Lonnie waiting in the car. "I'm sorry. I don't want to do this. I'm just sorry."

The wife settled in. The husband was sent off every morning with percolator coffee and a kiss. All the new glasses, the stainless flatware, the perfectly good pans, and the ugly plastic dishes were organized in the little kitchen's drawers and cupboards. Their clothes were suspended in the single closet, first his then hers.

The wife folded up the marriage bed in the morning, making it disappear under the sofa cushions. She showered and set her hair after he left, so he wouldn't see her in rollers. Every day she prepared a meal for two and when he came home from work they sat at the little kitchen table and ate awkwardly together, every slurp and clink enormous, as if eating were more intimate than what they did in the bed.

The wife arranged everything in tidy rows on the shelves. Her life was over, except for the living of it.

Every evening after supper we sat side by side on the sofa and watched the old basement television set my parents had given us. We watched comedy, mystery, variety, whatever was on, waiting, killing time, only waiting until it was time to open up the sofa. The evenings were thick with the unspoken waiting for Lonnie to climb on top of me.

One evening I switched on the end table lamp and moved over with a book. Lonnie slid over next to me. "Watch this show with me," he said.

"I'd really rather read," I said. "You might try it sometime." I shouldn't have said that, I knew, I meant to convert him, and that wasn't the way.

"I told you I would. Just not right now." He leaned across me and turned off the light. Then he got up and turned off the television. "Right now," he said, "old buddy Pecker wants to find a home."

He leaned the sofa cushions against the green easy chair and pulled the bed open. We took off our clothes and got under the sheet. I closed my eyes and pretended we were in the back seat together, parked in the middle of dark nowhere, with snow outside and steam inside. He was kissing me slowly, our tongues touching, and he was kissing my breasts and stroking my thighs.

In the bed he pecked my mouth and climbed onto me. His buttocks moved up and down for a minute, then tensed. My back was pressed against the rod under the thin mattress. He rolled off.

"Did you come?" he whispered. "Oh baby. You don't know how Pecker loves his Pussy. But I'm telling you."

The library card catalog listed the books, but they weren't on the shelf. With my left hand and its rings plainly on the desk and my face as blank as I could hold it, I showed the librarian a list of books.

"These can't be checked out," she said. "You have to use them here." *Use* them, she said, instead of read them. I felt my face flush, but I waited while she unlocked a cabinet. I hadn't meant to take them back to the apartment anyway.

"I'm working on a paper," I said. "For my psych course." The closest school was Katie's and my college, sixty miles away. She handed over the books and I carried them to a table in plain view. *Human Sexuality, Successful Marriage, Psychology of Sexuality*—I scanned their tables of contents, turned to the indexes, pretended to take notes. I was studying, doing what I knew how to do very well: memorizing and connecting, lifting out the odd pieces and writing them into sense. But I was faking it. Here were these hot clinical words—penis, clitoris, foreplay, orgasm, frigidity, ejaculation—but context evaporated as if they were mysterious scrawlings on a prescription pad. They didn't have any connection to the mess of me and Lonnie under the sheets, Pecker loves Pussy, the slimy wet spot, morning sickness, the stink of Cover Girl makeup, gestation.

Dear Chambrie,

You can't imagine how I miss you. You probably have a pretty good idea, but at least you have your classes. Are you rooming with Glenna? I walk on the beach a lot; it's nice living by the lake. The library's close enough to walk to, also. Mostly I just sit in this tiny apartment while Lonnie's at work and play our records and read a whole lot. I picture you yucking it up in the snack bar, making brilliant responses in class, dancing to the Apocalypse Jug Band, doing it with Josh on the tile. Just do it all twice for both of us, will you? You are going out with Josh, aren't you? There's no point in hating guys. This is all my own fault.

Don't worry about me. I'm past the point of doing anything rash. It's kind of nice being adored. Remember I told you how he smashed the crucifix when I broke up with him (tried to)? Was that a whole year ago? Poor pitiful moi. He glued it back together, can you believe that? He keeps it in the drawer with his socks and underwear. Pathetic.

We went to a movie the other night and in the middle of the show I looked over at him. There was this strange young man, very good looking, in a blue shirt unbuttoned enough to show some dark chest hair. This sounds weird, but you're used to my weirdness by now. All of a sudden it hit me that I'd washed and ironed the blue shirt, that I'm actually married to the stranger. I always knew I wouldn't find the right person to marry, I was such a reject, and I'd be a little ashamed of whoever it was. He'd be ugly or dumb or he'd work at a gas station, something like that. I was right, too. Still, he loves me and sometimes he looks like such a little boy I want to take care of him. Other times he's such a beautiful man (he'd kill me for "beautiful") and I think I do love him. Or maybe I'm just trying to make this a self-fulfilling prophecy. Dulcie White—sorry, Dulcie Saxbe—will turn out to love her husband. But it's sad, isn't it, that this is it. This will have to be the love of my life.

Can you stand all this disgusting, maudlin goop? Go flush this down the Yawper.

My mother came over yesterday and brought a teensy pair of pink booties with white button eyes and bunny ears. She said all kinds of people have been telling her that they had to get married or their daughter or their cousin did. She's finding out the whole town's secrets. You'd never believe it.

Can you come over here sometime? I couldn't stand to be on campus, even if I had a way to get there, which I don't. I really really really miss my chambrie. I better end this missive before I sink any farther into self-pity. It's turned out to be more suited for the Crepitator. Go and flush once more.

Beaucoup love from your Dulcie

We were in bed Sunday afternoon when my parents knocked on the door. We'd slept in, waking at the bells from the church at the end of the block and then falling back to sleep. By eleven I'd been wide awake, but when I tried to get up, Lonnie threw his arm over me to keep me beside him, and so I'd lain there frantically awake, bored, until I was ready to cry or to bite that imperial arm at the frenzy under my skin. I hated my acquiescence, but the payment for revolt would be a whole heavy Sunday of sullenness.

My parents were inside the short passage between the outside screen door and the heavy door to the kitchen.

"Don't move," Lonnie whispered. "They'll think we're not here."

"But it's my mom and dad."

"Don't move."

"Dulcie," my mother called. "We know you're here, Dulcie." Her voice might have been cajoling a child out of a dark closet.

"I'm coming," I called and leapt out of bed away from Lonnie. I grabbed my robe and went to the door. "We slept in."

Dad stepped back to the screen door. Here was his daughter in shortie pajamas coming from a man's bed, in the afternoon yet. He stared down at the gray-painted wooden floor.

"We wanted to take you out for Sunday dinner," Mom said.

"We slept in," I said again. They mustn't come in and see the bed open, the shades down, Lonnie in his underwear, nearly naked in bed.

"We'll go have a cup of coffee somewhere," she said. "We'll be back in a half hour."

When they returned we were clothed and combed, the bed was a sofa, and we all stood in the living room in awkward relief.

"Kath-y Jo-o, you stop that or I'll beat your head in." Linda, who lived across the alley behind us, was screaming at her kids again. "Kar-en Ly-hnn! Get back over here. Goddamnit, how many times do I have to tell you." She liked to give the names an extra syllable when she yelled.

Sometimes we'd sit on her back step and talk after our husbands had gone to work. I didn't have anything in common with her, except that we spent our days being wives across a cindered alley from each other. I was gathering experience, talking to her, collecting details like an anthropologist to tell Katie. Linda the Slattern, I thought of her. I gave her openings to reveal the sordid details.

But she was just a young woman whose husband plodded out the back door and into their faded blue car every morning, just a woman sitting half the day on her back step, smoking and screaming at her children. She teased her hair and wore pedal pushers. She didn't really have anything to tell me. She'd say she was going to use her new hot dog steamer for their supper or something like that. At ten she'd go inside for her soap operas—her stories, she called them—and the next morning she'd tell me the minute advances in plot and the dramatic if subtle shifts in relationships.

I saw that we were alike, really, both of us just marking time, not even with the anticipation that finally something would happen. Our lives weren't like our stories, in which the threads would in the end be twined, everything unknotted and untangled and woven into sense. Other people wound through their lives, trailing the motifs of their pasts. I pictured Katie with her good posture stepping straight out of a tapestry, trailing threads that wove into pictures behind her, so that, though she appeared to be stepping into thin air, she was really advancing into her story.

Linda the Slattern was only making it through another day, cereal for breakfast, bowls rinsed out, the husband out the torn screen door, children in the back yard, a cigarette on the back step, an hour of shadow stories, sandwiches, naps, steamed hot dogs, scraped plates, television, old buddy pecker, one more night, one more morning of backache from the rod under the thin mattress.

"My life is a tautology," I told Katie on the phone.

"Are you sure you're not just bored?" she said.

"No, I can see my whole life, and there's no sense to it. This will happen, that will happen, and so what?"

"But there is that baby growing inside you. I keep thinking how amazing that is. That's sense, isn't it?"

"Maybe," I said, and I could see how perhaps Lonnie and I had crossed to be the warp and the weft of this new picture. But then I thought of Linda's little girls, Kathy Jo and Karen Lynn, whose lives were fixed, who would start smoking at sixteen and get married to some factory worker and have babies and scream at them in some backyard, and over and over and over it flopped.

"Maybe there's no sense close up," Katie said. "But that doesn't mean it isn't there, does it?"

"What," I said, "are we getting into the ways of God here? More mysterious than we idiots here below can understand?"

"Our nada who art in nada," she said, and we started to laugh.

"Praise nada from whom all nada flows," I said.

"Oh, I miss you. We aren't nothing, you and I."

That's what Lonnie would say, I thought, though not about us. He isn't nothing, he'd say about somebody he wanted to put down, not seeing that the dismissal, as well as the double negative, raised the person up.

"I guess you're right," I said. "And if we aren't nothing, then it's too egotistical to think that other people are." I lifted my image of Linda's hunched figure from her back step and draped it in blessings. "Still—it's not like meaning is dropped down from above. Or predetermined. I mean, it's what we choose, right? It's free will, right? Maybe that's worse. Look what I chose, Ma."

"Don't," Katie said. "Don't do this to yourself."

"Anyway, it can all make sense and still be unhappy, right? Blessings in disguise and all that. Praise moi from whom all suffering flows."

"You're so cute when you're bitter," she said. I couldn't tell if she was laughing at me or crying.

Maybe Linda was in a spiral, not a loop. It was petty and judgmental to think I had her life and her daughters' lives figured out, just the same nonsense circling in on itself endlessly until they died.

"Do you believe I chose to have a baby?" I asked Katie.

"I guess you could have chosen not to," she said. "I mean, once it was there."

"It's funny, neither of my parents ever once suggested getting rid of it." Nobody said that ugly bloated word abortion, which made me think of fish belly white, of dead eyeless fish on the beach. Part of the truth was, we wouldn't have known how to arrange for an abortion. The other part was that I wanted my baby. I let it go with Katie, but what I wondered was whether I had somehow chosen a baby—even chosen this particular baby, which meant that I had been not compliant, just the stray victim of an accident, not just a passive girl in the back seat, but complicitous. It meant that I had first chosen Lonnie, or it wouldn't be this particular baby. And what had made me choose him instead of, say, Bruce at college? And what had made me choose that one last time to let him do it, when earlier it would have been a different sperm mating a different egg and later I would have ended it with Lonnie altogether?

When my husband pulled up, ready for his lunch, I said goodbye to Katie and opened another can of turkey noodle soup. I kissed him and left Linda, no more slatternly than I, sitting with her daughters across the alley, adorned with blessings and free will.

My mother drove over to take me to an obstetrician. She sat in the mustard-yellow waiting room while I lay back on the table with the white paper over it and slid my bare heels into the metal stirrups.

"So, Mrs. Saxbe, when was your last period?" he asked, stooping between my legs.

"I don't know."

"You don't know," he repeated. He looked up from between my legs. "How old are we, Mrs. Saxbe?"

Afterward, I told Mom how impatient and mean the doctor was, knowing I sounded like a child complaining about her teacher. I was mad at myself for crying in the examining room.

"He's the only obstetrician in this town," she said. She didn't say that

I should simply go home with her, that she'd take care of me as if I were sick, that she'd get me through it all. It wouldn't work anyway, and I could see that Lonnie would come after me, scenes would follow, I'd cry and get back in Lonnie's car, and it would all be so sordid.

The phone was ringing in the apartment but I couldn't get the door unlocked in time to answer it.

"It's Lonnie, anyway," I told Mom.

"Anyway?"

"He calls all the time. He never has any real reason, just wants to know what I'm doing or say he loves me."

"Well, that's sweet," she said.

I couldn't tell her how it was, how at any odd, unexpected moment, nervously expected by now, the phone could ring and Lonnie'd say, "How ya doing? Know I love you?" What was to be nervous about? If I walked to the library or over to the beach, I heard that ringing, ringing, ringing in the empty apartment, and when I returned, the rooms would be full of echoes. And then Lonnie would spend the evening sunk in silence and beer.

"When I was young, an older friend told me her husband would wake her up in the middle of the night to tell her he loved her," Mom said. "At first I thought that was so sweet. Then later on, I realized what an innocent I'd been. What he really woke her up for was sex." She laughed. "I don't know why that stayed with me all this time. Anyway, lately I've gone back to the original: He just wanted to say he loved her."

"If Lonnie woke me up in the middle of the night it'd be to make sure I wasn't in a dream somewhere without him."

"Oh, honey," Mom said. Neither of us wanted to acknowledge sex between Lonnie and me. I wondered how her reinterpretations of her friend's comment paralleled the stages in her own marriage. And I wondered how the friend had said it—bragging to a younger girl, with pride? or complaining about interrupted sleep? and then with affection in her voice or annoyance? If marriages had stages, would Lonnie and I move out of this one?

"What ever happened to your friend?"

"That was Flo Feister. You babysat for her a couple times. She and Jack couldn't have a baby and they couldn't have a baby, and then suddenly after fifteen years they had Jackie."

"Maybe he finally quit waking her up in the middle of the night and tried it in daylight."

We laughed the way Annie and I used to giggle in high school at innuendoes. Mom and I couldn't mention what Lonnie and I had done and were doing, but my state allowed a sort of girlfriend intimacy. I wasn't sure if it was sex or pregnancy or marriage that had done it. Or maybe, I thought and wanted to cry, it was my loss of potential: Now I was a housewife who would have babies and never finish school. Now we were the same. Eventually we'd be talking about our husbands and their silences and the heaviness of them on top of us. I shook my head, not wanting to think how Lonnie and my father might be alike, and not wanting to see him on top of my mother.

"What's the matter?" she said suspiciously. She was afraid, I thought, that I might tell her.

"Nothing. It's complicated. It's okay."

"Well. Look, I brought you something."

Inside the white Jacobson's box were a package of size 0 undershirts, a kimono with pale green kittens on it, a yellow bib, and three pairs of rubber pants.

"Am I really going to have a baby?" I said. I was choked up again. "Tell you the truth, I hardly believe it."

"I ran into Judith Mercer in Jacobson's when I was buying these. I know she's going to tell Larry she saw me with my hands full of baby things, and everybody your father works with will know. But there I stood. And anyway, we're as good as the Mercers. Or anybody else. I'm not going to hang my head. I just told her all these goodies are for my grandchild."

I could picture Mrs. Mercer saying congratulations in a knowing way. "I'm sorry," I said, even more sorry for the shame I'd brought to them now that my mother was refusing to show it. When she'd been ashamed, I could be angry at her pettiness. Now that she was being publicly brave, I felt more sullied.

"Listen to me. It's the good girls who get caught," she said. "That's all. The bad girls know how to protect themselves." She looked down, shy. "In spite of it all, I'm kind of glad. Buying these baby things—I lost that baby, you know. Now there's another one."

"You didn't do this with anybody else, did you?" Lonnie said, his back to me as he turned the sofa into the bed.

"Oh Lonnie." I was weary. "I keep telling you and telling you. No no no no no."

He gestured at the sofa's transformation. "Wah-la," he said.

"Wah-la?" I laughed and then caught myself. "You mean voilà."

"You went out with so many others, though," he said. "If you let me, why not them?"

"I didn't. I swear I didn't."

He lifted his arm at the impatient protest in my voice, and I jumped back.

"Don't do that," he said. He held out his hand and inspected the palm. "You know I would never hit you." He dropped the hand. "It wouldn't make any difference. I just want to know, that's all. I'd forgive you."

"Well, there's nothing to forgive. Why can't you just forget it?"

He unzipped and stepped out of his pants and then underwear. He pointed at his penis sticking out against his shirt tail. "Voy-la," he said, proud of himself. "Come here. Pecker wants his pussy."

In only the long yellow shirt, with his hard black-haired bare legs, he was so different, so other, so male that I was hot and aware of my breasts and all my skin. I undressed and lay down with him. He wasn't stupid, either, I thought, he was just a boy whom I could teach or at least guide, if I did it carefully.

"There really wasn't anybody else?" he whispered. He sucked at my breasts. "Am I your baby?" he whispered. "Say I'm your baby."

"You're my baby." I could feel the hair all over his body against the length of my skin. I pressed my palms on his back. "You're my man."

Mrs. Saxbe came over one morning. Lonnie was due home for lunch in a half-hour. I hadn't opened his can of turkey noodle soup yet.

"I was just reading," I said, feeling as if I ought to be baking up a storm or scrubbing the kitchen floor. "Lonnie'll be here pretty soon. Would you like to sit down?" I felt ridiculously prim around her, and hearing my words come out snobbish rather than demure, I ended up exaggerating the formality.

"Here's some clothes I got my son," she said. "Three new pair of underwear and two new shirts. The kind he likes."

I set them on the kitchen table, underwear hidden beneath the shirts. I felt myself blushing—underwear from his mother.

"He'll appreciate all this," I said politely. "He'll be here soon to tell you so himself." I laughed in the bright, forced way my mother did on the phone. "I bet you don't miss ironing all those shirts of his, anyway."

"I never minded," she said. "Are you starching them?"

"No, they seemed all right."

"Use spray starch when you iron them," she said. "That's how he likes them."

"Thank you," I said. Her dark gray hair was thick and smooth. "You know I want to take good care of him."

"I know you do, honey. I know you do. It's just you're both so young. Lonnie needs someone to watch him carefully. He's ... well, I guess you'll see. If you haven't already."

"Well, he has to be a man now," I said. No wonder he was such a child sometimes, I thought. He'd been mothered too much. She didn't think I was capable of taking care of him. I wanted to defend him, his adulthood, his capability. "He's taking care of me, too, you know. He's taking fine care. He's working and supporting us. He's going to be a father."

Mrs. Saxbe looked down at her brown and yellow plaid slacks. Her sleeveless white blouse was loose like a maternity top. "Well, you just take care of him anyway. Iron his shirts just right and make him desserts. Lonnie needs sweet things, and watch he don't get constipated."

Embarrassed for Lonnie, I said, "He *wanted* to marry me, you know. I think he's old enough to know what he needs."

"Yeah," she said, "and I'm Queen Elizabeth."

"He knew what he was doing. He married me on purpose." I had lost my primness. "He got me pregnant on purpose so I'd have to marry him."

"Well, you had to spraddle your legs to get that way, girl," she said. She walked out and shaking, I let her go. Out the window I saw her waiting in her car until Lonnie drove up. They stood talking in the driveway.

When Lonnie came in, he put his arms around me. He was shaking, too. "Don't sweat it, my little wife. She isn't nobody to get worked up over. She just worries about me, is all."

CHAPTER 8

Say, man, what say we do something tonight? Stu Mason said. He was the other salesman. The store didn't hardly have enough business for the two of them. It's Friday, he said. T G I fucking Friday. Let's us take the wifeys out.

Stu had a few years and two kids on him. Sometimes Lonnie hated the mouth the guy had and the soft gut. Stu said, Janice's old lady gets the rug rats Friday nights. We could do the drive-in.

The cowbell on the back of the door clanged and a fat old broad came in. I'll let you have this one, Lonnie said.

Aren't you the gallant one, Stu said.

I'll go give my wife a call, he said. His wife. He said it every chance he got. In the bathroom mirror he liked to watch his mouth pucker up and then spread for the word.

He let the phone ring eight times. He figured she was taking the trash out back. Maybe she was shooting the breeze with the scrawny broad who lived behind them. He tried again at eleven-thirty but she didn't answer. Eight rings at noon and she wasn't there.

Old buddy? he said to Stu. Switch lunch breaks with me. I need to get home.

Stu punched him. Used to go for a nooner myself, he said, before Janice started hatching kids.

Something must have happened to his wife. He drove the Witch back to the apartment. He might find her on the floor. Something must have happened with the baby. She had a book that showed the baby's growth inside the woman. He pictured an upside-down fish with his own face. He thought of Dulcie on the floor with the fish flopping out and he ran the stop sign at the corner.

He yanked open the screen door and then stood in the entryway between the doors just listening. He was afraid he would hear her moaning. He was afraid he would hear the bed whomping. Nothing. He used his key.

She wasn't there. The bed was folded up. The towels were spread out over the top of the shower stall to dry. There were chocolate chip cookies on paper towels on the kitchen counter and he whonked down a few.

He grabbed a beer. She wasn't over at Linda's. The scrawny broad across the alley behind them. He drove to the library. He'd never been in there. It wasn't nothing like the humongous library at her school. Where he'd watched her before she was his wife. The blood pumped hard in him.

Finally he took the Witch back to the apartment and called the store and said he would be late. Quickie wasn't enough, huh? Stu said.

Just shut up, he said.

She should have been home. Ironing his shirts or starting dinner. He saw his mother slapping flour onto meat. Dulcie might be with somebody. She could have called one of her college pansies to come over and get her. He couldn't sit still. He needed to get a gun. He slammed his fist into the bathroom door and made a splintered hole and tore up his hand.

She showed up at two twenty-three. She held a fat book against her boobs. Like it would protect her from the bullets.

Lonnie? You scared me, she said. What are you doing here?

Where the fuck have you been, he said. He was shaking and the words came out slow, one at a time.

Nowhere, she said. Just walking on the beach. I sat and read for a while, that's all. What's wrong with that? Am I not allowed to take a walk on the beach now?

Am I not allowed? he mimicked. Don't get snotty with me. You're supposed to be here. I come home for you and you're not here. Who are you out screwing?

He'd had three beers, waiting for her. He took his nooner and she lay still for it and then he drove back to the store for the last hour.

Whew, man, Stu said. Don't let the old man catch you smelling like that.

They went to the drive-in outside Waterton with Stu and Janice Mason. They had this '59 station wagon with phony wood on the sides that looked like it had been smeared with ashes. Stu noticed him checking it out and said, You can't look a gift horse when your daddy-in-law wants to give you wheels.

Janice turned around in the front seat. How long you guys been married? she said.

Six months, he said and squeezed Dulcie's knee. They didn't know anybody in Waterton. They could say whatever they wanted.

Oh you're just newlyweds, Janice said with one of those high school squeals. I figured. Look at them back there, Stuey, all cuddled up and here we are with a mile of seat between us.

Well, you aren't glued to that window, are you? Stu said.

She scooted partway over and then turned around again. We've got two kids already, she said. And—Then she stopped. Oh nothing.

And what? Stu said.

Nothing, she said. Just nothing.

Stu's pink face got dark until the freckles practically disappeared. Oh man, don't tell me, he said. Oh man.

In the back seat he rubbed Dulcie's thigh. Nobody said a thing for three miles until they parked and Stu hung the speaker on the window. Then Janice said, You want to go to the little girls' with me, Dulcie? She was crying without making a sound.

Hey babe? Stu said. All soft. He held out a couple bills. Why don't you get yourself some ice cream or something.

When they were out, Stu pounded the steering wheel. Oh man, he said. Oh fuck.

What's going on? Lonnie said. First we're going to the movies with the wives and a cooler full of Bud and next thing she's bawling and you're beating on your car.

Listen, just take your old Uncle Stu's advice. Be smart. Don't go out without your galoshes on. I mean don't go in.

Galoshes?

Rubbers, you idiot. Wait a while before you start in having kids. Truth is, I'm nuts about the little snots, but you can rush things. You can overdo things.

The idiot burned him. But then he wanted to let Stu know he was a stud, too. Yeah, well, he said. You aren't the only one shooting live ammo.

Oh man, Stu said. He reached over the seat and punched him. You too, huh? They both started laughing. Well, congratulations, man. What can I say?

Dulcie and Janice got in with boxes of popcorn. They were laughing too. I guess we're all in this together, Janice said. They watched the movie and every once in a while one of them would bust out laughing again.

The second movie was one of those dark slow deals and he started feeling up Dulcie and kissing her like they were parked in the boonies. Janice and Stu were making out in the front seat, too.

They had the bookcase he'd made for her in Senior Shop filled up with her books. She was always always reading. Always disappearing from him, flattened out like a run-over cat, sliding into those books. At noon she said, You want the usual? turkey noodle? At supper she said, Sell lots of shoes today? Her face looked at him but she was gone.

He decided he would read all her books. Starting with the top shelf. He'd do them all. The first one was called *The Brothers Karamazov*. I'm going to read all these books, he told her. Starting with these brothers from Kalamazoo. She gave him a look.

Good, she said. But, you know, you might like something else better. Just to start with. She handed him another humongous book called *The*

Grapes of Wrath.

After supper he left the television off and went at it. The words wouldn't hardly fit together. The sky, weeds, a crust on the earth, colors, ant lions, a wind, people without names, dust. All jumbled up.

Finally he got a beer from the kitchen. That's two chapters, he said. I'll do some more tomorrow. He turned out the light. Come on, he said, sit down here with me and watch this show.

August was hot as a bitch. He made love to her every night with the windows open and the shades up but they were too far away for any lake breeze. He thought he could almost see heat shimmering over the bed like the highway in the sunlight. Their bodies slapped together and pulled apart with a wet noise like biting into one of those fat dill pickles. Like ninth-grade guys' armpit noises. The noises and the sweat—it was embarrassing.

He used to be soaked after practice. One time with the meet at Allegan coming up he'd kept on running and then he stretched and when he finally hit the locker room it was empty. He was soaked and the place was humid with steam and everybody else's sweat. In his locker he found somebody's English assignment. The cover read, Autobiography, English III, May 19, by Jess Springer. There was a big fat A in red ink and the teacher's note: You fulfilled the assignment more than adequately, Jess.

Jess Springer was this short guy with good shoulders. Lots of chest hair. He'd needed to shave regularly even when he was a sophomore. Lonnie had talked him into going out for track and sometimes they'd traded rides home after practice.

The guy had paperclipped a note to the English paper: Lonnie, this is dedicated to you. I didn't hand it in with a dedication page because I didn't want to embarrass you. You have helped me more than you know, and I want to let you read this. Love, Jess. P.S. Don't worry. I don't love you that way.

He jammed the paper into his gym bag with his sweaty clothes and read it back at the trailer in his room. Jess Springer was a queer. The paper said: I have been a homosexual for two years now and no one knows, just the minister and now you, Mrs. Bundy. My friends here think I'm cool. I go into Kalamazoo weekends where I have other friends, homos like me. I feel terrible. Sometimes I feel as if my arms are lashed to two horses and men are whipping them to pull in opposite directions.

The paper went on for pages. What did it have to do with him? How had he helped Jess Springer? It didn't have a thing to do with him. The paper was smeared and soggy from his wet clothes and he threw it in the barrel outside where they burned trash.

After that he always noticed how Jess Springer left the top two buttons of his shirt open. He wore these print shirts that nobody thought anything of with his thick hairy chest showing. They still traded rides home from time to time and never said a thing about that English paper. But Lonnie always started sweating. He'd get home with the armpits of his plain shirts soaked.

He'd slide off Dulcie when they were done and they'd shower together. They'd cozy up in the shower stall together. All that sweat ran right down the drain where it belonged.

Her friend Katie was back at school. At least he had got Dulcie away from her. But Katie got her faggot boyfriend to drive her over, and coming home from work he caught them leaving in this cherry Corvette.

Nice try, he said to Dulcie. She was turning into a little sneak.

What do you mean? she said. Katie just had Josh drop her off for a little visit. What's wrong with that?

Was the other fag down in the back seat? Bruce. He got into your pants, too. Didn't he?

No and no again, she said. She stamped her foot. Katie came over to visit me. I am getting sick and tired of all this, damnit. She was crying. Her face was all slimy with tears and snot.

Don't swear at me, he said. Come on. Go blow your nose. I don't want her coming over here any more. She just gets you all worked up. This can't be good for the baby.

They sat down and ate. Meatloaf and these scalloped potatoes. He'd rather eat hamburgers plain without whatever weird stuff she dumped in, but he said, Good dinner, honey. At least she was trying to cook. Meat and potatoes. That's what his dad always wanted.

Dulcie got up and put on a record while they ate. Katie brought this over, she said. We were learning to play this concerto together. I wish I had a piano to practice now. I've been thinking the church down at the end of the block probably has a piano and maybe they'd let me use it during the day, when nothing else is going on. You think?

Katie wants to be so generous, he said, get her to give you that Vette. Anyway, probably they keep the church locked up.

Sundays the Methodists woke them up with bells. One of these Sundays, they agreed, they ought to go to church. Wednesday nights he liked to shut off the television and go to bed early. He could hear organ music while he made love to his wife. So faith, hope, love abide. He thought he could hear the words in the organ music. These three. The bed whoomped and he heard wife, wife, wife. Wife abides.

He shut off the record player and watched a half-hour cop show, and

Dulcie washed the supper dishes. Are we going to the grocery store? she said. They stocked up once a week. He liked the way they walked up and down the aisles together. They were actually married and living together.

Could you just do it? he said.

What, by myself? You mean you're going to let me drive your car? You feeling all right?

I'd just like to sit here. I worked hard today. I must've shoved a couple hundred pair of shoes onto people's rotten feet. I'm tired.

Dulcie had left the dishes to drain and he dried the good plates his mother had given them for their wedding. Then he turned out the lights and put on Katie's record to play and sat in the dusk. He closed his eyes and saw these glowing hands. Four glowing purple hands playing a piano. Up and down and faster and faster. Like it was one of those player pianos and the hands were trying to keep up with the jumping keys.

Katie was queer for his wife and Dulcie was too blind to see it. He saw them once put their arms around each other. In the dark it was their hands on each other's back hot and glowing. His sisters used to give each other backrubs. First it would be Suzie face down on the bed and Marie's hands rubbing her, and him sitting there, and then they'd switch.

He picked up the record player arm and accidentally scratched the record a little. He held out his hands and pretended he was playing a piano. You sit there, little boy, Marie said. I'm the mommy and you're the baby, and you have to mind me. His fingers were glowing in the dark, it looked like. He took out his pocketknife and opened the thin blade and put the tip in a groove. He followed the groove around and around. Then he pulled the point of the blade across the grooves. It felt good, the knife on the vinyl, and all the glowing hands slithered away.

All day at the store he thought of his wife. He started out every morning in clean, pressed clothes. He took turns with Stu, one in the stockroom and one waiting on customers unless it got busy. Which it didn't hardly ever. The old man checked up on them and the register at odd times. Playing games with them. He didn't trust them. Lonnie practically got down on his knees the first few times. He called him Mr. Walsh and the old man said there hadn't been a Walsh since the war. Now he just said Sir. He hated the old man's smelly trousers and the hot-shit way he gave them their paychecks on Fridays.

The stockroom was dusty and high ceilinged but otherwise the small room was a safe, enclosed place. He liked shelving the shipments. The boxes stacked by size and style and color. Men's and women's and boys' and girls'. Sometimes he could push a headache down by lining things up and stacking boxes in the dim tight room.

On the floor he thought of Dulcie all the time. He took down the cowbell on the door. He hated the fat clang. But the old man Mr. Hot-Shit Sir made him nail it back up.

Folks like to have their arrival heralded, he said. They like to be paid attention to and waited on. I want you boys to make every last customer feel like they're royalty.

Yes *sir*, Lonnie said. He wanted to say, They're royal all right. Royal pains. Royalty with sweaty socks and smelly feet.

The cowbell clanged and a fat broad came in. Hello, gorgeous, he said. What can I do you for today? He straddled the padded stool and smiled and gave her a disgusting ped for her damp right foot and lifted the foot in and out of a dozen shoes. She was some old guy's wife, he thought. What did that husband think of his wife's private feet naked and propped up between Lonnie's spraddled legs? The nylon peds he'd started calling galoshes to Stu. It was like putting on a rubber, sliding the nylon onto a damp ramrod foot.

I need something in navy, the fat broad said. My Joe is being honored at a banquet next weekend and I need something to go with my good dress. It's too late in the year for my good white shoes.

Her eyes were zeroing in on his pants stretched between his legs.

At night he would touch Dulcie's good white breasts and kneel between her legs and pump his pecker in and let himself down on top of her.

The cowbell clanged and he felt the swelled-up sound vibrate into his head. This woman had a pack of kids with her. Hi gorgeous, he said and gave the kids balloons that had Walsh Bros. Shoes in puckered letters on them. His headache beat against his forehead. He saw Dulcie shutting herself into a phone booth and calling some guy. That Bruce maybe.

He showed the oldest kid how to check out the running shoes. Look, you want it to be flat when you put it on the counter. And see, you want the stitching to be straight. The mother was liking this. He took a pencil and pressed the eraser into the center of the heel inside the shoe. See, he said, you want the toe to just come up straight. See how this one goes twisted? That's no good.

Dulcie might be meeting some guy at the library or even at the Methodist church. He wouldn't put it past her to use God. Then they'd drive to the beach and she'd spread her legs for the guy between the dunes. When he got home he'd check her over for sand in her crack and for cuts, the kind you get from beach grass.

These are going to be training flats, right? he asked the kid. You want to try them on with your feet a little swollen. You want to go jog around the block a couple times while I take care of your mom and the siblings?

Can he do that, Mom?

The broad was grinning to beat the band. He liked that word siblings. Long ago on their first date Dulcie asked him if he had any siblings. He said no. He didn't know what siblings were but he figured no would work, whatever. I don't either, she said. All sad. Later she found out about Suzie and Marie but he just said they were his half-sisters and didn't count as genuine siblings.

He got red Keds and blue Keds on the kids and talked the mother into just trying these new hot-off-the-truck loafers for fall. He saw the woman's husband ramming his pecker into her to make all these kids. He saw one of Dulcie's guys kissing her and slipping her some tongue and unsnapping her bra. Bruce was slipping his hand up her skirt and she was spreading her knees. The kid ran back in panting and slammed the door. Lonnie got him to walk around and bounce in the new shoes. The mother bought the lot, training flats and Keds and loafers. Come back and buy you some spikes, he told the kid. I'm going to see to it we order star-shaped spikes. You don't want nail heads.

Stu came out of the stockroom when they left. Woowee, he said. I didn't want to interrupt an artist at work. Too bad the old man didn't witness that performance. You'd be written into his will.

He was going to lose his wife. He knew it. He was going to lose his wife.

He woke early with a headache. He got up to take a leak and had to hold on to the wall. His head was heavy enough to pull him over. He shut off the alarm and went back to sleep.

They woke at nine-thirty and he made Dulcie call the store. The old man was there and she told him her husband was sick. All sweet.

I'm not sick, he said. I just didn't feel good. She folded up the bed and he picked up his empties. He'd done a job on a six-pack the night before. Dulcie made scrambled eggs.

Don't get dressed, he told her. Just put on your swimsuit. Let's hit the beach while it's still halfway warm.

But you're sick.

I told you, I am not sick. It's just this headache. He put on his trunks. He believed the sun would burn up the headache.

They drove down the shore away from town and stopped in the parking lot of this public beach. The water was too cold for her. They walked down the beach toward the pier. The doctor said she should go for walks. Or that was her excuse. She wore her same swimsuit as the summer before. This blue two-piece. Her stomach was starting to bulge. She had on her terrycloth beach jacket.

The boulders piled up at the base of the pier looked slick but were actually smooth and dry. They climbed up and walked out the pier. There were fishermen sitting on both sides. Some fishing the choppy light blue lake. Some fishing the dark blue channel. They each one sat separate with all their pails and bait cans and waxed-paper lunches and coolers. White cords hung down into the water and he knew half-dead fish were strung through the gills on them. Nobody said a word. Just fished and smoked.

At the end of the pier they were alone and he put his hand under her beach coat on her stomach. So you noticed that, huh? she said.

Spray flew up through the holes in the pier with every wave. He put his arms around her from behind and God he loved her and they stood watching the lake and the sky fall together. White spray hit them and the water was sucked back down the holes and then the spray coated them. Spray and suck and spray and suck until the pier rocked under them.

CHAPTER 9

Lonnie came home early with a whole case of beer and a speeding ticket. "Goddamn fuzz," he said. "I wasn't even doing fifty."

He loaded the cans into the refrigerator. He wouldn't tell me how he managed to buy it. Stu Mason might be buying it for him, or maybe he'd found a liquor store that didn't check IDs.

"Well, that ought to last you a while, anyway," I said. Behind my back, a pull tab made its hateful slurp and snap.

"Yes, Mother."

"Supper's almost ready. Did you remember we have that pre-natal session at the hospital tonight?" I had on my new maternity blouse over blue slacks zipped only halfway up. We'd gone shopping together, with money from my mother, and bought the blouse and white paint to fix up the wicker bassinet his sister Marie had given us. We'd bought some undershirts, diapers, and gowns, which I'd washed already so the new material would be soft against the baby's skin.

"You know, you're really beautiful," Lonnie said, at the two-beer stage already. One more and we'd be in bed instead of at the first class at the hospital. Two more and he'd be playing his Byrds album at top volume.

"Sit down and let's eat. Come on. We don't want to sit with all the other new parents smelling of beer."

He gave me a look. He wasn't falling for *we*, when he knew I meant *he*.

"I think you're really beautiful," he said again. "So why do you have to put all that muck on your face?"

"Come on, baby, come here and eat." Maybe I could still pacify him and get him to the class. "It's just a little powder, that's all."

"And lipstick globbed all over your mouth. And that gunk on your eyebrows."

I pulled my chair close, with my knee against his, and handed him the bowl of salad. "Everybody wears lipstick, baby. You've seen me at night without my eyebrows. So you know without a little help from Auntie Maybelline I don't *have* any eyebrows, that you can see anyway. What's the big deal? You never minded before. You always said you liked the way I looked."

"Yeah, well, you're my wife now. And I think you're beautiful without any make-up."

"Eat up, baby. We've got to keep moving or we'll be late."

I hurried through the dishes while he sat silently on the green couch with another can of beer.

"Okay, I'm ready." I was too cheerful. "Shall we go learn how to have a baby?"

He fell sideways on the sofa and raised his head to drain the can. His adam's apple gulped up and down as he swallowed.

"You go wash that gunk off your face," he said, "and then we'll go."

After he'd fallen asleep in front of the television, I took my blue cardigan from my drawer in the dresser and slipped outside. I walked around the block twice and on the third time around I tested the Methodist church door, but he was right, it was locked. Leaves from the old elms scuttled down the sidewalk, and my shadow cast by the streetlights was thick and wavering. I made another circuit, watching the shadow quiver before me until I stepped into it, then watching over my shoulder as it shuffled behind me. It was so easy to ruin a life. I had always flowed along, as if nothing I did would take me from the current. When I was a child, we often drove over to Lake Michigan for summer Sunday afternoons, after church, and while my mother rubbed baby oil all over her body and stretched out on a beach towel with some fat paperback or her new Reader's Digest Condensed hardback, my father would swim out to the sandbar with me and play in the waves with me. He held his nose and sat on the bottom so I could climb onto his shoulders, and as he stood up, I rose out of the water as if I were being born, rising out of the safe pressure of the water holding my body and into the shivery, thin air, and just before I lost my balance I pushed off from his shoulders and dove. Underwater, I let the waves toss me around, and emerging into the bubbly light, I was all mixed up and had to turn all around to find my father. "Again, do it again, Daddy," I yelled.

Newton was right, though, and I hadn't really been impervious, propelled along but exerting no force. My actions pressed on other people and even onto my self. The third law of motion applied to me, not only to steel balls on strings. When I leapt from my father's shoulders, what had happened to him? I cried, "Again, Daddy," and he sank to the bottom for me. My words acted on his body, and he sank. But that wasn't the meaning of the law. What happened to him? He felt the furrows of clean sand on his knees and shins, the furrows plowed by the action of the waves, and he felt his daughter in her ruffled cotton bathing suit scramble onto his shoulders, and he felt the force of her body shooting down through his shoulders, his chest, his thighs—and was it grounded in his feet or shot through into the sand, so that he was propelled up with my leap?—and he felt me shoving off from his shoulders always.

Everything I had done shot forces into my mother and my father and

Katie and Lonnie and now this baby, and all their actions were cast into me, and what might look from the top of the elm like brown leaves tossed around by random wind was choreography, all the forces of sidewalk and brittle leaves and wind and photons pressing on each other, even if the choreographer was only Newton's Third Law of Motion.

I turned the corner and walked once more by the house with the chiropractor's office in front and our tiny apartment in back. Inside, invisible forces staggered and spun and recoiled. I was afraid to stop walking and go in, but in truth it didn't matter—I was caught up, and it didn't matter, either, that my own actions, even my own passivity, had helped set it all in motion. There was no way out.

My body was swelling, and now Lonnie was making me faceless. He would probably sand down my nose and chin and cheekbones if he could. Except that I had a past, except that I had shoved off from it, except that I had acted on Katie and on Lonnie, I might as well have been a smooth egg of flesh, I might as well have been invisible and bloodless.

The rooms were still dark but Lonnie was on the floor. He was on his elbows and knees with his face to the rug, hands to ears, and his rear end in the air. "Oh no, what's wrong?" I said and leaned over him. He looked silly, like a kid trying for attention while everybody admired the little brother, and my heart swelled in hot pity. Then, holding my hand above his back, ready to touch him, I thought: Something is wrong with him and I can be untethered. I was a terrible soul, and I shifted my hand back and spanked his rear end. But I was afraid and I did it lightly.

"What is wrong? Are you in pain? Do you want me to call a doctor?"

He moaned and fell flat on the rug and rocked his head. He was having a seizure, I thought, maybe a heart attack, and I did care, I was terrified—but if he didn't die he might be paralyzed or comatose and I would have to nurse him for years and he couldn't stop me from putting on my eyebrows and strolling to the library. His breathing was wet. "I can't stand it," he said. "Don't ever leave me." He rolled up, keeping his hands on his ears, and I could see his face slick in the dark. "Don't you ever call a doctor on me," he said. "This is what happens. I get these headaches." He grabbed on to me. This is what happens, he meant, when you leave. This is how I rope you back in.

"Let's get you some aspirin. Let's get you into bed."

He let me open up the bed and help him into it. I brought him a glass of water and two pills. He let me pretend to control him.

In the bathroom I sat on the toilet seat lid and opened my library book under the bare dim light, turning the pages carefully so as not to make noise with the crinkly book cover. After only three pages, I heard him moaning from the bed, and as I tried to read on, he turned up the volume. We both knew he was faking it. We both knew I had to answer it. I changed into my baby doll pajamas and got into bed, and moaning lightly, he pushed the blue flowered bottoms down and slid onto me. "Hold me," he whispered so that I had to put my hands on his back while he moved his hips up and down against me. His skin felt oily and his ribs, his spine, his organs all were loose and jumbled inside the skin sack. When he was finished, he stayed on me, pressing me into the thin mattress, pressing my blank face into his shoulder until I could barely breathe. I pretended to fall asleep but we lay there, exerting equal and opposite forces on each other.

I spread newspaper on the kitchen floor and painted the old bassinet white, two coats. I'd always believed I'd have babies. My mother said she'd wanted six children but she had lost the baby after me, a boy baby. Sitting on the floor to paint the bassinette's legs, I saw my mother sitting with me on a floor, making a cradle for my Betsy-Wetsy out of an oatmeal box. She'd made doll clothes, too, a corduroy coat with a fur collar, dresses with shirred fronts, sleepers with feet. They must still be stored in the attic or somewhere. I'd never thought, before, that all the attention might be sublimation. I was, what, five? when her other baby was born dead. I'd known about him all along. She'd known he was dead for two weeks before he was born. He'd been given a name even, Derek Walter. When she screamed in labor, the doctor had told her to be quiet. "There are women here having their first babies," he'd said. So I'd heard her stories. But I didn't know if he had a grave somewhere. I hadn't thought of the weight a dead baby would be inside you or the grief billowing out as you screamed. She had been only my mother, never a young woman enduring two weeks with a dead son in her embryonic sac, washing back and forth when she walked around, like a dead fish at the edge of the lake, eyeless and white, the flesh beginning to fall in soft decay from the transparent bones. It had all been just a story. My father had never mentioned the dead baby to me at all.

I saw my mother holding my hand in a ten-cent store and letting me pick out a present for the new baby. I bought a brush and comb set. Pale blue in a plastic case.

I saw myself, secret under the willow in the back yard, dressing a life-sized baby doll. Pansy. She had short tight curls. She had real baby clothes—rubber pants and sunsuits and booties. She had a pale blue brush and comb set.

Pansy had something to do with the dead baby. Maybe my mother had bought me the doll before, so I would have my own baby and not be jealous. Maybe, having worked up my enthusiasm for the new baby, she brought home the doll for me instead of returning from the hospital flat and empty-handed. I didn't remember the dead two weeks. If I squinted I could see her on the porch swing with me on her lap, my long legs dangling. I didn't remember anything, any crying, the crib free to anyone who'd carry it away, my father shutting himself up in the oily dark garage, my mother's grief turned inside out. I had to make it up. I didn't want to ask her about it now, not playing on the floor now, not with a live baby uncurling through its stages of development inside me.

Katie drove Josh's red car over to Waterton, skipping her biology lab, and we walked the single block of the downtown. "Can you believe it's actually Main Street?" I said. "What a metropolis. And so original."

"It's a sweet little town, really. Kind of sandy. But sweet."

"You try living here. I don't know anybody here. Not that I care. I just sleep all morning, these days. I feel like a zombie. I can't seem to get enough sleep. Lonnie loves it. He kisses me good-bye in the morning and says to stay put. I'm finally doing what he wants."

We went into Judy's Girls and Women and went through the rack of maternity clothes. "Looks like the Easter Bunny got loose and laid all his eggs in here," Katie said. We started laughing at the pastel baby blouses trimmed with lace and rickrack.

"Can I help you girls?" the clerk said, coldly, as if she knew we were making fun of Judy's clothes. She stepped over to us and made a little noise in her throat when she saw my stomach.

Outside, we hurried down the block, past Walsh Brothers Shoes. "I don't think that clerk believed I was really pregnant."

"Are you sure that isn't just a pillow under there?" Katie said. "I wish it were. I don't see anyone but Josh anymore. I don't go anywhere, just to class. I hate it when Glenna comes up to my room and pretends everything's still the same."

"I was so naive. I can't believe it. Her and her horses." Every night Lonnie was on me. I kept my eyes closed, but I could feel the tensing of his back and his rear end. "Did I ever tell you, when I was in ninth grade, we used to go on hayrides, and one time I was making out with this guy named David Appleton. He kept trying to get his hands under my jacket and my blouse. And I thought it was because his hands were cold."

We took Josh's car down the coast and stopped by a cottage boarded up for the winter. And winter was coming. The sky was gray and swollen with unshed snow. We walked down the dune behind the cottage to the beach. The lake was gray, too, and tumid, veined as if currents swarmed in the water.

"He ruined the Tchaikovsky," I told Katie. "Scratched it all up."

"Why would he do that?"

"I didn't ask. He'd just get mad and it wouldn't be worth it. He's jealous, I guess. Jealous of anything before we were married."

"Don't let him do this to you, Dulcie. Please don't."

"I can hardly blame him. Why did I go out with those other guys and then park with him? I almost went to bed, even, with Bruce, and I knew I was pregnant. I even married him in that pink dress I bought for the dance with Bruce."

"Don't. You didn't do anything to feel guilty about." She was crying. "You didn't do anything wrong."

"I don't know why I let him do it in the first place." It was something I'd allowed him to do, not anything I'd really done. "And then to keep on—"

"I'm never going to," Katie said. She sobbed and hiccupped. "You taught me that, anyway. No matter how steamy the windows get, it's not worth it."

"He loves me, though. He keeps saying he loves me. So quit. I've done enough crying for both of us. So you don't have to. Come on, now. Look. I want to show you something."

I stopped on the gray beach and pulled down the stretchy panel of my maternity slacks and showed her. There was a thin brown line on my stomach, running straight down from my navel.

"Should I come in with you?" Katie said in the driveway. Even through the double doors and storm windows we could hear the Righteous Brothers in full cry. *Bring it on back.*

"You'd better not. But you don't have to worry. He wouldn't hurt me."

Lonnie had all the lights off and the blinds closed. The sofa was opened, and he lay face down on the bed. The record was playing at full volume. The rooms must be ready to explode, I thought, with the pressure of the tambourine's giant chink, chink and all that lamentation. *You've lost that lovin' feelin', now it's gone, gone, gone.* At the end, Lonnie got up and lifted the needle back to the beginning of the song. I turned on the kitchen light and sat at the table trying to read. I wished the landlord would knock on the door and complain. But I was afraid, too, that he would knock on the door and witness all this shame. *And I can't go on.* Lonnie was kicking the mattress steadily.

CHAPTER 10

He called in sick the day her mother was coming to get her. The idea had been, he would tool over when he got off work and they'd eat at her parents'.

You're going to lose your job if you keep doing this, she said.

She had on her same baby dolls. She said he kept the heat up too high for her winter nightgown. Her belly was getting big. In bed he had to sort of hike up on his elbows so he wouldn't squash the kid. Her hips were spreading out, too. And she finally at long last had a genuine set of hooters.

It was all his doing.

They would name the kid Benjamin Lon Saxbe the Third. He wondered if he could make it Bernadine if it turned out to be a girl. This snooty guy at school everybody called Tray because he was a third. He had no idea why. He wouldn't call his son Tray. Even to be funny. Himself, he'd never been a junior, either.

Well, she said, I still have to hit the laundromat. Don't forget I'm going over to my mom's and then you're supposed to meet me there.

Don't break it, he said. She didn't get it. The laundromat? When you hit it? Don't break it?

That's lame, she said.

Why couldn't you do the laundry at your folks'?

I am not about to drag all our dirty clothes over there, she said.

I could help you this morning, then. Drive you over and carry the basket for you.

I thought you were supposed to be sick, she said. You'd better get back in bed, hadn't you? I don't mind walking, anyway. It isn't far and I can get our stuff into a couple pillowcases.

After she left he took a leak. He didn't need to shave, he thought, just to stay home. Even if he did let her go to her parents' and then meet her he didn't need to shave. Not for her parents.

She'd left this dirty little bag on the back of the toilet tank. She was in such a hurry to get out, she'd forgotten it. He unzipped it, and a rotten sweet smell hit him. He dumped it in the sink. There was a red pencil with a red cap, a greasy bottle of medium-ivory make-up, a compact exactly like his mother's, he thought, and a lipstick. He'd seen his mother flip open her compact like Captain Kirk using his tricorder to call the Enterprise. She used the little mirror and smeared on her lipstick and rubbed her lips together.

His face felt greasy under the beard stubble. He couldn't stand being dirty. Maybe he really was getting sick.

Dulcie had sure rushed out. She was happy to get out. Happy as a gopher in soft dirt.

He uncapped the red pencil. The lead was soft brown. He wrote Dulcie on the mirror. He put a brown heart around it. With the lipstick he wrote Lonnie inside the brown heart too. He dumped the mess of her make-up back into the bag and zipped it up. He dropped the bag on the bathroom floor and stepped on it. He heard something plastic go. He put a sock on and his right cordovan and stomped on the dirty bag until it was flat and pink goop was coming out of the zipper.

He wasn't about to shave but he turned on the shower and watched the steam fill up the bathroom and try to eat the heart off the mirror. After he was in the shower he found he still had on his underwear. He soaped up all over and ran the bar of soap down inside his underwear. He stood under the hot hot water until it rinsed clear and then he turned both handles off together, fast so he wouldn't get his nuts scalded or frozen either. Cold showers he didn't need. He left the soaked underwear on the shower floor. Let her figure it out.

Happy as a gopher in soft dirt.

He wiped the towel across the mirror. But light, so the heart and the insides only smeared. Like they were trying to beat feet out of there.

At the laundromat he watched her through the window. He was shivering in his old varsity jacket with his wet hair. She was taking clothes out of machines and piling them into a grocery cart. The soaked clothes would be heavy. She wheeled them over to the dryers. She'd already made her phone call, he thought. She sat on this kitchen chair with her back to him. Any minute Bruce would be pulling up and would drive her out to the boonies to put his hands all over her and his prick up her while Lonnie's wet clothes flopped around in the dryer. Or she was waiting for him to call her back on that pay phone on the wall by the soap machines. Dulcie held a book propped open on top of her belly.

His wet hair was stiffening in the cold and giving him a headache. He walked back to the apartment trying to keep his head steady.

Their baby was probably going to have dark hair, Dulcie had said. He had dark brown hair and brown eyes but she had blonde hair and blue eyes. She'd learned in biology something like dark was dominant over light.

He went through the entire apartment, pulling out drawers and checking underneath and standing on the kitchen counter to check out the top of the cupboard. She had secret letters or phone numbers or money hidden somewhere. In the closet was her big leather suitcase. The combination lock was set for her birthday, he knew, and inside he found her college clothes. He pulled the string to turn on the closet light and shut the door. Here was the yellow sweater he had given her, and the yellow skirt. He sat on the closet floor and held the sweater to his face and stroked it. Bruce also had put his arm around her there on the sweater and touched her breasts there and put his hand under the yellow skirt. His pocketknife was sharp, his dad had taught him how to keep it sharp when he was just a kid, and he slit the skirt first and then the sweater and sliced them up in the closet.

Finally he got up and dumped the shreds outside in the trash can. In the bathroom mirror the heart was still running away. Yellow fuzz from her sweater was caught on his whiskers.

He was naked in bed when she got back. She left the lights off and unloaded the pillowcases. Come here, he told her. Pecker wants Pussy.

But my mother will be here soon, she said.

I guess she knows we do it, he said. He thought of Mrs. White walking in while he was putting it to her daughter and watching his ass in the dark. He said, Take off your clothes. It won't take but a few minutes. Speedy Gonzalez here.

And she was dressed and waiting when Mrs. White knocked and practically falling out the door. I'm ready, Mother, she said. Lonnie will be over for dinner. She hollered it so he'd be sure to get the message.

He heated up his own turkey noodle soup for lunch. He took a long heavy nap and woke up sweating like when he was a kid and his mother put him down for summer afternoon naps. That was the way she said it: I put him down for a nap. He'd heard her through the coating of hot sleep. That was sometime before she went to the hospital.

He took another shower. He drank a can of beer. He decided to shave after all. His face itched. And he was going to his father-in-law's. He wasn't worried about what the old man would say. He didn't give a good goddamn. Dr. White wasn't really the old man. He wasn't a real doctor, either. Not the kind that could figure out what was wrong with you. Just some college kind of doctor. He never said much and it was hard to read him. Lonnie wasn't afraid of him. But he decided to shave.

The sky was covered with clouds that looked like smoke. He took the interstate, doing eighty most of the way. Dulcie kissed him at the front door, quick so her parents wouldn't see. She had on new pants and a striped blouse hanging down over her belly. Her mother had made her a dress and bought a corduroy jacket and a bunch of new clothes. She showed him.

I bought you a new blouse, he said. I was going to get you some more stuff.

I know, she said. But I've been needing maternity clothes. Don't look like that.

It gives me pleasure to buy clothes for my daughter, Mrs. White said. Look at it that way.

Halfway through the dinner, which was some funny kind of chicken and asparagus, her father came out with it. Lon, he said, all serious. Dulcie's mother and I would like to make an offer. We'd like to pay your way through school.

But—I already graduated, he said.

The university, I mean, Dr. White said. We know you could do it on your own. But it would take a while that way. Consider it a loan, if you'd rather.

He couldn't say a word. He sat there with a cloth napkin on his thighs and too much silverware on the table and too much light.

Give it some thought, Dr. White said and squeezed his lips together.

Rhubarb pie? Mrs. White said. Still warm? A la mode?

Dulcie was all hot over the idea on the way home. Did you take the SAT or the ACT? she said. We'll have to find out what the university wants to see. I can help you. I can type your papers. Heck, I can write them for you, if you want. Well, that wouldn't be right. But I could help you study. What should you major in, I wonder? You wouldn't have to decide the first year, anyway.

He didn't know dick about any of it. SAT. ACT. Papers. Major. He couldn't do it.

I thought of barber college, he said. Except I couldn't touch all that greasy hair.

Barber college? You're kidding.

His mother used to ride him about getting a trade. If you think I'm going to clean rich broads' houses all my life just to support your narrow butt, you've got another think coming, she said. Listen to your mother when she's talking at you, his dad said. You could go to trade school. Be a barber or an electrician or mechanic. Or plumbing's good. Or you could marry a rich woman. Like I did. He winked.

Listen, Dulcie said. I'll help you. You can do it. Don't underestimate yourself.

At home he cracked a beer. He picked up her library book. It had a red library cover, no picture for a clue. He looked at different pages. What the hell was going on? He couldn't believe it. But there it was. The book was about some cathouse.

What are you reading this crap for? he said. This why you've always got your nose stuck in these books? For the filth?

That's William Faulkner, for your information. You should try reading him.

He threw the red-covered book from the living room to the kitchen. Her purse was hanging on the bathroom doorknob. He pulled out her wallet and chugged the beer and found her library card. He ripped it in four pieces. He bent the metal piece in half. He burned the pieces in the sink.

She sat at the kitchen table crying. She wiped her face with the striped blouse. He could see her watermelon belly when she hiked the blouse up.

At the store he kept smelling the women. He sat on the stool across from them and when they put their feet up their smells escaped from under their dresses. Their damp stockings smelled too.

Once when it was raining his mother had picked him up from school. What's that smell? he said in the car. Smells like cat food.

She said sometimes when women needed to bathe they smelled kind of fishy. She said she'd been down on her hands and knees all day.

He'd shut up. He'd never guessed the smell was coming from her. But she didn't even care. He beat feet to his room as soon as they got home.

But Dulcie had deodorant and body powder. He'd bought this perfume for her on their three-months' anniversary. Love Potion #8. It was a joke. It was also powerful stuff. You could smell her a mile away.

The old man at Walsh Brothers chewed him out royally. Your enthusiasm for the job has slackened, he said. You're becoming less than reliable. You're such a personable young man, and you do a good job of selling when you try.

Don't try to con me with that psychology, he said. I don't have to take this crap. But he waited until he was out the door to say it.

He felt like he was the one going to have the baby. He'd stayed on the can for a half hour until Stu pounded on the door and said they had people getting antsy out front. His mother said he'd been a constipated baby even. He was premature and she couldn't nurse him. Which he was glad to know. The formula bound him up, though.

He stopped at the drugstore on the way home and got those chocolate squares his mother used to get him. At the checkout there was this plastic football that said Daddy's Boy on it and he bought it too. The kid had to be a boy. He felt it kicking from inside. Dulcie held his hand on her belly sometimes for him to feel it. He'd have brown eyes and he'd play football. He would if he was Lonnie's kid. He might be somebody else's kid. Bruce or somebody else might have put it to her.

He walked all bent over from the Witch to the back door. He was all cramped up. He handed Dulcie the plastic football and eased down on the couch. That's for my son, he said.

CHAPTER 11

Lonnie took the garnet ring my father had given me last Christmas. He wanted it, he said, because I hadn't given him a wedding band. He wore it on the little finger of his left hand. "Do you know how ridiculous that looks?" I asked him. "That lady's ring on your big hairy hand?" The truth was, he hadn't exactly taken it, he hadn't uncurled my fingers and forced it off, but he kept insisting and then he fixated on the idea that I didn't want him to wear it because some other guy had given it to me. At my parents' after dinner, I said, "Dad, will you tell my husband where I got this ring?" But Lonnie said on the way home that of course my father would lie for me.

What did it matter?

The baby had quickened. I loved that: The baby had quickened. The first time the baby turned over, like a seal, like an otter, sleek and wet and boneless under the skin of the water, I burst into tears. I tried to tell Katie what it was like, the scary thrill of that smooth roll inside you, and she said it sounded like a bad case of gas. I remembered the women in the waiting room when I'd first gone for the pregnancy test, sitting with their palms on their stomachs, with their eyes shiny and unintelligent as cows' eyes. And now I held my hands spread on my own flesh to feel the flutters and the kicks and the rolls—the quickening.

"There's this way you could prove it to me," Lonnie said.

He was eating his turkey noodle soup while I made him a second cheese sandwich. For once he liked my way better than his mother's, buttered bread grilled in a frying pan instead of Bernadine's slab of Velveeta between dry toast spread with mayonnaise.

"What do I need to prove now?" I said, and immediately regretted the thick patience in my voice. I turned the sandwich over. The top was dappled golden brown. I'd grown keen to his voice and hands and habits, and sometimes I could distract him before the suspicions swelled in his head. They were like bubbles in his brain, and only I knew they were there, and now and then if I was paying attention I could soap them so they couldn't get enough air to swell up.

"What does she need to prove?" he said. "Oh nothing much. No big giant deal. Only that it's my kid in there, that's all."

I stood behind him and put my hands on his shoulders. "I've told you—"

"And told you and told you," he finished. "Yeah, well then prove it. Tell that doctor you want a blood test. Soon as the kid's out, you want a blood test."

He shrugged my hands off him.

"You don't really love me at all, do you?" I said.

He turned fast in the chair and grabbed me. With his face against my stomach, he said, "Don't you say that. Don't you ever say that. I love you so much I can't hardly stand it sometimes. That's how come I have to know."

"Let go. Your sandwich is done. You don't want it to burn up, do you?"

Cheese had oozed out into the frying pan. I flipped the sandwich onto a plate. The bread was burnt slick and I gave it to him black side up.

After he left for the shoe store, I made myself a sandwich, the textured bread golden and perfect.

I didn't practice the embarrassing question. I slept long in the days before the appointment, and when I had to go out, I thought I was invisible, an enormous invisible matron in dark maternity clothes. The question was like something small and solid in my jacket pocket. I didn't need to finger it. When I handed it over to the doctor, Lonnie would have to know the truth.

I waited until the doctor was finished with my body and my pants were up and my shoes on and I was sitting on the patients' side of his desk.

"All right, Mrs. Saxbe," he said, "looking good. Looking real good."

"I need to make a request," I said. "When the baby's born, would you do a blood test?"

"Well... blood test?"

His pencil cup was the ceramic torso of a pregnant woman. A handle was attached to her swayback.

"A paternity test," I said. "My husband needs to know."

He picked a pencil from the white pregnant body and bounced it on its eraser. "We can do that. But, you know—"

I stood up. "I don't want to know anything. I just need you to do it."

"Your parents live close, isn't that right?" he said. "They're nearby to help."

Later after supper I told Lonnie I'd asked for a paternity test.

"Paternity? Does that mean I got to buy a bunch of baggy clothes?" he said. "Anyway, I just wanted to see if you'd ask him."

"Who's this?" Lonnie said. "Bernard Fink. *Fink?* Another one of your boyfriends?" He was going through my address book.

"Bernard Fink was my piano teacher. Give me back my book." My mother had given me the blue book, with a scroll of white birds on the cover, before I'd left for college, and I'd copied into it the significant names to carry along with me. I'd added nobody but Glenna and Katie. Lonnie was already there, even before I left.

"Did he fuck you? Did he?"

"He was my *piano te*acher."

"And I'm Queen Elizabeth. Who else is in here you don't want me to see?"

I grabbed the book but he held on, and so I let it go. What did it matter? The blue book with its white birds wasn't my childhood. I let it go.

"Quit your bawling," he said. "I hate that. Is that the Fink's kid you've got in your belly, is that what's going on here?" He ripped pages from the book and hurled it into the lamp on the end table. When the lamp didn't crash over but only wobbled, he shook me by the shoulders and shook until I went loose.

In the midst of this Katie knocked on the outer storm door and called, "Hey Saxbes! You guys home?"

"Oh no," I whispered. "She can't see me like this." Shame flooded me. "Tell her I'm taking a shower. Tell her I'll be right out."

In the bathroom I started up the water. I heard Lonnie say, "Well, hey, gorgeous!" My face was wet and blotchy, and I scrubbed it and stuck my head under the faucet. I was protecting myself, not Lonnie, not letting her see me a shapeless red-faced mess. Or I was protecting us: She shouldn't know about that hot panting intimacy. I had loved Katie, and we had been intimates in our little practice room with two pianos, in our little dorm room with the matching bedspreads and the Picasso and the Renoir on the walls, we had been as naively intimate as those girls, the one dark-haired and the other blonde, primly lolling together on the river bank. My new intimacy was hot and messy, with his thick fluid oozing out of me onto the sheet every night, with all my slobbering tears, and I wanted to keep Katie on the innocent side of the river.

I combed my hair and rubbed my face dry and opened the bathroom door, but she'd already left.

"I said you weren't here," Lonnie said. He'd pulled his shirt out of his pants and unbuttoned it. "I said I was just about to take a shower."

I went straight back to the bathroom. I heard the refrigerator door and then the wet snap of a tab top. I sat on the toilet lid crying with my face in the wet towel, helplessly outraged that he'd sent Katie away, and then I dropped the towel and cried with my face up, letting go, fully participating in the melodrama. Just as the crying was growing forced and I was noticing the clotted dust on the ceiling vent, Lonnie kicked the door and said, "Get on out of there now. Give it up. Let's go to bed."

I thought he would pull me against him and make up, but he flung my full pink nightgown at me. He'd stripped to his underwear and opened up the bed. The apartment was overheated, the way he kept it. He watched carefully while I took off my clothes and put on the nightgown.

"You think you're such hot shit," he said. "Hot shit on a gold platter. You think you're too good for me." He said it thoughtfully, working it out in his mind. "You don't like my company. Well, come here. I want to show you something."

He opened the door and pushed me out and slammed the bolt into the socket. Through the glass in the door he said, "I wouldn't want to force myself on your royal highness. I don't guess a little cold could hurt you none."

The space between the door into the kitchen and the outer storm door was like a tiny porch, enclosed but unheated. It was full fall, and I began shivering right away in the cotton nightgown. I watched him remove another can of beer from the refrigerator. He stood in his underwear with his hard back to me and tipped his head back to drink.

I supposed he wanted me to tap on the glass and look pitiful and beg to be let in and swear again and again and again and again that I'd never let anybody but my own beloved baby husband touch me. I sat on the braided doormat. The apartment lights went out and I heard the bed take Lonnie's weight. I decided not to cry anymore. What did it matter? The door was closed on Katie now. I had lost her. I took a full shuddering breath. I could never go home and be my parents' daughter again. I sat in the brittle cold, on my little stage, so sorry for the shivering girl, in trouble and cast into the cold night in only her nightgown, full of the tragic scene.

My mother had seen bruises on my shoulders when I tried on the red wool jumper she'd made me. "I was afraid of that," she said. She tried to hug me but I stayed straight and stiff and I wouldn't look at her.

"Men can be like that, sweetheart," she said. "So aggressive. Does he get enough sex? That can make a man mad, the frustration."

"*That's* not it," I said and wouldn't look at her.

"Dulcie, sweetheart. You can leave him. *You* could do that. I never had anywhere to go. But you could come back home."

"No I can't," I said.

If Lonnie didn't let me back into the apartment soon, I'd have to run outside across the alley, barefooted in my nightgown, and see if Linda was home. I could make up some story. Say Lonnie was gone somewhere and I'd stupidly locked myself out. But then what? I couldn't stay all night at Linda's, not without telling her the truth, which was that Lonnie and I were trash, low-life trash, our motors run on jealousy and burned-up library cards and sex. I didn't know Linda's husband. What would he do? Go kick in our door and give Lonnie a man-to-manning about proper treatment of the little ladies or punch him or sit down with him for a beer and a good laugh? Or maybe Linda would call the police. I lay down on the doormat and pulled my knees up. I shook with exaggerated shivers, as if Lonnie were watching, though the shaking was involuntary. I was ashamed. I would call the police before I'd call my parents.

Stop that shivering, I told myself. Do you want to hurt the baby? I pulled the dirty rag rug around my stomach and breathed in the cold and made my body go limp until I was hardly shaking.

I made up a story.

Lonnie arrived home early. He slapped another speeding ticket down on the kitchen table. He helped himself to a can of beer. "I can't eat no more grilled cheese sandwiches," he said. "Let's go out." So we took the highway to get out of town. "Got to blow some of this carbon out," he said. Suddenly at high speed we sailed into the guard rail and crashed through and tumbled down the embankment, almost joyfully, like a child rolling down a grassy hill. The car landed upside down and I was hanging by the safety belt and let myself down carefully but Lonnie, unbelted, had been hurled out. Some people who had seen us crash climbed down and found him. "You don't want to look, ma'am," they said. And everybody was so sorry for the poor young widow, carrying his child.

A light went on inside. I heard the toilet seat hit the tank and in a minute, I heard the flush. I closed my eyes and stayed still, so I didn't know if he checked on me, and then the bed took his weight again.

No.

We took the highway out of town. "Got to blow some of this carbon out," he said. I pressed my fingers into my shoulders to make the bruises hurt. Suddenly at high speed I reached over and wrenched the steering wheel and made the car crash through the guard rail. I'd been to the library and read up on physics and figured out the precise angle of impact, the precise speed, the precise angle and tension for my body. I laughed, exhilarated, as the car rolled over and over, and I watched him fly through the window. Hanging from my safety belt, I let myself down carefully and climbed out the window. She didn't have a scratch, they would say. I found him impaled on—what? a steel spike, a steel spike left from construction work on the highway. He was already dead. He had died instantly. Except for the spike emerging from his chest and the blood dripping around it, he looked like the old Lonnie, my walking, talking boyfriend, and I considered kissing him but I didn't. And everybody said oh the poor young widow but at least she has her baby and her whole life ahead of her.

After I'd killed him, I was numb for a little while. But then my teeth started chattering and my thighs shook against my stomach. I felt damp, as if sweat were congealing. Maybe tonight would be the first snow. The baby was shivering under the rug, I thought, and then it was so still I thought it might have died. I would have to carry it all the way, as my mother had my dead brother, but I would have to leave Lonnie then and go home so my mother could get me through the time with that stone weight inside me. I wondered what had killed her baby. Then my baby kicked and a sob leapt out of me. I had to pound on the door and beg and promise, or run across the alley, do something, before the baby did freeze.

The door opened. Slowly and softly. I didn't move. "Are you asleep?" he whispered. He lifted the dirty rug off me. "Come on in. You can come in." He was still whispering.

I rolled up and stepped inside past him. He didn't try to touch me. I went to the bathroom in the dark and washed my face in warm water, and got under the covers on my side of the terrible pull-out bed and refused to shiver until the blankets and the hot room settled me down. For the first night since we'd been married he didn't touch me and whisper that Pecker loved Pussy and climb onto my body. I didn't give him anything. He didn't say he was sorry, and I didn't forgive. He had gone too far. We had gone too far, and we knew it, and we sank into the silence the way a child who has cried too long finally settles into soft, righteous sleep. This is the end of all that, I thought. Now we will just be young expectant parents. I'd place his hand on my stomach when the baby kicked, and we'd think of names, and then the air-breathing, crying baby would be in the white bassinet, and all our lives would drift ahead, maybe a little disappointed but warm and unbruised. What did it matter? What made me believe it would be anything else?

CHAPTER 12

He knew she was sneaking around. Calling guys up. Writing secret notes. Meeting them. Probably Katie was pimping for her.

He counted the pages of blue paper in her stationery box. He tore a sheet from the kitchen pad and logged the numbers.

```
letter paper27
envelopes18
stamps10
kitchen pad84
change dish:
   -nickels7
   -dimes3
   -quarters3
```

When he left for work every morning, he took to balancing a matchstick on the outside sill of the door. Whatever she did, he would know. He would know if she went out to sneak around. He would know if she put it down in writing. If she mailed it. If she used a pay phone. And then he would catch her.

Monday night the old man nabbed him on his way out. Mr. Phony Walsh. Stu had split already. Split like a banana. At noon Stu said his little wifey was at her mother's with the rug rats for a week and he had a banana in his pants. Guess that makes you some kind of a fruit, Lonnie said. Me, I got a snake. A one-eyed trouser snake.

Mr. Saxbe, the old man said. Lonnie. Sit down. For just a minute. Then we'll get you on your way home. But we seem to be having some problems.

The old man plunked his butt down on the padded stool like he was ready to measure Lonnie's foot. He guessed he'd found out about the bounced check. But that didn't have nothing to do with the store. So the register must be short again. How come he right off thought it was Lonnie? It could have been the great straight Stu Mason just as well.

Mr. Saxbe, he said. You've called in sick an awful lot. Or you're late. Or you leave early. Or you take a long lunch. I've tried to be patient here. I know you're young. I know you're starting a family.

Sweat was soaking into the armpits of his shirt. He hated that hot and cold feel. Stu had been bitching to the old man, he figured.

I've been here, he said. He looked the old man straight in the eye. Like they said to do in voc ed. He said, Stu's been feeding you a line. To get on your good side.

Mr. Saxbe. Mr. Mason isn't a factor in this discussion. In point of fact, he defends you. Why I can't fathom, since he's been doing your work for you. Now you listen up.

Lonnie stood. He didn't have to listen up. I have to get home, he said. I'm sorry. Sir. I won't let it happen again. Sir. Right now my wife is getting ready to have my baby. Sir. She needs me to be with her. Sir.

The old man shook his head. I was young once, he said. You needn't take that tone. But you need to learn that when you take the money you do the job. Sit back down. I'm not finished. I'm trying to teach you something here.

He could save it if he sat and kissed ass. If he said, Oh thank you massuh sir. He itched all over, his skin itched and his insides itched, and he knew if he said a thing it would come out bad. He'd say, You old fart, you noodle dick, you couldn't never get it up to make babies of your own. Or he'd just punch him out.

I can see I'm not getting through, the old man said. So take this as the final warning. This is an ultimatum, Mr. Saxbe. Expecting wife or no. You are going to be out of a job unless you shape up. Now go on home and think about it.

He stopped and bought a case. He popped a can in the car and sat in the driveway to finish it. Go on home and think about it. *Now you can just go sit in your room and think about it. You can sit in your room, young man, until you can control yourself.* Inside he kissed Dulcie. He needed something. I had a hard day at work, he said. Take care of your baby nice, he said.

He drank a can while he watched her in the kitchen. Supper was hot dogs. She cut slits in them and put in slices of cheese and put them under the broiler. One night she'd made pancakes. For supper. I'm doing the best I can, she said. Meat costs money. But he liked the hot dogs. These are good, baby, he said. The old lady never fixed these.

She smiled at him with her lips together. That meant she was worried.

Listen, he said, everything's okay. Okay dandy swell. Take your pick. Old man Walsh thinks I'm hot stuff. He's wanting to give me a raise. He said that just tonight.

He downed another Bud at the table and watched her do the dishes. She had to stretch to get at the sink, her belly was so huge.

He came up behind her and kissed her neck. Come on, he said.

Now? she said.

He opened up the bed. He needed something. And then he'd get down to some serious drinking. Ultimatum schmultimatum, his dad would say. Walk like a man, my son, his dad would say. He laughed, thinking of his dad singing with the Four Seasons.

He figured his dad hadn't ever seen his sisters in the bedroom. He said one time, Daddy how come the girls like to rub? His dad said, Yeah, sounds like a pack of pups in there. Sugar and spice, schmice.

The doctor said he should quit six weeks before the baby was due. Which was now. Or last week. Anyway, that was her word only. That was what she said the old quack said. Her and that doctor were in it together. He'd fake the blood test too.

Walk like a man. Walk like a man, my su-uh-uh-un. He didn't like the Four Seasons. Frankie Valli sounded like he'd been goosed. And liked it. Fuck like a man, he thought. Oh fuck fuck fuck. Like a mah-ah-ah-an. Fuck like a man, Dad says I can, fuck like a man and cu-uh-uh-um.

Afterwards Dulcie took a shower. She came out with her hair in wet strings. She was growing it long again. She had on her nightgown. She finished the dishes and then got into bed.

I know it's early, she said. But this is nice. I feel cozy. Huge. But cozy. Reading in bed is one of the great pleasures of the world.

By eight she was out. He turned off the stupid phony detective on television. Dick, the idiot was called. Private dick. He couldn't hardly believe it. A private dick. He was trying not to laugh out loud. She needed the sleep. She was all the time sleeping. At least he knew where she was when she was zonked out.

He helped himself to another Bud and stepped out back. Snow was coming down. The sky was light with snow clouds. He held out his left hand. Don't melt, he said out loud to the snow dropping onto the back of his hand. But it did. It dropped like little white bugs and right away it changed into water and ran down the hairs on the back of his hand.

He shut himself up in the space between the outside door and the door to the kitchen. Just to see what it was like. He squatted. He couldn't bring himself to sit on the dirty foot-wipe rug. It wasn't so bad in there. It was practically warm. He'd want to put black paper over the window into the kitchen. Otherwise he liked it in there. He wished Dulcie would wake up and find him there. See? he'd say. See? It's good in here. It's warm enough. You weren't so all-out mistreated.

He felt like he was covered with wax. Dulcie had a book from the doctor that showed a baby just born with this white junk all over it. He felt like the snow was coating his skin all over.

He knew what Dulcie looked like under the covers in bed. Under that nightgown. Her belly button poked out. You could see veins in her tits.

She looked stretched tight all over. This brown line like the seam on his mother's stockings went straight from her belly button down to her hair.

He drained the can and sat on the painted wooden floor. He loved Dulcie White so much. She was a tight big egg. He remembered a picture from eighth-grade health. They showed the guys this filmstrip in the dark. The coach pulled the shade on the door so any girls in the hall couldn't look in. The picture was this round egg with eyes and lips. Curled eyelashes and red lips. The egg was cheek to cheek with this little sperm with a tail. The sperm was grinning to beat the band. Oh baby oh baby. They had little hearts above them. He'd never forget that stupid picture. They'd all laughed like strangled idiots and the coach got mad and turned on the lights.

He fell over on the floor and pulled up his knees. He was sick. Now he looked like a fetus, he thought. He hated that word fetus. Fetus schmeatus. Fetus meatus. He was going to puke. Dulcie was in there under the covers just sleeping away. Dreaming of some guy putting his meat into her. Some private dick. Lonnie was cold. The cold felt good. Like he could freeze out the sickness.

Last year his mother got hold of some pills that made him sick. She gave him a pill after supper one night and said it was vitamins. Then he had a beer, just one fucking beer, and he puked his guts out on the kitchen floor. She made him clean it up. The next day she told him. You drink too much, she said. You keep on drinking and I'll put that medicine in your food. You'll learn what drinking does to you.

He was stone cold furious and he quit eating her food for three days. He opened up his own can of soup and built himself a bologna sandwich and just sat at the table with her and her hamburger casserole and his dad and the green beans from a can. His dad said, Well, Bernie, I guess you've taught him a lesson. And anyhow, ain't it better if he's doing it at home, not out in the boonies?

Starting a family, the noodle dick had said. You're starting a family. Like it was a choice. Like in shop you could say, For the next project I'll start a bookcase. What you started, you could finish. You'd sand it and stain it and Mr. Atcheson would grade it. Starting a family was not for sprinters, though. One time Coach had filmed them. He could still see himself in gray and white running on his toes, his knees high, his bent arms swinging, leaning forward. Now check out Saxbe, Coach said, see how he's going all-out straight. There's no weaving there. Then he reversed the film and the little gray Lonnie's knees jumped up and he was yanked backwards. Everybody laughed at him. You look like a ruptured duck, Jerry Angus said.

He started to heave. He held it down. The film ran backwards in his head. He crawled to the outside door and dragged himself up. Outside was warm and it was snowing thick and wet. He kneeled and his guts heaved. He'd seen dogs like this, retch, retch, retch, bringing it up one level at a time until they opened their mouths wide and it came gushing out. Oh Christ. He kneeled in the warm snow. Oh Jesus shellacked Christ. Don't start what you can't finish, Mr. Atcheson used to say. Build you a bookcase before you start a house. Finally he puked onto the snow. He saw his hunched back and his shoulders shaking and then the film reversed and the puke flew back into him and he did it again.

He piled snow on but it melted on contact. He did not want to face that mess of hot dog and beer in the morning. At the trailer his dad would have a shovel. Here he didn't have a single tool. He found a stick and spread the mess around and stirred it into the dirt and leaves and snow.

Inside, Dulcie was still zonked. She hadn't even missed him. He was in this for the distance. He rinsed his mouth and got into bed with her. He still could not believe he was in bed with Dulcie White. She was on her back with his baby inside her. Her mouth was open and she made these little snores. If he was starting a family, then it wouldn't be just this one baby. He couldn't hardly breathe beside her. A dozen or a hundred sticky white fetuses crawled all over him. He sat up fast and breathed deep. He liked the 100-yard dash. He liked the 220 best. But he sank back down and put his bare leg up against her and closed his eyes and breathed through his nose and ran a film of himself. His head was up to watch the horizon. His arms were loose. His feet were close to the ground. He took the weight on his heels and rolled it onto the balls of his feet. He ran the film forward and forward and forward.

I got a killer headache, he told Dulcie in the morning. You call Stu and tell him I'll be in later on. Call him now at home.

He got up to take a leak. The headache was right in the front of his forehead. He felt top heavy.

Lonnie, feel this, she said. All surprised and too loud. She grabbed his hand and put it on her belly.

I *feel* like junior in there, he said. There was this picture in her book of the fetus with an enormous head. That's how his head felt. He wished he could float, too, and wouldn't have to hold up his heavy head. The fetus had a narrow butt and webbed fingers. Now he could feel the kid through her nightgown. It kept making these little jumps. Over and over.

What's going on? she said. Why is he hopping like that? You think something's going wrong?

She didn't care about him and his pain. Kid's just practicing his dribbling, he said. We got us a basketball player, is all. You gonna call Stu for me or not?

From the bathroom he heard her on the phone. Talking all sweet. He remembered Stu's wife was away. Right now Stu could be telling Dulcie about the banana in his pants and she was loving it.

By the time he wiped the rim and flushed and washed his hands, she was off the phone. What was that all about? he said.

She had both hands spread out on her belly. He's had kids, she said. I asked him about this hopping. She giggled like an idiot. You know what it is? The baby has the hiccups. The hiccups!

When he woke mid-morning, the headache had moved back an inch and shrunk. But it was still heavy. Smaller but just as heavy. He shaved and cut himself and showered in the hottest water he could take. In his clothes he felt hot and scraped and raw.

At the store Stu gave him his mother's look and shook his head. He only said, That was cute. Your wife didn't know the kid could get the hiccups.

Lonnie tried to stay in the stockroom the rest of the morning. At noon he told Stu to go on, get out of here, he'd make up for coming in late by staying through both their lunches. He was too sick to eat, anyway.

He was cramming size sixes onto this fat broad's feet when the old man came in. She had little feet but they were fat. He was trying not to gag at the fatty smell from under her dress when she put her fat foot on the stool. He needed to get her out of the door. But the old man wouldn't rag on him with a customer in the store. So he said, Let me see if we've got this in a D. Her feet were practically square.

The fat broad was gone when he got back with a pile of boxes.

Hey, where'd she go? he said. I was going to sell her these bedroom slippers and call them the new fashion in women's flats.

You don't demean the customer, the old man said. What you should have done is what I in fact did: You do the expeditious measurement, without calling attention to it, you confirm the style she wants, and you special-order. You do not tell the customer she has square feet.

He didn't know he'd said it out loud.

You weren't here at nine, the old man said. You weren't here at ten.

I'm sick, Lonnie said. I'm sick but I'm here anyway. You should appreciate that. I'm even putting in extra right now. I'm skipping my lunch break.

You're not sick. You're hung over. You smell like a brewery. You're sweating beer. I can smell your vomit. I'm out of patience with you. I've bent over backwards, but that's it.

Stick it up your ass, Lonnie said. You old fart. You old noodle dick.

He said it, he said it softly, he was shaking, and he stepped to the door. He didn't think he could take the terrible cowbell clang if he opened the door.

Wait just a minute, the old man said. Here. Here's a check for last week. Now we're square. I hope you get yourself straightened out, young man. For your own sake. For the sakes of your wife and child.

The old man was like the guidance counselor at school. Who Mrs. Sanderson had made him see. He never knew how come. Nothing Lonnie said could make him hot and mad. He was always so goddamn calm like he had all the answers in the world and you didn't know dick. The old man was like that. They had all the answers but they wouldn't tell you. You got a little pat on the head when you figured out any part of it. Good boy. Goood booooy.

He took the check. He couldn't say a word, he was so hot and sick and raw. The old man had been going to fire him no matter what. He'd had the check ready. It wouldn't have mattered what Lonnie did. He could have opened the joint at six in the a.m. and sold a thousand dollars' worth of cordovans. He'd have been shitcanned anyway.

He ripped the cowbell off the door and threw it at the counter. And he was out.

He cashed the check at the liquor store before the old man changed his mind and put a hold on it. He took a case of Bud. Me and the wife are having some friends over, he told the guy at the register. It was the one who'd sold him yesterday's case. Nobody at the store looked at ID. Me and the wife are having a little party, he said. A little get-together.

He drove back down Main and parked across from Walsh Brothers Shoes. He went into Judy's Girls and Women. Hi gorgeous, he said to the clerk. What would be good for a girl going to the hospital? I want to buy a present for my wife. She's about to have my baby.

She sold him a pink flowered robe that had a pink ribbon to tie at the neck. He carried the box out and beeped his horn and waved. He thought he saw the old man at the window.

The headache was killing him. The sound of the horn had smacked right against the pain. He touched his finger to his forehead. He made a tiny circle. If he could make a tiny hole, the pressure would rush out.

The match he'd left on the sill was on the ground now. Dulcie had opened the door. She wasn't home. Now when he needed her she was out running around. A blue notebook was on the couch. On the cover it said The Chambrie Poems. The first page said, Dedicated to my best friend, Love forever, Katie. Jess Springer had dedicated his English paper to Lonnie. His homo paper. He turned the pages. None of it made any sense. It was nothing but blue-ink words lined up to look pretty. Katie the queer. Katie the cunt.

He lay down on the couch, squashing the notebook under his hip, and tried to sleep off the headache. He heard her open the door at four-thirty. He saw the red Corvette back out.

That's not very friendly, he said. To just drive away. Your best friend just dumps you in the gravel. You should have invited her in.

She took in the bent blue notebook and the white box with the store bow on it. We saw your car in the driveway, she said.

Soon as you get rid of me, you and Katie hit the town together.

We just went shopping, she said. Not that I bought anything. She got us a sweater for the baby. There's nothing wrong with any of that. What do you care if I go downtown with Katie?

She held out a yellow sweater. It had a hood. There was a white rabbit on the front. She stood there with her other hand on her belly. Staring him down. That was Katie's effect on her.

I don't want you running around, he said. He wondered what all they'd seen downtown.

I'm not running around, she said. Soft and slow. Like the guidance counselor again. Let's reason this out together, the guy had said. She stared at him. She squeezed her lips together until they disappeared. He slapped her. He slapped her across her stiff mouth. She stared at him and stayed tight. He held back not to really hurt her, just to teach her. He slapped her and slapped her. Finally she looked down. Finally her mouth was loose with blood.

CHAPTER 13

After he hit me, he slammed out. I thought he'd rush away, spewing gravel and slush, but he only sat in his car. I watched him through the Venetian blinds and I was glad. When Lonnie yelled, the baby jumped, and now I stroked him and rocked my body for him. "Hush little baby, don't you cry," I sang. "Mama's gonna buy you—" Something. I didn't know the words. I didn't even know where the song came from. "Mama's gonna buy you an alibi," I sang. That didn't make any sense. Those weren't the real words. An alibi for what? Lonnie's head was down on the steering wheel and I thought I could see his shoulders bucking. Good, I thought, you cry. I'm not crying. Not for you. I lay down on the sofa. At least when he hit my face, he wasn't hurting the baby. It felt good to cry, to cry calmly against the rough upholstery. "I'll never let him hurt you," I said to the baby. All the pressure in him, and all the pressure in me, had been released with the slaps. Now I was soft and washed—dulcet again. I pulled my knees up to the baby and surrounded him. He hadn't been kicking much in the last few days, but the doctor said that was because his quarters were getting cramped. A doctor must have told my mother the same thing. When she surrounded her baby, she must have believed she had soothed him to sleep.

Lonnie sat alone in his car, going nowhere, and I was glad. I didn't fall asleep this time. I had been sleeping all the time, as if I were buried in snow, and the frozen didn't care about anything—books or suppers or buried babies or mothers or anything—and Lonnie's slaps shook me out of the sleep.

Suddenly my pants felt wet, and I pushed up from the sofa. I knew one of these days my water would break. Those were the odd words—how did water break? I pictured silvery amniotic fluid running and pooling like mercury. But it was too soon for that. Maybe it was blood and maybe thawing out meant losing the baby—more odd words, for if he emerged now he would not be lost, he would be exactly right here, a bloody blue unfinished baby—and it would be Lonnie's fault. I was afraid to pull down my pants and look. It would be our fault, for didn't I know the cocky words—What's it to you?—and didn't I know the defiant stare to force his hand to my face? Nobody could ever know what happened. My mother had lost her other baby, nobody's fault, and there was a story that went with it, but no one could ever see the slippery cable of umbilicus between Lonnie and me or be told that I was the guilty one. I had fallen into Lonnie's lust in the back seat and into my own sort of numb concupiscence, which was deceitful and more wicked than his hard obvious flesh. He said I was a whore, and I'd wanted to answer back but hadn't dared, that he should check the dictionary, if he could read, that whores took money, but maybe whoredom was the truth, for hadn't I taken everything anybody offered, taken it all carelessly as my due? I took my father's money, I took my mother's unconditional love—*oh please dear God if you only let her live*—I used Lonnie as my walking, talking boyfriend when nobody wanted me, I took his devotion and played with it, and maybe I'd been a whore for Katie even, entwining our selves, supersaturating our little rooms until we breathed each other's lives—and then betraying her. I took it all, just as if our lady's presence were sufficient reward. Yes, you may touch, our lady said, and I'll accept all your coin and grant you nothing. I sat in my wet pants on an ugly used green sofa, and I hated hated hated myself. I started punching my shoulder. If the baby weren't in me, I would pound my stomach. I was afraid to pull down my pants. I was glad he had hit me.

I stopped punching my shoulder when the outer door opened. He crept in and knelt on the floor at my feet. "Oh God, your face," he said and put his arms around my legs. "I've been out there praying," he said. "I honest to God prayed. Which I never done. Oh God, Dulcie. I am sorry. I love you so much. I am so sorry. I don't never want to hurt you." He rubbed my legs. "Oh baby, baby, baby. Forgive me. I swear to you. Never again."

I put my hand on his head. "It's all over now," I said. "But I'm afraid something's wrong."

"But I promise, Dulcie. I am promising. Please. You can't leave me."

"With the baby. I'm really afraid something's wrong with the baby."

He sank and his hands slid to my ankles. "Oh God oh God, I didn't do nothing to hurt the baby, did I?" His shoulders twitched as if he couldn't cry anymore. "What happened?"

"I think I'm bleeding. I was afraid to look."

I let him take me into the bathroom. Everybody knew what it meant when a woman was bleeding. I never thought I would say to any man, I am bleeding. This wasn't the same blood. All the blood meant no baby, though. Lonnie slid down my maternity pants. I gave in to our intimacy. I wore my underpants low so the elastic didn't press into my stomach. He knelt and eased them down to my ankles. "I'm so big I can't see my feet," I said. "Tell me."

"They're a little wet, but it's not blood," he said. He bent over and sniffed. "I'd say you pissed your pants. Smells like piss."

"It's too soon for the water to break." Now I wouldn't be embarrassed when the involuntary gush came. "I think that'll be a lot of water, anyway."

He took off my pants and washed me with warm water and brought me clean underpants. We knew I must have wet my pants when he hit me, and now that we knew what we could do to each other, we were too intimate to be shy.

"Sometimes I think I'm going crazy," he said. "I figured out a long time back my mother was crazy. I heard you can get it from your parents."

This was his secret. He was afraid he was insane. Paranoia, schizophrenia, dementia praecox, non compos mentis, genetic, congenital, acquired—I wouldn't give him the words. He scrubbed my underwear in the sink and the intimacy allowed him to tell the secret, which I guessed I'd already known. "You're not insane," I said. "You're all right. You'll be all right. I'll help you be all right."

I could help him. He wasn't stupid, and now that he was malleable, and now that I saw how the slender, terrible Dulcie had used him, I could soothe him and smooth him into the good and bright boy he was at heart. I could teach him grammar.

"Let's wash your face," he said.

In the mirror I saw my red cheeks and my split lip and dried blood at the corner of my mouth. I was glad it showed, for an instant righteous the way I was as a child when the handprints showed after a spanking, and then glad for the evidence of our change and our intimacy.

"You know what, let's do something," he said. "Go get something to eat and go see a movie. Comb your hair and get your coat. I'll get the car warmed up for you."

The next day my lips were puffy and the bruises were dark purple, and in the next week they deepened to black and grayed and then turned dirty yellow. "We're fair-skinned," my mother used to say. "We bruise easily." Once she fell out of bed in her sleep and hit the metal wastebasket and ended up with a black eye. She used to go to the beach with leg make-up on to hide her veins and her yellow bruises. Lonnie had thrown away my make-up, so there was no hiding the bruises, but my washed, marked face made me feel oddly purified. Lonnie was gentle and solicitous. We were done with the childish complications. We were moving into our adult life, husband and wife, expectant parents.

The morning after, Lonnie said he had the day off, the boss had given him a day off as a bonus, and we drove down the coast and made a day of it. We ate a McDonald's lunch, with chocolate milkshakes. At a shopping center, we wandered from store to store holding hands. In the Sears infant department, we bought a tiny blue suit with feet, receiving blankets, and a diaper pail.

In the evening, my mother called. Why didn't we come have Christmas with them? We could even come over the night before and go to the Christmas Eve service with them, and then spend the night. Lonnie put his hand under my maternity blouse, and I slapped it away.

"What's going on there?" my mother said. "Here, let me speak to my son-in-law."

I went into the kitchen and put away the air-dried dishes. I heard him laugh. "You're something, Mama White, you are really something."

"Mama White?" I said after he'd hung up.

"She said to figure out what to call her." He'd been calling her Mrs. White. Dad was Dr. White. "Her idea was Mother White. I told her it sounded like a nun. And anyway I already had a mother. What I needed was a mama."

He opened the refrigerator.

"Lonnie? Oh please don't. Not tonight. Come in here and sit with me. Let's just be cozy."

I had the idea that I could read to him as part of the improvement program. I'd decided I'd apply to the university for him for next fall.

He came back with a can of beer. "Now don't give me that look," he said. "I just said I didn't need another mother. This is just one beer. You can allow me one beer, can't you?"

"All right. But there's a price. You have to let me read. I mean aloud."

"She drives a hard bargain," he said and sat beside me with his feet on the coffee table, taking tiny sips from the can with his little finger stuck out.

I'd decided any fiction would seem too much like children's story hour, at least in the beginning. And he wouldn't have patience for obscure poetry or anything too pretty. I began at the beginning of *The Rubaiyat*, trying to read in a normal voice, remembering the high school embarrassment at dramatic, impassioned readings.

He closed his eyes. Once he said, "Make it a jug of beer." I was afraid he'd laugh at "the wild Ass," but he let it pass.

"'I came like Water, and like Wind I go.'" He repeated the line. "That's me in there. How'd your husband get in there, baby?"

That makes you all the harvest I reaped then, I thought. Oh well. Of course, he wasn't all. There was my watermelon crop. At least he was listening.

When I came to the Secret of Life—"While you live/Drink!—for once dead you never shall return"—I changed "Drink" to "Love." Why give him an excuse? He stretched out on the sofa, his feet up on the armrest and his head on my thighs. "I don't have a lap anymore," I said and stroked his dark hair. I loved the picture of us. I read on.

Soon he was asleep, his breathing deep with a little flourish of snore at the end of each intake, his mouth ajar and wet on my thigh. I read on. *The Eternal Saki from that Bowl has pour'd/ Millions of Bubbles like us, and will pour.* For years I had loved these poems. But why? All of us trapped under the inverted bowl, asking and asking, knocking our stunted wings against the blunt sky, learned that the only way out was down into the dead earth. *The Flower that once has blown for ever dies.* I wondered why I loved the despair. Dust moved me more than skylarks. And the drink-up answer to the despair was—well, was Lonnie snoring and drooling on my leg. *Carpe diem* was pure vanity, the bloated, sodden body crashing through its day until it fell face down and went out trying to breathe mud. But I read on.

The next morning Lonnie went back to work and at noon returned to eat his turkey noodle soup for lunch. One day I'd tried vegetable soup but he said he couldn't eat any garden, he liked only turkey noodle, and so every day at 11:45 I opened the can and dumped the yellowish noodles and the fatty broth flecked with meat strands into the saucepan. I could hardly stand the smell, but I had to stay in the kitchen to make his sandwiches. The fat globules moved on the surface like amoebae as the soup heated and then broke up and mated before melting into streaks.

I sat down across from him while he ate. "I was thinking," I said.

"Yeah, well, don't strain your brain," he said. He laughed, and so I did too.

"Anyway, I was thinking maybe we should get a Christmas tree. Just a little one."

He looked surprised. "Sure, well, why not? We never had one, for years anyway. We have Christmas at my sister Suzie's. But what about your folks? I thought Mama White wanted us over there."

"Don't call her that. And besides, you don't have a tree just for the one day."

"We always did. When I was a kid. It'd be up in the morning. I'd get my Santa stuff and we'd eat a great big dinner. The next day the tree'd be gone."

What, did Mother Saxbe boil up an extra package of hot dogs for the great big dinner? I thought. I stood up to look out the window, ashamed of myself. Judge not, my mother used to tell me when I'd sneer at all the lowbrows in the world. You don't know what goes on in their lives. You have no idea.

"That's kind of sad," I said, picturing little boy Lonnie, slicked-down and waiting beside the one-day tree. "It was always a big deal at our house." If they had enough money to get a tree, they could have had it up for a couple weeks. Maybe it was a space problem in that trailer. Lonnie'd had a shrunken childhood, I was seeing. So now he took security where he could find it, in a soup ritual. And in me.

Mid-afternoon, I was holding my old raccoon-collared coat closed around my belly, walking on the salted street instead of the icy sidewalk, when Lonnie passed me. We recognized each other the way the doctor and I had once at the grocery store, uncertainly and a bit embarrassed, out of context. Lonnie stopped the car and backed up. He reached over and opened the passenger door.

"Just where do you think you're going?" he said.

"What are you doing here now? I thought you were at work."

"Get in here. Come on. In." A car beeped behind us and he rolled down his window and raised his middle finger. The tires spun, kicking back gravel and salt, and the car behind us pulled around and passed us. The driver was shaking his head and pointing his index finger at us like a gun.

"I was only going to the library," I said. I'd told the librarian I'd misplaced my card, and she'd made me a new one which I kept hidden in the pocket of my corduroy jacket, and I checked out only one book at a time, keeping it under my sweaters on the closet shelf and reading it during the day. Now that Lonnie and I had settled down, though, I meant to go back to reading in front of him.

"I come home early with a surprise," he said, "and this is what I find. My wife out whoring around."

"Oh Lonnie. I thought we were better. I thought we were past this. I thought we were going to be all right." My voice sounded thin and high.

"Quit your whining," he said. "We'll be all right when I can trust my wife. You think you're so mistreated."

My lip was scabbed and the bruises on my face were purple. Neither of us had mentioned them for two days. I wanted him to remember. I wanted to return to our peace. "Well," I said, "maybe there was a little mistreatment." I leaned over so he'd look at my face.

"That wasn't nothing to get worked up over," he said. "You just bruise real easy."

He drove fast, and the car spun a half turn when he tried to turn into the driveway beside the apartment, so that he had to back up and then pull forward too slowly for the requirements of his mood. He handed me a paper bag from the back seat. "Take that inside," he said. I hoped he hadn't bought me a present. I didn't want anything from him, and I didn't want to thank him or apologize. I didn't want to be guilty again, guilty of walking the streets while he was out buying me a present. I didn't even want it to be baby clothes. This was my baby. I was the one with the baby.

Lonnie opened the trunk and lifted out a three-foot fir tree. He held it straight up, one hand on the sawed-off trunk and the other sunk in among the needles, and carried it across the backyard to the alley. He took the lid off one of the trash cans and released the tree straight into the can. I did not stop him or rescue the tree. I didn't know which of us was more aggrieved.

Inside he dumped a dark green shirt and dark green pants out of the bag.

"That tree was half your surprise," he said. "The other half was I got me a new job."

"You mean you quit the shoe store? Just like that? Aren't you supposed to give two weeks' notice or something?"

"You don't know nothing about it," he said. "The old man insulted me and I don't have to take that."

"Insulted you? What did he say?"

"Maybe it wasn't me he insulted. Why don't you just let it alone."

"What's that mean? You mean he insulted me?" I pushed up from the sofa. "He doesn't even know me."

"Just settle down. Let it alone. I took care of it."

I wondered what he'd done. When he left, I could call the shoe store and find out. Mr. Walsh could tell me his insult, for I was too enormous to be ashamed anymore. I could explain. I could apologize for Lonnie.

"So you defended my honor," I said. "So what's the new job?"

"I'll be making more. Fifty cents an hour more. They gave me this uniform."

I'd already thrown away the receipt with the bag. He'd had to buy the dark green uniform. I let it be. What did it matter? If he made more money, we could eat better suppers. I could buy my parents a Christmas present. We could save money and wouldn't have to depend so much on my father when Lonnie started school.

"So what's the job?" I said.

"At that foundry down near Benton Harbor. I can be foreman in a couple months."

He was out the door at eight in the morning, wearing the dark work clothes he called a uniform. I'd made him a couple sandwiches, since the foundry was too far and his lunch break too short for him to come home for his soup. Next he'd be acquiring a black metal lunchbox and heavy work boots. "Judge not," I said. The baby moved when I spoke, as if he were petting the inside of my skin. At least Lonnie was taking care of us. He's not afraid of hard work, my father might say to another man.

I was scouring the bathroom sink when Linda knocked and called out. I dropped the rag flecked with whiskers and let her in.

"You caught me cleaning the bathroom," I said. "Whiskers and shaving cream all over the sink. Yuck."

"Whiskers! That all? I don't care about whiskers. It's the way men pee all over the toilet I hate. I hate cleaning their pee and cigarette ashes from all over the toilet."

"Yeah, I know what you mean," I said. "Men." In truth, Lonnie didn't miss. Or if he did, he wiped up after himself. But he left whisker stubs in the sink. "Hey, sit down for a while."

"Oh girl, I can't. The kids are down for a nap but not for long. No, the thing is—I seen that tree in your trash and if you're just dumping it out, I wanted to ask, could I take it?"

She was embarrassed to be asking, I could tell, not wondering why we'd thrown it out.

"I wish you would," I said. "It shouldn't go to waste. It's a good little tree for your daughters. It should have occurred to me."

"You didn't want it?"

I could have said that it was too small or that we were going away for Christmas. I could have protected myself from speaking the truth. But I said, "We had a fight and my husband threw it away."

I didn't know why I'd said "my husband" rather than "Lonnie" or just "he." Maybe with that word the fight seemed normal, merely what married folks did sometimes, benign.

But she said, "I seen you had a fight." She nodded at my face. "Del smacked me once. Once only. This was before the kids." She backed from the kitchen table to the door.

"What happened?" I said. My voice sounded raspy, and I cleared my throat.

"This buddy of his puts his hand on my ass, and I laughed. I shouldn't'ta laughed. But criminey. Soon's we get home Del smacks me in the face. You noticed that little scar on his cheek? I cut him. I just took my paring knife and cut him. 'You ever touch me again,' I tell him, 'I'm not going to hurt you back,' 'cause I could see where that would go. No, 'I'm gone,' I say. That's all. 'You touch me, I'm gone. Out of your sorry life.'"

Lonnie and I were just another mean pair, married in our teens, starting to drop babies, all of it predictable and miserable, and now the drinking and the hitting and the promising must be part of it, too. I'd never known a woman who'd been hit by a man. But here was Linda just like me.

"He said he'd never do it again," I said.

"Okay," Linda said. "But girl, you better learn to duck." She opened the door and backed into the foyer.

"I wouldn't dare do anything back to him," I said. "Besides—"

"You tell me you deserved it, I'll smack you myself. Don't feed me that. Listen, I'll just get that tree and talk at you later."

She was in a hurry. She wanted to get back to her little girls and her own shabby house. She wanted to get away from me. If I hit Lonnie, he'd punch me all the harder. He said he'd never hit me again, but already his contrition had faded into my thin skin, so easily marked. I watched Linda struggle to pull the tree from the trash can. I should go help her, I thought, but I watched her tip the can on its side and work the tree out. She righted the can and shook the tree and carried it across the alley. Lonnie could kill me. I hoped the little girls wouldn't find bits of garbage in the tree's branches.

He came back filthy, his face and arms and clothes mottled black, the hair on his arms coated with grease, as if he'd tried to camouflage himself. There were circles of clean skin around his eyes. He had the bitter stink of greasy black metal.

I saw right away that it wouldn't do to tease him, to call him Dulcie's pet raccoon, or to praise his hard work. He grabbed me and held me tight, and I knew that I had to stand still for it, though he stank of grease and sweat and my white blouse would be ruined.

"It was bad, huh?" I said.

"I can't do this," he said.

He showered while I put supper on the table. He came out steamed and scrubbed red. I handed him a beer. In the bathroom I tried to wipe his grease from my cheek and hair. I wanted to change my blouse, but he'd be mad if he found it soaking in the sink like an accusation. His blackened clothes were wadded in the white plastic wastebasket.

We ate supper, he drank beer, we sat together on the couch with the television on, we said nothing about the dirty job. I didn't know if he'd been fired or quit, but I knew he'd be sleeping in the next day. Once he caught me pressing the bruises on my cheek, and he said, "Quit that" and pulled my hand from my face as my mother might have. We opened the sofa, and in bed he sat on me and did it, though the doctor said he shouldn't anymore. I was so big he couldn't lie on me, at least.

On the way to church with my parents Christmas Eve, two terrible things happened. The sky and the ground were white from the afternoon's snow, and the four of us encapsuled in Dad's car seemed separate—bright in Christmas clothes, and safe—from the other cars traveling the sanded streets, from the muted buildings downtown and the mounded snow banking the streets. But then my mother said, "Oh no, look out," and we saw a large dark dog start across the street.

"It can't hear you," I said, knowing she wasn't telling my father to watch out, knowing the dog would be killed.

The car several lengths ahead of us hit the dog. When I didn't see the body, I thought maybe the dog had made it across the street after all. But then I saw it under the car, a black shape caught and tumbling as the car drove on, and at last it was released in front of us. Dad tried to swerve but we hit it. I felt the thump and lift as the right tires went over it.

"Listen, it was already dead," Dad said.

Then we saw blinking pink-red lights in the snow up the street, and the cars ahead of us slowed until we were right behind the station wagon that had hit the dog. I counted five heads in the car, but none of them turned around. The people must have felt the dog tumbling beneath them. A man holding a lantern waved us around a wreck only a block from the church. As we passed two smashed and steaming cars, two men lifted a stretcher into the back of an ambulance.

"On Christmas Eve," my mother said.

I looked back at the hunched, stunned creatures moving around the wreck in the pink light.

CHAPTER 14

He hated how her belly stuck out over the pew in front of them when they had to stand up to sing. She was so enormous. Move back, he told her. She held the hymnbook open in front of him. She thought she was the holy Virgin fucking Mary or something. The accident had spooked him. That brown blood beside the Camaro. Which was totaled. Dulcie and her parents were just singing away. He kept his mouth shut.

The preacher had a big bald head. He had on one of those choir robes. The church was all dark. Except for these fake candles on the walls. The guy was talking in this phony voice about the Son of God. *And an angel of the Lord appeared to them, and the glory of the Lord shone around them, and they were filled with fear.* He probably didn't have on any pants under the choir robe. He probably wore boxers. What did he know about the Son of God? What did he know about fear?

The totaled Camaro was just a year later than the Witch. The church was like a cave. With this high-up ceiling. He couldn't hardly breathe. He was cold. These people all around him weren't nothing to him. A bunch of fancied up wax things. He needed to be closed up in his Witch. With the bucket seat like God's hand holding him.

On Christmas afternoon they were going over to his parents'. That was the plan. The agenda, Dulcie's father called it. What's the agenda? he said. His parents wouldn't have a tree. The Whites had this huge fucking big tree with nothing but silver balls and blue lights all over it. And all these fancy packages under it. Mostly for Dulcie. There were a couple with his name on the tags. He had looked.

How come blood turned brown on snow? It was probably just the dark and the cop car's light going in circles. Probably it was still red if you were close enough.

There was a big huge cross up behind the preacher but it didn't have a Jesus on it. His private Jesus in his underwear drawer had long faggot hair. You could tell his feet were nailed down, the way he didn't all the way sag. He wasn't dead yet. You could see this look on his face. This look like he knew every tiny thing and he was just so sad he couldn't take care of it because here he was nailed down. Like he knew your dad couldn't breathe right from the war. And your siblings used to play baby with you and nobody cared. And your mother was just too big in her men's work shoes for a trailer. Like he'd seen her in the nuthouse. All of a sudden he had a flash of his mother strapped down getting zapped by electricity.

Maybe Jesus was sending him the flash. He grabbed for Dulcie's hand. He wanted to run his thumb over Jesus's hanging down head and feel that face.

In the morning Dulcie's mother made them sit on the floor to open presents. They took a break halfway through to eat coffeecake. He'd heard of coffeecake. Mama White, he said, this is like nothing I've had before. With my parents, it was nothing but eggs and more eggs. We never got dessert for breakfast.

I fixed you pancakes, Dulcie said. I could have made coffeecake if I'd known you wanted it.

His presents were a blue v-neck sweater from Dulcie and Jade East from her parents. He couldn't figure how she'd got any money. He thought he knew every cent. He'd brought along the pink robe for her and she ripped the ribbon off the box. There was a game with a zillion little pieces for the both of them. I had to give somebody a toy, Mrs. White said. Next year we'll have a little one to buy toys for. She looked straight at him down there on the floor with his knees out Indian style. She winked.

He figured she must have heard last night. Dulcie had cried. Oh not here, she said. Not here in my old bed. Anyway, we're not supposed to do it so close to the baby's birth. But then she quit boo-hooing and he got it over with. The headboard kept hitting the wall.

They're a good-looking pair of kids, Mrs. White said. Aren't they, Walter? We're going to have a beautiful, brilliant grandchild. If it's a boy, maybe—maybe you could name him Derek.

For a second he thought she was about to start bawling. But then she got up and went into the kitchen. In a little while he heard more coffee perking.

Dr. White handed him an envelope. This is for both of you, he said. There was a hundred dollar bill inside.

He closed his mouth and swallowed. He felt how he'd looked there for a second with his mouth hanging open. Thank you, sir, he said. This is generous of you.

Dulcie leaned over to check out the envelope and he folded it and stuck it in his back pocket. This was man to man. No matter what he said about the both of them. He wondered if Dr. White ever had to put Mrs. White in her place.

He wanted a beer but he had to sit in the living room with Dr. White while the wives made a big racket in the kitchen. Dulcie's face had got fat with her belly. The bruises just looked like smudges now. He wondered what she was blabbing to her old lady under all the racket. She had this habit of putting her middle finger on the leftover bruises and moving it around and pressing. Like she wanted to dent the smudges into her puffed-up face.

Him and Dr. White sat in these two hard brown chairs. That looked like the covering was some old guy's sport jacket. He hoped his dad would have stocked up on Bud. There wouldn't be anything open on Christmas.

Dulcie's old man was saying something about some Green Berets in Vietnam. How the enemy hid in caves and tied snakes by the tails inside the openings. Had he ever heard of such a thing?

I wished you hadn't told me that, he said. They sat there man-to-man in the hard chairs. Geez, snakes. That's enough to give you nightmares.

Say, Lonnie. Have you given any more thought to the university? I'm not trying to put any pressure on you. You'll need to be thinking about getting the application in, though.

Those snakes, Lonnie said. He shook his head. Sometimes he felt like he had snakes like that inside his skull. Just hanging like they were nailed onto the bone.

Listen, son, did you hear me? the old man was saying. I'm going to be needing to sell some stock, but we can do it. Don't get me wrong. We want to do it. But we want to be working out the agenda.

He wasn't never going to be a son to this man. Hundred dollars or no. Stock or no. He respected Dr. White, for sure. But he couldn't see him freezing his can off in the bleachers just to watch him play ball. He wouldn't drive to every high school track in the state just to stand around with a bunch of jerk-off kids and idiot parents and then follow the bus home. He thought he could tell his real dad that deal Dulcie'd read to him, like wind I go, and he wouldn't say boo hi nor howdy but just hear it.

Is anybody hungry? Mrs. White said. She was all peppy. He waited for her to break into a Battlebush cheer. Anybody work up an appetite opening presents? she said. Rah rah rah.

Dulcie lit candles on the table and they all clinked water glasses and ate this humongous fancy meal.

What's this called? he said. Mama White, you're going to get me fat.

It's stuffed pork roast, she said. Her face was all red.

Afterwards she handed him this silver tool. You can do the honors and snuff the candles while we clear the table, she said.

It didn't take a rocket scientist to figure it out. He put the silver cup down on the flames one by one. Snuff snuff snuff. Smoke streamed out and he waved it away before she could see he'd done it wrong.

They sat around and shot the breeze with his parents at the trailer. Finally his dad said, What about those items in that fancy paper I seen in the bedroom? You going to bring those out, Bernie? Or am I sleeping with boxes instead of woman tonight?

So his mother brought out this armload and sorted out the stuff for Marie's and Suzie's. Lonnie opened his. It was three pair of underwear. Dulcie's was towels.

Oh, we needed these, she said. This tan will go with the bathroom. Thanks a lot.

They hadn't given anything to any of the parents. Dulcie wanted to, just a token gift, she said, but he told her nobody expected anything from them.

He cracked another Bud from the refrigerator. He saw his mother and his wife look at each other. You two don't need to be flashing looks between you, he said.

Nobody's paying any attention to you, Dulcie said. Don't be paranoid. I was only going to say we ought to bring in those lemon bars my mom sent over. I guess we left them in the car.

So, he said, you hear I'm going to college? I'm going to learn how to be a rocket scientist.

I don't know what to do with you, son, his mother said.

Nobody knew what to do with him. Not the Whites. Not his wife. Or his dad. Nobody at school or even his coach. Join the crowd, he said. I don't even know what to do with my own self, half the time.

They were all supposed to go over to his sister Marie's and eat dinner. But he begged off for him and Dulcie. I am just not up to those wild kids, he said. Dulcie needs to be taking it easy. In her condition. He winked at his dad like Mama White had winked at him on the floor.

I don't want you out driving with all that beer in you, his mother said.

At least the roads are cleared by now, his dad said. But your mother has the right idea. You may as well stay here for the night. And not drive all that way back to Waterton.

I made a big pot of stew to take over to the girls' for supper, his mother said. I'll dish you out some of it and Dulcie can heat it up.

Your mother makes a stew like nobody else, his dad said. Real special.

You get some of that in you, she said, and soak up some of that beer.

He and Dulcie watched some Christmas shows with fake snow and some movie stars and their little kids singing and horsing around in the fake snow.

I can't believe your mother gave you underwear for Christmas, she said.

After a while they ate some of the dessert her mother had made.

Now I'm stuffed, she said. We should have eaten that stew first. Is your mother going to be hurt that we didn't eat her dinner?

He thought of her coming home and finding his empties. Yeah, I guess she might mind some, he said.

Let me heat it up and we can try to eat some.

She got the dish out of the refrigerator and took off the plastic lid. There was a crust of solid white fat on top of the brown meat and gravy.

Ooooo, I don't think I can eat any of this, she said. Though I'm sure it'd be good once it was heated.

I'd barf it right back up, he said.

They stared into the bowl together, and then she started giggling. Barf, she said. What a word.

He got to laughing too. Spew, he said.

Disgorge, she said. Regurgitate.

Puke. Pray to the porcelain god.

I've never heard that, she said. Ha! Pray to the porcelain god.

He took the stew bowl out of her hands and got out a spoon. She followed him down the hall. What are you doing? she said. She was still laughing.

He spooned a chunk of meat into the toilet. Followed by a piece of potato and a string of onion.

I can't believe you're doing that, she said.

He plopped a carrot in and flushed.

Oh that's disgusting, she said.

They were both cracking up. He spooned in half the bowlful and they had to use the plunger to get it to go down.

At least your mother will think we loved her stew, she said. But I tell you what, I'm going to be asleep when they get back. I'd never be able to keep a straight face.

He sat up in his dad's chair drinking beer and watching a sloppy Christmas movie after he tucked her in to his bed. Then he turned out the lights and shut his bedroom door and fit himself into the single bed with her. His mother had put out a sheet and quilt for him to sleep on the couch. He thought he might wake her up but then he just settled for getting up against her. He woke up when his parents came back. He thought about going out and giving them a hard time for getting in late, for a joke, but he stayed put.

Well, Benj, he heard his mother say, will you come look at this? You could hear everything in the trailer at night. He heard the plunger working. Splooge. Gulp.

Now why did they—?

Waste—You'd think *she'd* at least —

Pair of kids. Just a pair of kids.

Dulcie slept through it, at least. He hoped he could hustle them out in the morning before his mother said anything. He felt sick. He was afraid he'd puke for real but then he thought, down, snakes, down, and he fell back asleep.

CHAPTER 15

Lonnie had already started work as an inventory clerk in a new discount store just outside town, and we'd used the Christmas money from Dad for rent and groceries, so I didn't think he was only venting his frustration the next time he hit me. He had his reason—this time I couldn't say what had become of thirty-five cents from the ashtray where he kept change—and he ripped my red jumper and bruised my shoulder and arm. He stopped when I fell backwards into the wall, scared he'd hurt the baby, I supposed, and I thought I could use that move to stop him next time, at least until the baby was born.

If I didn't go into labor soon, the doctor was going to induce it. I cried after Lonnie tore my jumper, and I caught myself against the wall before I went down, as if my whole body were a fleshy sponge around the baby. But I was hardly inside my body, and he could barely hurt me. I was an angel of myself outside in the snow looking through the Venetian blinds. I was not really alive anymore. Women died during childbirth. There was Hemingway's Cat and afterwards her Tenente walking into the rain. Right now I was fading into my own angel, who felt a little cold but that was about all, retaining my porous skeleton to support and feed the baby.

After Lonnie left, I wrote a letter to Katie, before I faded completely. I played the Beethoven Ninth, trying to stay awake long enough to ask her to make sure the baby was saved. She could take care of it or give it to my parents to raise or even find a good childless couple to adopt it, but Lonnie couldn't have it or his parents either. Whatever she had to do, take the Saxbes to court and get an order for psychiatric examinations of them all, or steal the baby, she had to promise.

I hid the letter under my sweaters on the closet shelf, and put on a big old summer blouse of my mother's. I hung the torn jumper on the back of a kitchen chair. I wanted him to see it when he came back. Then I thought maybe he wasn't going to come back. Maybe he'd driven back to his parents and was already asleep under his old plaid bedspread. Once he'd told me he wanted to make a lot of money and buy his parents a double wide. Once when I mentioned that my mother always picked up the house before the cleaning lady came on Thursdays, he looked dark and said I'd never be allowed to have a cleaning woman, no matter how rich we got to be.

I was Mrs. Saxbe and so was his mother. That was very strange.

I lay down on the unopened sofa, with a blanket over me. I didn't need the whole bed, without Lonnie, and besides, I could only sleep on my back now.

Lonnie was just driving around, no doubt. If he didn't go home, where would he go? He didn't have any friends around here. Neither of us did. Sometimes I wanted only to be all alone inside the three rooms with the snow outside. Sometimes I was such a tiny fat molecule inside a bubble that I believed my parents and Katie had never known me, or maybe that they didn't even exist, and I was desperate to sit them down beside me on the ugly green sofa.

The other Mrs. Saxbe might be pulling a blanket over Lonnie right now, I thought. I was numb and almost asleep, and for a moment, it was pleasant and even a bit interesting to see him in his bed at home, as I might have pictured him when we were still in high school and everything was still mysterious. But when I closed my eyes, I was ashamed. It had been terrible, flushing her food down the toilet in that trailer. I was glad she hadn't caught us at it, but now that collusion was between me and Lonnie. What were the Saxbes thinking of me, who couldn't take care of Lonnie and hold him with me? Maybe they were glad, as I, huge as I was, winked out and released their son.

When I woke at two-thirty, the windows were full of the silver-gray light of snow and Lonnie was still gone. I'd been sleeping in my mother's old sleeveless blouse and underpants with the waistband low under my stomach. I put on knee socks and shoe boots and my raccoon-collared coat, and went outside to see if maybe Lonnie was asleep in the car—and simply to be out in the snow. The night sky was murky white, and the snow was falling neatly on bushes and driveways and roofs and empty cartons beside trash cans. It was warm on my face and hands and knees. It fell carefully, rounding edges and covering gravel, lowering branches to the ground. Once I had been my mother's and my father's little white-haired girl, curtsying in a pinafore my mother had made, and sitting on my father's arm as if it were a ledge, laughing coyly at the photographer, and dressing a big doll in real baby sunsuits, and rising on my father's shoulders and diving into Lake Michigan. I must have been their living doll. My father made me a sandbox beneath a grape arbor. I remembered the dusty smell of purple grapes. My mother made me a blue dress with smocking and a white collar. Lonnie had taken that daughter and rubbed his dark-haired body all over her.

Something must have happened to Lonnie. The snow was waking me, and when I started shivering I went back inside. The baby jumped when the door slammed behind me. "I'm sorry, baby," I said and rubbed my stomach. "Baby, what's happened to your daddy?" Now that he had left me or been killed in a car wreck, I was sick. I sat shivering in my coat and looked in the phone book. I thought I might throw up. Waterton had no hospital. If he was dead, where would he have been taken? Maybe to the Benton Harbor hospital, where I would go to have the baby. I called information for the number and then tried the hospital. No Benjamin Lon Saxbe had been brought in, dead or alive. Helmholtz's Funeral Parlor was the only listing under "mortuaries." I dialed and immediately put down the receiver before even the first ring. What would I say? Herr Helmholtz, is my husband in your parlor? A parlor would have shaded light, a smell of old roses, a basket for visitors' cards, and doilies on the furniture. A-tisket, a-tasket, Lonnie's in a casket.

I went into the bathroom and knelt before the toilet for a long time but nothing happened. Maybe this sick tightening and turning in my stomach was labor. How dare he leave me alone with that? The baby struggled as if trying to turn. The baby knew what was happening. Lonnie was in a ditch somewhere. My mother used to wait up, angry, when I was late getting home. For all I knew, she always said, you were lying in a ditch somewhere. The warm snow was covering his body, smoothing all his edges. Herr Helmholtz was draining the blood and Lonnie's body was collapsing on a stainless steel table.

I retrieved my letter to Katie from under the stack of sweaters on the closet shelf. I read it again and added a P.S. *Katie, you're the best friend in my life. You know I love you. Please forgive me.* Then I put the letter in an envelope and wrote across the seal: *For Katie Leeview only. Anybody else who opens this I curse as crazy forevermore.* Maybe Lonnie would believe I had the power. I knew he was afraid of being called crazy, or of being crazy. I hid the letter in the pocket of my spring jacket stored in my suitcase.

Beyond sleep, I tried to read and paced the three rooms and drank the rest of the milk and turned out the lights and watched out the window. By four the snow had stopped. I hoped the drifts were high enough to trap me. Girl gives birth in snowstorm. Widow delivers own baby. I couldn't call my parents in the middle of the night, in the middle of my own craziness. Girl bleeds to death but snowstorm baby lives. No one was at the dorm switchboard and Katie could do nothing anyway.

At six-thirty the phone rang.

"Hey, wife," Lonnie said.

I gave him a few seconds of silence. I hated the tears that shot to my eyes. "What happened?" I said then. "Where were you all night?"

"I'm in the slammer. You'll have to come get me out."

"What? Where are you?"

"The police station." His cocky voice shrank. "Come get me. Bring that grocery money."

"Well, but you have the car. What happened to the car?"

"I can't talk," he said. "Just come."

So I washed my face and dressed in the good blue dress my mother had made and brushed my hair back over my shoulders. I wouldn't be a barefoot slut.

I called a taxicab and said, briskly, "To the police station." The driver looked as weak and drained as I felt. I sat straight in the back seat. "Quite some snow last night," I said, just like a grown-up, though the roads were already salted and in the daylight the snow looked limp.

The policeman at the desk looked at my pregnant stomach first. "You Mrs. Saxbe?"

"What happened?"

"Picked up for DWI. Around one-thirty."

"So, he's been sleeping it off?" That was the television phrase, and I thought he might laugh at me.

Another policeman led Lonnie through a set of doors, past me. He looked like a guilty little boy, in oversized white coveralls.

Then he came back in his own brown corduroys and V-neck sweater and yellow shirt, and he paid some money and agreed to appear, and the policeman at the desk shook his head and handed me the car keys, and we walked out into the salted snow. Lonnie's face was stubbled and he smelled not like stale beer this time but like pure clear alcohol. This must be what they mean, I thought, when they say someone smells like a distillery.

He didn't make me call in for him this time. I heard him say, "Looks like it's time to start pacing that old waiting room. Yeah, cigars. Thank you, sir. Appreciate that." His voice was quiet and sober.

"I'm not ready to go to the hospital, you know," I said. "Although I thought maybe I was in labor. About four in the morning I thought so."

"Rag on me later," Lonnie said. He pulled open the bed and dropped the blinds. "I don't have the strength for it now."

Once he was asleep, I lay down beside him. His skin smelled like alcohol and salt. I didn't have the strength for anything, either.

Early Sunday morning, I woke to the whoosh of water in the percolator.

"I can't believe you're up," I said. "What's going on? It's only nine."

"I'm feeling holy," he said. "We should go to church."

"What, did the prison priest convert you?"

"It wasn't prison."

He hadn't said much about the night in jail, and I was afraid to ask and set him off. I pictured a cell with bunks chained to the wall and a lidless toilet, and Lonnie in the prison coveralls holding onto the bars and watching for me to come save him.

"Okay, let's go to church," I said.

Lonnie made fried egg sandwiches with mustard, his father's favorite breakfast, and we dressed and walked down the block to the Methodist church. In front, the sign this week said *A little child shall lead you to the Kingdom.*

"I hope that doesn't mean I'm going to give birth during the sermon," I said.

My husband held my arm and we entered the steamy vestibule.

In the afternoon Lonnie's boss at the store called. "It was false labor," Lonnie said, and I wondered where he'd heard the term. "Guess Junior's not ready to face the cruel world. No. No, sir. All right."

"That was nice of him to call," I said. "On Sunday afternoon."

"The old fart holds these stupid pep rallies in the morning before they unlock the doors. This isn't nothing but part of the pep. Team spirit. What a crock."

"He probably just wants to know if you'll be at work in the morning."

"You got that figured right, babe," he said.

"Well... are you going back to work in the morning? I mean..."

"'Course I'm going to work in the morning. What, you think I'm not gonna take care of you and my kid in there?"

For Sunday dinner I prepared pork chops the way my mother sometimes did, with mushroom soup sauce and rice. It looked nice but the meat was dry. It was like eating wood pulp in gravy.

"I ain't a big fan of rice," Lonnie said. "Looks like maggots. One time there was this dead dog—"

"Hush," I said. "We're eating."

"Trying to, anyway."

We looked at each other, fibers of meat on our forks, and laughed. We were all right. We were a pair of kids trying to keep house. We knew what we were. The food was plastic and the sauce was paint. *Oh, Mrs. Saxbe, what a lovely dinner you have prepared. Why, thank you, Mr. Saxbe. Would you care for some tea?* The baby moved, but it was still a game. The baby would actually be born, would actually come out of me, but then we three would play house, the Mommy and the Daddy and the baby doll dressed up in real baby clothes, so serious, so silly, a sufficient way to live.

"We could play that game we got for Christmas," Lonnie said. "That'd be something to do tonight."

He was trying hard. The night in jail had changed him. We'd been subdued all Saturday afternoon, after the intensities of Friday's fight, of jail and whatever had led to jail, and of my bad night waiting for him to appear, or not. We'd been somber and courteous with each other, and the heaviness was almost pleasant. After supper Lonnie had taken the three beers that were in the refrigerator out to the trash cans beside the alley.

Today we were beginning to lighten. He wasn't drinking beer or holding me beside him for some stupid television show or starting the insidious questioning that would lead to me and Bruce in a back seat or bed, the safe mild questions—Had I seen *Midnight Cowboy*, what was my favorite song by the Lettermen, how did I used to get across town for my piano lesson, was Katie going to marry Josh—the questions that I could see skipping like stones on water to the accusations but that I was powerless to stop, once the mood was in him. I knew when the worm of the mood was in him before he did. No answer was correct, any lie or truth or placation bounced equally on the flat water, and as with the petting we used to do in his car, the worm fattened until it exploded into raw white pictures of me and someone else naked.

Until the tightness of watching for the worm, of trying to guess the right answers, eased, I hadn't even known how rigid I'd been.

"I feel good today," I said. "We're going to be all right, aren't we?"

He looked at the newspaper while I cleaned up the kitchen. The chiropractor subscribed to a paper to have it in his waiting room, and he let us take Sunday's.

"Okay, babe, you figure out how to play this and explain it to me." The game box was designed to look like a thick leather-bound book. I eased down to the floor and set out the board and all the little plastic pieces. It was a complicated game with forbidden moves and a hierarchy of tokens. Little fence pieces were pegged one by one onto the board to make various sized corrals to capture the opponent's men.

"I think I have this figured out," I told him. "But would you get me a glass of water first? I don't think I can get up from this floor."

"The floor's as good a place as any," he said and leapt up with the extra pep of a healthy person in a sickroom. He brought back two glasses of Coke. "Should we have a little background music, my dear?" he said in a mincing voice.

"Whatever is your desire." I guessed he'd play his favorite Byrds album, but he dropped the needle and Beethoven's Third roared out.

"A wee tad loud, m'dear?" he said and adjusted the volume. "Three's my lucky number." He dropped to the floor so vigorously that the record skipped. "Prepare to be beat."

I wanted to correct his grammar. I wanted to look him in the eye until he heard the literal meaning. He was a bit too roused with his conversion, and I wasn't quite ready to forgive all, at least not until I'd been asked. But I sipped my Coke and smiled at this husband. He was trying so hard. And it was a relief to be fat and boneless on the floor.

It took only twenty minutes to win the game. He turned the record over for the Scherzo and sat back down. "Okay, that was beginner's luck. Now I'm warmed up. Done my stretches and now I'm gonna sprint."

"Good metaphor," I said.

"Don't you teacher me, Dulcie."

I could have won before the final movement even began. He couldn't get the rules down, which tokens could move in which ways. I made a couple stupid moves to slow the game.

"You sure you want to do that?" I said when it was obvious he was going to advance right into my territory.

"Just shut up. I don't need your help."

"Okay, then." I popped the last fence piece into place. "I own you now." He looked puzzled, and I laughed. It was terrible hot laughter. I tried to keep it down.

"I can't concentrate," he said. "That stupid racket." He jumped up and ripped the needle across the record's grooves. "Oops," he said. "It slipped. Solly, Chollie."

I sat enormous and weak on the floor. I hated him.

"Just because you can't win a game," I said.

He turned the board upside down and the tokens fell off. He stomped on them. "Oh yeah? I guess I win after all."

For a moment we looked in silence at the bright smashed plastic. Anything could happen next: He could laugh or he could kick me, or I could start crying once again.

I said softly, "Sometimes I think you really are crazy."

He picked up the game board and hurled it across the room. It hit the wall and plastic fences flew. He grabbed his jacket and slammed the door behind him. The glass in the window shook but stayed intact. I stayed on the floor, not crying. I'd driven him out, maybe to protect myself and the baby, maybe just because I hated him. At last I got onto all fours and pushed myself up. I turned off the lights but left the door unlocked. If I locked him out, he could smash his way in and be furious enough to kill me. *If you ever leave me, I'll kill you*, he'd said, and locking him out might be the same as leaving him. From the dark apartment I saw him by the alley, bent over the trash can. Then he kicked it and turned it over, and garbage scattered on the old snow. He found the cans of beer and carried them away. I heard the car door slam, but he didn't drive away. The keys were inside, beside the television. He was crazy. When Katie and I took Psych together, we thought how exciting it would be to work out the puzzle of dementia and see straight into the sicknesses and cure them. Here was craziness in the flesh and instead of trying to work it out I was frightened of the patient, and even through the fear I provoked him.

Marriage was as complex as derangement, but I should have been able to study it too and memorize its stages and its categories. My parents' marriage hadn't been this deranged, though. I didn't think it had been, anyway. Their life had been like everybody's parents' lives, all in order from the bouquet tossed carefully toward the next bride to coffeecakes and church on Sunday mornings to a pink baby, all systematic in the big tedious white house. But my father had fallen asleep and burned a hole in the dark green MSU blanket while I was being born. I thought I could smell burnt wool like singed chicken feathers. My mother and I had made our ways around the man. He was a man. *Does he get enough sex?* my mother had asked when she saw my bruises. *That can make a man violent, the frustration.* Wasn't that what she'd said? She'd had her own bruises and her own dead blue baby. This was all crazy. Lonnie was crazy, he was crazy, he was crazy, and I was crazy too.

CHAPTER 16

He got in the back seat of the Witch. He wasn't going anywhere. The keys were in the house. Also the slammer had spooked him. He chugged the first beer. He'd wiped the cans off in the snow but he could still smell garbage. They were cold, at least. Thank God and January for small favors.

He pulled up the car blanket and took it easy with the other two beers. There wouldn't be no more, once he'd drained them. He wasn't going to buy more, either, so there wouldn't be no more at all. He'd been a poor sport. You weren't supposed to show a thing when you lost. You said to the man from the newspaper: Albion played a good game. A real good game. You could shake your head. Your shoulders could slump a little and you could clam up but that was it. Dulcie'd been a poor winner, though. Battlebush gave us a run for our money, the winners said. We had to fight for the points. They could shake their heads, too. Dulcie made a big deal out of wearing this old raggy blouse without sleeves, in the middle of winter yet, just so he'd have to look at her bruises. You won, he wanted to tell her, so let it alone. You bruise easy and you won, so be a good sport.

He liked the back seat. He wasn't even cold, what with the blanket. He never sat in the back seat. He was always driving. Except when him and Dulcie used to park by the lake or out in the boonies. He wished she'd come out and get in the back seat with him. Except her belly was so humongous they wouldn't fit. He would pop her bra and kiss her tits. That was one thing, she had real tits now. That's good, baby, she'd say. I like that. Which she never did say. He put his hand under the blanket but then he stopped. What the hell. He was a married man. He couldn't hardly believe the baby was going to come out through that part of her. His son was in there, way up there, all the way in her.

Something hit the window and he jumped and spilled the beer on the blanket. Son of a bitch it was the cops again. He wasn't drunk this time. What the hell. Then knuckles hit the window again and he saw it was Dulcie's white face with her nose pushed flat against the glass. Oink, oink. He reached over the seat and cranked down the window. Scared the shit out of me, he said.

Lonnie—she said, listen, I'm scared, forget all that stupid stuff, I'm afraid I'm going to have the baby now.

You didn't call the cops? he said.

No, why do we need cops? Just come in, I'm freezing, maybe we need to call the doctor.

He was in the driveway. He wasn't even driving. They couldn't put you in the slammer for Sitting While Intoxicated. His son was about to be born. He wasn't intoxicated anyway.

Inside they sat together on the couch and she read from her book. There were three signs, it said, contractions, the water breaks, and bloody show. I can't do this, Lonnie, she said. Contractions were like cramps. Jesus knew, he'd had cramps when he was constipated. It hurt like holy hell but you could stand it. Contractions started above the small low bone in the pelvis. She opened up her robe and they tried to find the small low bone. Her belly button stuck out. You look like a balloon, he said. That's where I blew you up and tied you off. Some guys after a meet once filled a toilet stall in the locker room full of blown-up rubbers. He couldn't remember if they'd won or lost that day. Coach never said a thing but they heard pop, pop, pop, flush and pop, pop, pop, flush until the stall was empty.

He didn't want to be around for all the water and that bloody show.

Well, I thought I was having contractions, she said. It felt tight and it kind of hurt, but not like in the movies. You know how in the movies the woman always gasps and screams and everybody goes crazy?

He spread his hands on her. She was tight as an overinflated football.

Listen to this, she said. It says being born is like pulling a turtleneck over your head.

They sat for a long time with all their hands on her belly.

Well, I thought something was happening, she said. Are you mad that I dragged you back inside?

Maybe she'd been faking the pains. He didn't care. She wanted him inside with her.

I'm sorry, she said.

No baby, it's me is sorry.

She was supposed to see the doctor the next day anyway. He'd gotten two hours off to take her. They were supposed to see if they wanted to induce labor. He liked that word. Induce. It was in the same category with abide.

He untied the ribbon at the neck of her robe. He rubbed her tits and hefted them and kissed them. He tasted something sweet.

You don't want to be doing that now, she said.

He tasted the other one.

She put her hand on his back.

Am I your baby? he said.

She did a silent little laugh. I guess you are, she said. She rubbed his back.

The kid was upside down now, the book showed. He closed his eyes and started floating. He felt for her other hand and pulled it over. He wasn't hard. When he started floating out and turning, he opened his eyes to stay on the couch.

The kid's entire whole body was up in her. He filled her up. The kid owned her.

Let's try to get some sleep, she said. Who knows, it might start during the night. Or they might decide to induce it tomorrow. We'll need the sleep.

He moved her limp hand but when he lifted his, she pulled away. He was swelling. He could fill her. Couldn't you just do that? he said and pulled her hand back. He doesn't own you, you know.

Who doesn't? What are you talking about? Do you think we could just sleep?

You're mine, he said. You're my wife. He stood and took down his brown cords.

She pulled the cushions off the couch. She thought he was just going to roll over and go to sleep. She wouldn't even touch him. Her hands were too holy to touch him. He opened the bed, all right. When she was down, he pulled her panties off. Oh Lonnie no, she said. We can't do that any more. He got down beside her but it didn't work sideways. He was hard enough now to hit the moon but her belly was too big. The kid was in the way. He tried to roll her over.

We'd hurt the baby, she said. We don't want to hurt the baby now, do we?

If not now, then when? he thought but did not say. That was his son. He would never hurt his son. But he would let him know who was boss. His kid would know who was who.

I'll just put the tip in, he said. That won't hurt anything. He almost laughed. That was always the line. I'll just put the tip in. You'll still be a virgin. Nothing can happen. Don't worry. He himself had tried it on Donna Fortner in tenth grade.

Don't give me that, she'd said. Old Donna. I'm not all that dumb, she'd said.

For a flash he thought Dulcie had said it. But she had been all that dumb. She thought she was such hot shit in the brains department but she was dumb. Look at her here on this stupid fold-out bed fat as a hog and starting to bawl.

He'd cried the first time his sisters made him take his pants off and they'd liked it. Lookit, Suzie said, the baby's crying. He needs his diaper changed.

Don't, Lonnie, please please don't, Dulcie was blubbering. You'll hurt the baby. I have to go to the doctor tomorrow. He'll know.

He pushed her knees down and sat on her and held his arms rigid to keep his weight off her, and he believed he felt his son's head. Later, he thought, I'll laugh about butting heads. And he was heavy on her and he wanted to push his entire body inside her.

He went to work for a couple hours and then drove her to that doctor's. He looked at the beat-up *Sports Illustrated* that was in the waiting room for all the men who sat there like idiots while their wives spraddled their legs for the doctor. The nurse came out and said, Mr. Saxbe? Doctor would like to see you.

Christ. He'd hurt the baby. Oh Christ.

Sit, sit, the doctor said. He was old. It was like in the Battlebush counselor's office, the man on the important side of the big desk, and Lonnie treated like a bad boy on the other side. Now he was going to be getting the royal reaming out for last night. He wondered what Dulcie had told him naked in the examining room.

She's under a lot of stress, the man said. The baby's clearly term. We're going to go ahead with this.

Say what? he said.

You'll be a father by tomorrow, the man said.

You mean—induce? He was glad he knew the word. He hadn't hurt the baby. They were going to do it now. He would have his real Dulcie back tomorrow.

The two of you go home and pick up her things and then drive on down to the hospital. They'll get her started and I'll see you later on this afternoon.

But—then what?

Then prepare yourself to wait. Bring something to read. It could be a long time. But she's young and healthy. No need to worry.

How long? he said.

Well, I can't predict, you know. But it's a first baby. Could be twenty-four hours.

She had her bag already loaded up with the robe he'd given her for Christmas and this little blue deal for the baby and a flannel blanket. A receiving blanket, it was called. That was funny. Receiving blanket. He pictured his arm with the blanket over it receiving the spurted-out baby like a football.

In the hospital she disappeared in a wheelchair and he sat like an idiot in this corner room, him and this other guy. My wife's having my kid, he said, but the other guy just said, great, man, and didn't say a thing about why he was there. Somebody must be dying, he thought. Finally they turned on the TV and watched an old Dobie Gillis. He looked around for a *TV Guide* to see if they could catch some hoops or something. Downstairs they had this cafeteria that smelled like sick people and he had a cheese sandwich and a piece of cherry pie about as old as the Dobie Gillis show. He went back up to the corner room and the other guy was gone. He wondered what he should do at night, go home or try to sleep in the plastic chair. He didn't want to think about what had to be happening to Dulcie. Before they wheeled her away, she wouldn't say a thing and she was breathing fast and wiping her eyes.

It'll all be over with pretty soon, he'd told her. Before you know it.

I never did understand that expression, she said. Before you know it. What does that mean?

How do I know? he said. I ain't no rocket scientist. But it'll be okay. It's just like pulling a turtleneck over your head.

But he couldn't hardly believe that. She was little, he knew that better than the doctor or anybody. There was bone in there. Bone was not like a sweater.

Before he could even get hungry for supper, this nurse in a green apron deal said, Hey Saxbe! I mean, Mr. Saxbe. Guess what. You're a daddy. She should have tried out for cheerleader.

He couldn't say a word. It wasn't supposed to be over yet. Finally he said what he was supposed to say: Is she okay?

She is absolutely a perfect doll, the cheerleader said. Fingers, toes, the works, all there.

Dulcie's fingers? Say what?

He called his parents and then Dulcie's. He even called Katie. She gave a yip and yelled, Hey, Glenna, you're an aunt.

Dulcie was in this room with two others. A nurse pulled a curtain around the bed.

He sat beside her. You did it, he said. You did it. He stroked her bare arm.

It wasn't a turtleneck, she said. That was a lie.

But it was quick, he said. The doctor said it would be tomorrow.

It was tomorrow, she said. Tomorrow and tomorrow and tomorrow. It was a decade. An eon. Infinity. Her eyes kept closing. This is my only baby, she said. For ever and ever.

He got to look through a glass window at this squinched-up red thing. What made it his? It had a plastic band around its arm. It twitched the arm up and he could read it: Girl Saxbe.

For the second time he slept alone without Dulcie. The other time was that iron cot in the slammer. That time he was zonked out. When he woke, he got up to piss and someone had puked in the john and he was wearing some coveralls that reeked.

He heated himself up a can of turkey noodle soup. He was going for a sandwich but all he could find was a plastic bag with two slices of moldy bread in the refrigerator. Dulcie needed lessons from his mother. She knew how to keep house. He didn't think he'd ever seen Dulcie dry-mop the kitchen floor. She didn't starch his shirts either.

He couldn't sleep. Dulcie was zonked, probably. He sat up in bed with the TV going. He'd picked up a six-pack after he left the hospital. He was a father now. He was allowed. He was entitled. He could celebrate.

It was okay to have a girl. They'd have a son another time. It might be easier to daddy a girl, anyway. They'd have to name it after his mother.

He missed Dulcie. Still, sitting up with a cold one all by his lonesome wasn't too bad. It was a relief, tell the truth, sitting there limp under the blankets.

In the morning he didn't wake up and he had to peel over to Barnett's without breakfast. He guessed he had an excuse, anyway. He took his morning break early and went over to the snack area and ordered donuts.

This girl Judy from Housewares dropped her big butt down across from him. She was always hanging around. Probably she didn't know he was married. She was okay but sometimes she made him feel sick and he had to get away from her. He knew she had a thing for him.

My wife's in the hospital, he said. Just had my baby.

Oh! Judy said, and clapped her hands, all worked up. Well, Daddy! she said. Boy or girl?

She chewed an ice cube from her Coke and he had to get up before he hit her.

What? she said. What's the matter? Didn't you get what you wanted? Or—oh, I am such a jerk. She smacked her forehead. There's something wrong with the baby.

No, it's okay, he said. It's what I wanted. It's just—my break's over, is all.

He made it to the back room under the stairs where he had a desk which was a wide board set across two file cabinets. His chair was a metal stool, too high for the desk. He started in on the week's numbers: nails, paintbrushes, sandpaper packets, electrical tape, turpentine, hammers, saws, and he compared the totals with last week's and made out re-order slips.

He had to call the doctor and find out if the kid was his. Dulcie wouldn't let him forget that test. A girl wasn't a kid, he thought. The baby. The child. The daughter. He'd made Dulcie ask for the blood test and now he had to call and find out the baby's paternity. What was he going to do if the daughter wasn't his?

In the workroom he was surrounded by broken vises, dented paint cans, opened packages of screws, and a mess of candy wrappers and stained paper cups and empty pop cans.

What was he going to do if the baby was his?

The man was Dulcie's doctor. She'd been alone with him all those months. She'd asked him to do the test and she'd conned him with her tears. He'd lie for her now.

He went upstairs to the stockroom for a can of sand-colored wall paint some old biddy wanted. He leaned on the railing and looked down the stairwell. He braced himself against the iron railing—it would be so easy to lean his shoulders down and then the rest of his body would follow. He backed away before he couldn't stop himself.

In the afternoon he cut out early and drove to the hospital. She was sitting up against a heap of pillows with a book in her hand. That figured. She was wearing a hospital gown, not the pink deal he'd got her. Her face looked sort of flat and for a flash he thought of Judy's round made-up face. Maybe he could let Dulcie wear make-up again.

Hey, babe, he said.

Hey yourself, Daddy, she said. Did you see her today? They brought her in to nurse, and I think we're getting the hang of it.

There were two other women in the room with the husbands leaning on the beds.

She's got dark hair, it looks like.

She sure does, Dulcie said. That reminds me—the doctor came by and he said to tell you he'd done the blood test. They just prick the heel. You're supposed to call and find out the results.

Well? he said. What are they?

You're supposed to call. I didn't ask him.

Why not? he said. Afraid?

My God, Lonnie, she said, won't you ever stop?

He pulled the curtain around her bed so those other husbands holding the wives' hands wouldn't see Dulcie crying.

The check on his old account had bounced. He forgot about that Saturday night when he stopped at the package store. The manager was pissed.

We've been selling to you underage and here you show your gratitude by writing checks on non-existent accounts.

One check, he said. Big deal.

He slapped a ten on the counter and told the pissant what he could do with it. There were other stores.

On Sunday afternoon his parents drove over. His mother heated up this casserole she'd brought along and a can of peas. She had a chocolate cake too.

Did she have a hard time, son? she said.

It was over like that, he said and snapped his fingers. She just slid out like a pup.

She nodded like she'd figured that. Not like you, she said. With you I like to died.

They'd brought this red and white suit for the baby. Your mother just knew it was going to be a boy, his dad said. So what're you going to name her?

It was going to be Benjamin Lon Saxbe the Third, he said. He wanted his father to know that. I'm thinking maybe Bernadine.

His mother took the laundry basket of his dirty shirts to their car.

We'll be back next week, she said. Got to hold my grandbaby.

CHAPTER 17

My mother'd had to be induced, too, while Mrs. Vanderdyke from across the street stayed with me. My mother screamed and screamed and the doctor said, Shhh, there are women here having their first babies. Mrs. Van put her false teeth back in and tried to make me mind, but I pretended I was suddenly deaf. I pointed to my ears and shook my head and mouthed "I can't hear you," apparently struck mute as well. My father must have come home after the dead baby was born, but I didn't remember.

I had to ride in a wheelchair, though I could have walked. It was out of my control now. It would be done to me. It would happen to me. A nurse took off my blue maternity dress and hung it up. She fed my arms into a backless white gown and helped me onto a bed. Another nurse came in with a needle on a tray. I couldn't stop shaking. My skin was hot and tingling, just waiting for the stretching and the tearing.

"Someone's leaking," one nurse said to the other and handed me a Kleenex.

I wanted my mother. Lonnie didn't have anything to do with this. I didn't care what he was up to. He could go drink himself blind and deaf and dumb. The two nurses injected me, they broke the water, they shaved me, they gave me an enema, and I wanted my mother. When I was seven years old and in the hospital, I'd had an enema. A nurse had brought a box covered up on a tray, and she said, "I'm going to give you an animal."

It wasn't a mouse or a little rabbit in a wooden slatted box and I must have cried at what she did to me. My mother told me later they bought me the Dale Evans wristwatch because I'd heard I was supposed to die of leukemia. A dying person wouldn't need to tell time. A little dead girl wouldn't wear Dale's ticking gun finger.

By three, gentle contractions began. They said my husband could come in for a while but I shook my head. I still wanted my mother but I was doing it. I was doing it alone. The pain was blunt and the doctor came in and reached in to feel the baby and said something, dilation, and I was doing it.

"My mother had a dead baby," I said to the nurse.

"Well, you're having a live one," she said. "I can guarantee that. That's a live one in there who wants out."

I spread my palms on my stomach. With the contractions, it was like armor. The baby was an animal in a wooden box. It must be terrible to be in there, I thought suddenly. It must be a storm in there. Amniotic rain must be whipping the baby and the cord kinking and twisting and the sac caving in, and if it was awful to think of being the turtleneck, how much more terrible must it be for the formed head to shove itself forward and forward toward the impossible unblinking opening? The poor baby was being punished for me or by me. The pains were long and the loosening was brief and brief and then the pains welded solid. My legs trembled and I had never had a pain in my whole life before this never ever. I couldn't breathe to scream, all right all right this was the punishment. This was too much, too fast, too soon, I'd worn pinafores and played the piano, let me hear you tinkle those keys, my father used to say, I'd stretched into my body and let Lonnie—and I blinked out that stupid back seat—and this was the punishment all right for my betrayals all in nineteen years and I was dying and the baby was stuck and drowning in me.

They lifted my rigid body over to a table and wheeled me down a hallway, to delivery, he said, and my whole length and wrap of skin dilated, cannot believe, she said, and I was deep in the red of my rigid body and I was gone, out of the body above the unturning wheels, into my mother's baby when he thrust his heels into her and shook and died, and I collapsed into my body and draped myself over the baby. They turned me onto my hands and knees and the baby swung from me and there was a needle in my spine and they turned me onto another table and stroked my bare heels into stirrups and covered me in sheets.

"Better?" the doctor said. "Now you can relax and enjoy it. See that mirror? Look—you'll see the head appearing."

"She doesn't know how lucky she is," someone said. "Can you believe this is a first?"

"Speedy Gonzalez," he said.

In the convex mirror I watched the dark swirled head rise from between my legs, and the shoulders angled out, and then in a rush of water the body was out.

They laid it on my stomach and suctioned out the nose and mouth and the baby bleated.

"Little girl," someone said. "A sweet little girl."

"She's all white," I said. She was covered with caked white powder. Her hands were blue.

"That's vernix," the nurse said and lifted her and wiped her and smoothed the wet hair on her head. And this had nothing to do with shame.

The rest was mysterious, too—sitz baths, stiff dizzy walking, bleeding onto the pink bathrobe—but I wasn't afraid. The two others in the room said these were their second and fourth babies. They were large women with wide bottoms and full rich breasts that knew by shape what breasts were for—of course, of course. They weren't really meant for making a shape beneath a yellow sweater, for sitting tight in A cups, for a boy's hand. They were for the babies. They were the babies' udders. What did it mean that boys always wanted to touch them?

"Bet you had a hard time, honey," one of the women said. "Them narrow hips."

"It wasn't too bad," I said. I didn't tell them it had taken only two hours. I didn't say that for penance it should have lasted for two days and then killed me or that if I'd had Dale's gun I would have killed myself if it had gone on ten more minutes. But we all smiled at each other. We all knew the truth.

A nurse pushed a chrome cart of babies into our room and handed out three. I watched the other two, the real mothers, open the fronts of their gowns and loosen the babies' blankets.

The baby had thin dark hair swirled into a curl over an ear. The head was too big for the body. The eyebrows looked like smears of charcoal. Her hands were pink. She was wrinkled and blotchy. She looked worried. She was looking at me. Her eyes were dark blue and they didn't look quite finished. I touched her cheek and her lips kissed and she turned to my finger. I opened my gown and we tried it, all new, all shy, her fingers pointing and curled like Buddha's, her squashed nose perfect for breathing against my breast, and the suction began.

A nurse brought in the birth certificate and laid it on the tray across my bed. She needed a name for my daughter.

"Think about it, if you need to," she said. "I'll be back."

The boy's name was supposed to be Benjamin Lon Saxbe III. I meant to call him Benjy. The girl's name was supposed to be Bernadine for his mother and the middle name could be Lindsay for Mama White, Lonnie said, if I wanted that instead of Mae. I wanted to name her Katie. Katie Lee. She was my baby. How could I call her Bernadine? But she was my baby. It didn't matter. On a sheet of yellow legal paper, I printed it: Bernadine Lindsay Saxbe.

Let him be satisfied now.

Lonnie showed up at noon the next day while a nurse was handing out the babies. He pulled the curtain around my bed.

"I sneaked away from work," he said. "They'll never miss me."

I held my unbuttoned nightgown closed. "Well, be careful," I said. "You don't want to be fired." I adjusted the baby so her face touched only my arm.

"Junior there looks hungry," he said.

"Junior? You can't call her Junior. Not a little girl."

She rooted for a way under the sleeve of my gown. I touched her cheek and she turned her head toward my finger like a plant, time-lapsed photographed, curving toward the sun. I let her find the finger.

"Sure," Lonnie said. "Bernie Junior. I like it."

Finding the finger dry, the baby opened her mouth and bleated. Her puckered face turned red and her fists flailed as if she wanted to pound us both. Milk soaked my nightgown and I pulled the sheet up over my chest.

Lonnie stepped backwards. "This wasn't one of the all-time great ideas, I guess," he said. "Listen, I better peel on back." He came quickly to the bedside and kissed my mouth.

"Okay, see you tonight at visiting hours," I said. "Or you don't have to drive all the way back if you don't want to."

"Why? Who else are you expecting?"

When he was gone, I pulled back the sheet and opened the wet gown. I led the baby's mouth to my breast.

"Package for Dulcie White," Katie said and stepped briskly into the room. She was wearing a candy striper's apron. "Sorry, I mean Dulcie Saxbe." She handed me a box tied in yellow ribbon.

"How'd you get in here?" I said. "They don't allow anybody but the fathers."

"Pretend you don't know me," she whispered. "Helene Davis on the second floor is a candy striper at the hospital. Her father is rich so he makes her do volunteer work. She loaned me the outfit. You can't believe how I missed you. What was it like? I want to know every little pain. Was it absolutely horrible? My poor chambrie. Open the box."

Inside was a tiny yellow suit with a duck on its front. "Yellow," I said. "I love it. She can wear it home. Weren't we silly back when we thought we could paint a nursery yellow and hide out and have the baby?"

"Can I see her?" Katie said. "Before I start bawling?"

We moved slowly through the hall, the new mother leaning on the candy-striper.

"Lonnie said you were naming her Bernadine. Really?"

"His mother. What can I say?"

"But you can't call her Bernadine, can you? I mean, Bernadine—it sounds like some old witch from a Southern swamp."

The baby was sleeping on her stomach right in the center of the nursery crib. Her fringe of hair was dark brown against the white sheet.

"I wanted to name her Katie," I said.

A nurse stopped behind us. "Candy stripers don't work in maternity," she said. "What are we doing here?"

"Just a minute," I said. "She's helping me."

"Dulcie," Katie said, "I wanted to tell you—."

"Good-bye now," the nurse said in a singsong voice and led Katie away.

"I'll come over as soon as you're home," Katie said. "Kiss Deena for me."

Alone I hobbled back to my bed in my ugly blood-stained pink robe.

On Saturday, washed, with clean limp hair, clothed in the maternity dress I'd worn to the hospital, I sat in the husband's chair by the bed and waited for Lonnie to come and take me home. The other mothers had left the day before and the room was empty. The baby was still in the nursery crib. I was acutely awake. The newly made-up beds glowed, and the stainless metal bars on the beds were so shiny they were almost liquid. I wouldn't have minded staying. On the bedside table, a brown-edged rose floated in a glass bowl—from Katie and Glenna—and the books and magazines from my mother were stacked. I'd try to keep the books, but it wouldn't break my heart if Lonnie threw them out, since in the past few days I'd read them all. The plastic of the chair felt silky to my hands. Everything was stark and slick and antiseptic.

Under the loose dress my body was thin again and full breasted, though the brown line running straight down from my navel had not disappeared.

Then Lonnie came into the room's sharp focus. His eyebrows were bushy, his stride was slightly bow-legged, and the backs of his hands were hairy. He was coarse and blurred, and now in a wheelchair with my baby in my precise arms, I had to leave with him.

In the afternoon, after Lonnie had gone back to work, his sisters brought their girls over to visit the new cousin.

"Now you three be quiet and calm," Suzie told them. "Don't disturb the tiny, tiny baby, you hear?"

But they romped about the apartment's two rooms, bounding beside me on the couch, then fooling with my neat line-up of baby powder, oil, Q-Tips, washcloths, and diapers. In the kitchen they searched the refrigerator and the cupboards.

"How come you're nursing her?" Marie said. "I tell you what, I wasn't about to do that with Mitzi."

"I read that it's supposed to be better for the baby," I said. "To get all the right nutrients and minerals."

"At least you don't have to sterilize bottles," Suzie said.

Marie started giggling. "Yeah, but does she have to boil the nipples? Ouch."

They'd brought practical presents: a bottle warmer, diapers, and bibs.

"So what does Lonnie think?" Suzie asked. "About you having her on the tit?"

The little girls had the pans out in the kitchen.

"Remember when we used to dress him up?" Marie said. "That one time we did him up like a gypsy?"

"Yeah, we made him wear that purple skirt you had. And Mom's off-the-shoulder blouse and these hoop earrings."

"Your full petticoat," Marie said, laughing. "He was so cute."

Suzie touched my leg. "God, girl, don't tell Lonnie. He'd die."

"We used to mess around with him. Lucky he was too little to remember. God, we were so bad." Marie was still laughing.

"That was kid stuff. All kids do that stuff," Suzie said. "I bet even the snow queen here played doctor."

A child screamed in the kitchen. "Mom! Sissy hit me, Sissy hit me."

The baby woke in her painted bassinet and began a rhythmic muted crying.

"You go separate the monsters this time. It's your turn," Suzie said. "I forgot how tiny a newborn cries."

Sometime, I thought, I could ask them about Lonnie, and maybe figure out what happened to him and why their mother left him and his father for that year, or whatever it had been. But now wasn't the time, with all the children yelling and the milk rushing into my breasts with the baby's crying. They thought I was a snow queen. What? Chilly and aloof, I supposed. Maybe I was. After they left, I sat in the rocking chair and fed her and sang little songs I didn't even know I knew. *Mama's little baby loves shortnin' shortnin', Mama's little baby loves shortnin' bread.*

She would be my only child. She was so tiny and refined compared to Suzie's and Marie's unwieldy children. My body was warm for her, and I would raise her to be the same intact little person she was now.

Lonnie brought egg salad sandwiches in wax paper for supper. He'd bought them at the store's snack bar. He heated a can of tomato soup, adding water instead of milk. I let him wait on me and do the dishes afterward.

He unfolded the couch early and moved the bassinet to my side of the bed. "She sleeps all the time," he said. "She's okay, isn't she? I mean—she's not some retard?"

"She's just a newborn baby. Of course she sleeps a lot. She's perfect.

Besides, the doctor would have told us if anything were wrong." I was worried that her head was too big, though. Still, Lonnie's mother had a big head. Lonnie's sisters hadn't noticed anything, and they didn't seem the type to keep quiet out of tact.

Lonnie moved close under the covers. "I was one lonesome fool with you gone," he said. "Next time we have a baby, we'll just skip the hospital."

"Next time *we* have a baby," I said, "we'll take turns. You can have it."

"Babe, I would if I could, I really would. That's how much I love you," he said seriously. "Besides, I'd be in all the news and we'd get rich."

I tried to laugh quietly at the notion of Lonnie with a pregnant stomach, wearing huge shirts and Levi's with a zipper in a stretch panel in front. "I guess you'd have to have it caesarian," I said.

"I put your pillow against my back," he said. "I pretended it was you. This bed was too empty. I don't never want to sleep without you again."

"Well, you have to wait a while for anything besides sleeping."

"Well, I know that," he said, hurt. "Can't I just miss you?"

"You know what? I missed sleeping with you, too," I said. I was surprised but it was true. He was not going to climb onto me, and his body was warm against me. Sometimes I wished he would be one thing: a jealous nickel-counting, record-scratching child, or a nice, clean-cut young man, as my mother still believed he was at heart, or the husband who ripped my jacket and hit me—and why was it that ripping the corduroy jacket was as bad as the bruises?—or a malleable boy who followed me everywhere and fixed tomato soup for supper. I wanted to settle myself with him—to love him despite it all, or to tolerate him and settle into a life, or to hate him and—and what? take my baby and run? It was all mixed up, the boy taking me for pizza shifting into the man in shirttails scraping the cookie dough out of the bowl shifting into the child who heaved a game board into the wall shifting into this real male body beside me who had flowed into me and made the one and only and singular baby shifting into the one who made me ask for a paternity test and then wouldn't request the results shifting as if a knife were drawn through him as through cake batter to marbleize it.

At two o'clock the baby gave a muffled cry and I sat in the rocking chair and nursed her. The radiator spurted minute sounds. In the middle of the night, with Lonnie asleep and my baby in my arms, nothing was any clearer or simpler, but nothing really mattered, either, nothing but the shut-down absolute purity of sitting up in the darkness with the baby sucking and breathing.

CHAPTER 18

The courtroom was jam packed like the bleachers at a home game. Except it was more like church, with pews and holy whispers and the judge's altar. Lonnie sat in the second row next to an old guy with long gray hair who had on a gray trenchcoat like a weenie-wagger. On the other side of the old guy was some girl who looked to be maybe a junior. She had her yellow traffic ticket on her lap like she didn't want anybody to think she was a thief or something real bad. A ticket wasn't nothing.

First these guys in suits went up in pairs. These were the rich guys and their lawyers, he figured. Then the judge started in calling names with the A's. Anderson. Atchley. These guys went up one at a time. There was a big map taken from a plane on the wall behind the judge's bench. There was a flag. The walls were crusty piss-yellow. The rods of fluorescent lights on the ceiling flickered and hummed. You didn't get that in church. After a half hour the judge was only at the D's. These two stenographers sat on either side of him just chewing their cuds. His mother hated anybody to be chewing gum. Like a cow chewing cud, she always said. These stenographers at least were chomping away with their mouths closed, but he thought he could hear the noises inside their mouths anyway, all wet and popping. Garrison and Gentry and Harvey and Iverson one at a time went up and bowed and scraped before his honor. He was a bald man who thought he was God.

Lonnie thought he was going to fall asleep. The courtroom was hot and woolly smelling. There were yellowed shades over the windows and a dirty no-smoking sign Scotch-taped to the wall. Jasper and Koslowski and Kurtman. There were initials scratched into the back of the bench in front of him. R.B. G.C. B.B. You didn't find that in church either. Lionel and Lloyd went up and got sermoned.

His royal fucking honor got to the S's after a couple hours and Lonnie went up and just stood and took it. There wasn't no choice. Up close the judge had about six long hairs growing out of the top of his head. He almost had to laugh at the hairs. He was about to blow up, he was so full of heat. God fined him three hundred bucks and gave him a probation officer. He had a week to come up with the three hundred. I could have fined you a thousand dollars, God said. Or you could go to jail. I'm trying to wake you up here, young man, before you kill somebody.

It ought to be you, he thought. You in that blue shirt under that fruity robe. If he'd been one of them with the lawyer like Jesus at his side, the hairless old judge would have had him up there hours ago and just patted his back.

Yes sir, he said, I appreciate that, sir. He didn't know where the three hundred would come from. Dulcie's father had already paid for the hospital. After the car payment and the rent and the hamburger Dulcie fed him and the gallons of expensive milk she was guzzling and the junk she was buying for the baby, diaper pins with duck heads on them for Christ's sake, there was no way he could come up with three hundred in a week. His honor's *shirt* probably cost a hundred dollars and he probably ate steak every night. But it wasn't just the three hundred, it was the Yessir, oh thank you for sparing me, your honor, would you like me to lick your shoes while I'm down here kissing your ass. He couldn't hardly stand it, he got out a *thank you sir*, he rubbed his itchy hands on his thighs, he turned around and beat feet out of there before he choked the holy shit out of the hairless wonder sitting up there high and mighty in that black robe.

He woke in the middle of the night. Dulcie wasn't in bed with him. He had dreamed he was chasing an invisible man through some kind of marketplace, like in Mexico or someplace, like someplace in his old grade school book, with carts and stalls and mobs of peasants. He could just see the bare outlines of the invisible man. He chased him, knocking over baskets full of fruit and gourds, falling into carts full of beans that spilled everywhere, bumping into women so the melons in their aprons rolled on the dirt road.

He didn't move. When his eyes were used to the dark, he could see Dulcie sitting in her rocking chair. She was nursing the baby. He wished she wouldn't do that. What was the point? Why couldn't she just feed her from a bottle?

In the dream the invisible man was after Dulcie. Then all of a sudden they were out in the country and Dulcie was down in the grass and the invisible man was on top of her. Her red peasant dress showed right through his body. Then he faded out all the way. But he was still there.

Dulcie was rocking away. Her hair was growing out and it hung over her face. It was a good thing he'd woke up or he'd have had a wet dream. The glow-in-the-dark alarm clock read two-thirty. Dulcie was whispering, Mama loves you, oh your mama loves you, do you know that sweet baby?

The invisible man made him sit in the grass and watch. I'm going to do things, he said. You won't see me but I'll tell you. Now I'm undoing her blouse. Now I'm kissing her. When you see her move I'll be inside her.

Something was going to happen. His guts were hot, like he was going to blow up, the way he'd been in the courtroom trying not to laugh at the judge's hairs growing out of his bald head. Dulcie was crying in the dark. He could hear her. The rocking chair rasped when she rocked back and she sniffed and wiped her face on the baby's blanket. He couldn't take it. Something had to happen. He closed his eyes and pictured the invisible man in the dark and tried to go back to sleep.

On Sunday the idea was to go over to his parents' and then hers. Show the kid off. Get a free dinner out of the deal. Dulcie had him hold the baby while she got the bath ready. Marie'd given them this pink plastic bathtub. She set it on the kitchen table and put a pillow beside it. She put out all this junk, soap and powder, a diaper and plastic pants. She poured a couple inches of water into the tub and dipped her elbow in.

He kind of liked holding the baby. I could wash her this time, he said.

Oh well, Dulcie said. Let me just do it. We want to get going pretty soon, don't we? She took the baby and undressed her on the pillow.

You look like a little girl, he said. Playing mommy to your doll.

The baby's dark eyes kept watching him all the time Dulcie washed her and dressed her. Her arms and legs jerked around like she couldn't control them. Her forehead was wrinkled. She looks mad, he said. Check out those fists.

At the trailer, his dad went for the baby right off. Dulcie didn't have no choice but to hand the kid over.

Hello there, little Bernadine, he said. How's our little Bernie?

Kind of looks like me, don't you think? Lonnie said.

His mother held the baby then. Oh precious, she said. Our little bitty precious.

Now that the baby was born, Lonnie couldn't do no wrong. Maybe nothing would happen. Could be, everything would work out. He'd get a decent job and him and Dulcie would get their own place and he'd make her pregnant again and his mother would look at him like she was looking at him now, like he was God's gift, and nothing would happen.

The baby started crying and Dulcie took her into his old bedroom and shut the door. That was okay with him. He didn't think none of them wanted to watch her whip out the tit. I couldn't nurse you, his mother said. Like she'd only said a hundred times before. You were premature.

He was just as glad. He didn't want to think about sucking his mother's tit. He wondered if she'd done it with Marie and Suzie. But he didn't ask.

He got his dad out to look at his car and asked him for the three hundred. He told him about the ticket and the judge who treated him like pond scum. But he kept the night in the slammer to himself. Like always, his dad let him have the money.

I'll pay you back, he said. I'm just borrowing this.

His dad always said, Don't worry about it, son. But this time he said, I'll be expecting it. It's about time for a lesson in responsibility. Now that you're playing with the big boys.

On the way over to Dulcie's parents' he finally had to tell her how her old man had paid the hospital bill. He hated it that he couldn't even pay for his own kid. I'm going to pay him back, though, he told her. It isn't charity.

Her parents made fools of themselves over the baby. They had all these presents, too, clothes and stuff, and a fancy blue stroller.

I don't see how that'll fit in my car, he said. This was just great: now Dulcie could go tramping all over town.

We'll see what we can do after dinner, Dr. White said. I bet between the two of us we can figure it out.

The baby slept on the couch and they all ate about a five-course dinner. At dessert Dulcie's mother gave her a card and when she opened it up a twenty fell out on the cherry cobbler.

That's to go shopping, she said. Buy yourself a new outfit.

Oh you don't know how sick I was of maternity clothes, Dulcie said. This is great. Though I may wait until I'm really back in shape.

Well, I want to see that outfit when you get it, her mother said. She was staring at him when she said it. That pissed him off.

Don't you trust me, Mama White? he said. It was a joke.

She looked at him all serious. Dulcie's father and I want to make sure that—

Lindsay, Dr. White said.

All right, she said. I'll mind my own business. Who can eat more cobbler?

Outside they collapsed that baby stroller and got it into the Witch's trunk. You know, young man, Dr. White said, all quiet and nervous, we can't have you hurting our daughter.

Say what? Hurting her? Who the fuck said—

Now, son, you're not to use that language— The old man was shaking. Damn. The old man was scared.

I'm not your fucking son, he said. I'm my father's son. I wouldn't touch your precious daughter. Anyway, don't tell me you never laid a hand on your woman.

No, the old fool said, who—? He turned around and crawled back to the house. Lonnie slammed the trunk.

They drove back to Waterton in silence. He felt like he'd run the two-mile without stretching first, been disqualified for a false start, and come in last anyway, his socks around his ankles and his tank shirt soaked.

You'd think it was summer, Dulcie finally said. If you only looked up.

The sky was blue and clear. But the trees were bare. Crusted black snow was heaped along the roadsides.

Yeah, well, it's only February, he said.

CHAPTER 19

Katie drove over without calling first. "I was pretty sure you'd be here," she said. "I read in one of my mother's magazines about post-partum blues. I wanted to make sure my roomie didn't have them. So I said to heck with Shakespeare and borrowed Josh's car and—voilà."

She took off her coat and laid it on a kitchen chair. She wore a straight wool skirt and a cream sweater with knit drawstrings at the wrists and neck, tied in loose bows. She looked thin.

"You look like a model," I said. She was beautiful now. Josh must have been in love with her.

She held out her arms and spun around in the kitchen. "The complete coed," she said. "Don't make me laugh."

"Don't make me cry."

"Where's the baby? Can I see her?" She looked around as if the baby were in a cupboard, and I saw my own kitchen. A saucepan half-full of turkey noodle soup was on the stove, left from Lonnie's lunch, and a plastic bowl with a fatty yellow scum still sat on the table with bread crumbs around it. The linoleum floor was dirty.

"She's sleeping. Come see."

Katie stood silently by the wicker bassinet with her hands together, as if she were praying to the baby.

"She's so perfect," she whispered.

The sofa was still open, and I yanked the blankets off, shoved them in the closet, and folded up the bed.

"You don't have to whisper," I said. "She sleeps through anything."

Katie sat on the edge of the sofa. Her dark hair was still long and straight. I'd washed my hair earlier but not set it, just pulled it into a low ponytail with a rubber band. My breasts felt enormous in the heavy nursing bra. My blouse was stained with milk leakage.

"So. Tell me about school." I sat at the other end of the sofa.

"There's nothing to tell. It's just the same."

I wished the baby would wake up.

"Except me," Katie said. "I'm not the same. At first, when I came back to school in the fall, I was even mad at you. I knew it wasn't your fault, but I couldn't help it. I was mad at you."

"And now look at me," I said. "A real slob of a housewife."

"Josh wants to get married. After we graduate, anyway. He wants us to join the Peace Corps."

"That'd be neat," I said. "The Peace Corps. You'd have to write to me, all about your travels. Your wild adventures. Everybody you help."

"Josh thinks this whole country is going to heat up. That's what he says, heat up."

Except on Sunday, I didn't read a newspaper. "Maybe it's just Josh who's heating up," I said, as if smut could conceal ignorance, and was right away ashamed. "I didn't mean that," I said.

"Well, you're right, he is. But I—oh, I can't even talk about it. I'm so scared and I just can't—do anything."

That was my fault. I'd shown her what became of girls who did it. I might as well have taken one of those caulking guns and sealed her off. And I couldn't even tell her she was wrong.

Katie waved it all away. "He's a pacifist, you know. He thinks we're going to be in a war. Anyway, I came over for *your* blues. And to see that little one."

I went over and picked up the baby. She came out of sleep with a little hum.

"What is that, a baby or a cat?" Katie said. "Deena, the amazing purring baby."

I handed the baby to her, and she held her stiffly on her lap. "I wouldn't dare have a baby," she said. "See, already you know what to do. You're a good mother right away. I'd be too afraid."

"You might change your mind later on. But I always thought I'd have children. Just not quite this way."

"Josh doesn't want kids, either."

That surprised me—not that Josh didn't want kids but that a man would have an opinion about it. "Lonnie didn't so much want children," I said, "as he wanted me to have a baby. Or he wanted me to be pregnant so I'd have to marry him."

"You know, we're going to have to get Josh and Lonnie used to each other. Later on we can live near each other, and they'll have to get along. We can all go to Europe together in the summers."

Josh and Lonnie would never ever be friends. It was impossible that we'd go to Europe. I saw the four of us at the Arc de Triomphe. I saw myself holding a man's hand, and I changed him into Bruce. I kept the baby and put her in a pack on Bruce's back, and there we all five were in the Alps.

"It seems impossible," Katie said. "This creature was inside you, and now here she is. I couldn't do it. She's exquisite. She is. But I'm never going to have any babies." She crossed her legs and hunched over, preserving herself.

"You know what my mom said? Oh, she was sweet and brought me a bunch of books and baby stuff. But she said I should have suffered more. I should have been in labor a lot longer."

"She wouldn't say that. Why would your mother say that?"

"To pay. I was a bad girl," I said. "She took it back. She didn't really mean it."

"Oh that makes me mad," Katie said. "You're so forgiving."

"Well, I *was* a bad girl. And she was in labor a really long time and for what? To deliver a dead baby."

"*I* never want you to suffer. I want you to live happily ever after. I want us to be true friends forever and ever."

When Katie left, I laid the baby in the bassinet and cleaned up the kitchen, set my hair, and put on my old watch-plaid kilt and a sweater. But it was all over. I was living out my pathetic life. This was it. Katie and Josh would go to France for their junior year, and after they graduated they'd learn Hindi or Swahili and teach villagers how to irrigate their fields and read to their children.

She was gone from me. She'd come to see me for a while yet, off and on, and she'd send birthday presents to the baby for a couple years. She'd write from France and maybe still sign the letters *Love, Chambrie Katie*. But she was gone from me. I didn't blame her. It was my own fault. I could have stayed with her in our little dorm room, and maybe we really could have performed the Tchaikovsky piano concerto at graduation, and then it would be the two of us going out into the world. I took the rollers out of my hair and combed it out before Lonnie was due back from work. For a second I let it be Bruce, who was returning from his research position at the university, and I saw him kissing me and lifting the baby high, and he said, "How's our little girl? How's our little Katie girl?" But Bruce and I had gone out together only to go with Josh and Katie. We never would have been in love. I'd never sip a drink in a Paris café. I sent Katie off without me, I let her go, I waved from the dock as the ocean liner lurched out into the harbor.

"Quit feeling sorry for yourself," I said in the kitchen. "You're the one with the baby." You had to stay on shore with a baby, I thought. And so what? I worked chopped onions and ketchup into a bowl of hamburger and patted the mess into a loaf pan and every fifteen minutes poured off the orange grease. When Lonnie came home the table was set, the meatloaf was done, and the green beans were heating on the stovetop.

"All right now," the doctor said after my check-up. "What are we doing about birth control?"

"Birth control? You mean—I don't know. I read that nursing would... I mean, take care of that."

He looked at me intently, and I blushed. Of course he knew what Lonnie did to me. Everybody knew. "You *are* pretty safe while you're nursing," he said. "But you don't want to take chances, do you?"

The baby was asleep in her infant seat on the floor. Now that she was here, I wouldn't have any more babies. *She* was the baby and that was all. I shook my head.

"I'd like to start you on birth control pills," he said.

"Lonnie says—I mean, my husband thinks they aren't safe."

"No, they're ninety-nine percent effective," the doctor said. He took a plastic wheel of pills out of a desk drawer.

I'd never be able to hide them or pay for them. "No, he thinks they haven't been tested thoroughly, that's all," I said. *No wife of mine is gonna be a guinea pig*, he'd said. What he really wanted, I thought, was to take chances again. *I'll kill you if you ever leave me*, he said. If one baby didn't leash me to him, then two babies would, or three, or four.

"Well, that has to be your decision," the doctor said. I didn't know if he meant that I should make up my own mind or that he wouldn't interfere with what Lonnie and I decided.

At the front desk the nurse handed me a small white paper sack. I opened it in the bathroom at home and found a thin can of spermicidal foam and a clear plastic tube. *Spermicide* made me laugh. We'd discussed the Latin suffix -cide in seventh-grade English, I remembered. Insecticide, herbicide, homicide, fratricide. Nobody had mentioned sperm killer then. I pictured the wet spot on the sheet with a dozen little sperms floating in it belly-up, tongues hanging out, little Xs over their eyes.

Lonnie handed me the mail at noon, a diaper service ad and a letter from Glenna.

"Hey. This is addressed to me."

"No shit, Sherlock."

"Then why did you open it?"

"It's just from Glenna. So where's lunch? I gotta get back."

"You're not supposed to open other people's mail. Didn't your mother teach you that?"

He slammed the refrigerator door. "What, Glenna sending you secret messages? Setting you up with dates? That the deal?"

I shivered as if I'd swallowed a piece of ice and could feel it moving down my esophagus.

"Bet you wish that was you," he said. "Admit it. Parties and all. Buying some fancy dress for the Washington Ball." He did a mincing hop and made his wrist limp.

I got out the bread for his sandwich. "I'm not envious of Glenna," I said, my back to him. "We have a baby. We're doing fine. Don't you know I'm happy with you?" I spread mayonnaise on the bread, hoping he heard the words and not the cold in my voice.

Mustard on the other piece of bread. Two slices of bologna. I hated the rubbery flesh-colored bologna. No lettuce. *I ain't a rabbit, Dulcie.* I'd make myself a peanut butter and jelly sandwich after he left.

"Sit down, eat your lunch," I said. Sandwich on the table. "I don't have the energy for an argument. And you don't have the time. Just... please, don't open my mail."

He dug his fingers into my shoulders and I tried to duck away. "Your lesbo buddy claims to love that guy Rick." He shook me. "You gonna tell her all about making out with him and fucking everybody else too?"

He shook me until my neck went loose.

He shoved me away from him. I caught myself on the kitchen counter and knocked the mustard jar onto the floor. We stared at the mess of mustard and glass and for an instant we might have started laughing. But the baby gave a cry and I stepped over the broken jar past Lonnie to pick her up.

"Leave her there," he said.

I backed along the wall away from him. He came after me, and I circled the room faster. The baby wailed. Suddenly Lonnie dropped onto the sofa, as if he'd seen how ridiculous we looked. He opened his arms.

"Hey, baby, I'm sorry," he said.

I went to him, and when I was in range, he whipped his arm back and slapped me solidly across my face.

The snow thawed for two days, and on the third day I wrapped up the baby and pushed her in the stroller down the block. If Lonnie called, he'd be angry that I wasn't in the apartment. The thaw had left the sidewalk covered with fine black dirt. I had the infant seat and my old piano music on the stroller's awning.

The church's front door was locked, but the side door was open. I parked the stroller in the hallway and called, "Hello? Hello? Anybody here?"

There was an organ in the chancel, but I didn't dare touch it. I found a piano downstairs in a low-ceilinged room with rows of folding chairs and a platform stage. The whole church seemed empty. I set the baby in her infant seat on the floor and played a soft scale. Nobody appeared. I spread my fingers and dropped my hands onto the Pathetique's opening chord. The sound was muted. This was what I thought of as a parlor piano, with soft slow keys. I used to like rec room pianos, old uprights with a gaudy sound and clattery action. My own baby grand had a firm and bright sound that I believed was best on Beethoven. It wasn't my baby grand anymore, though.

On this church piano, my fingers were slow and fat, and I couldn't press hard enough on the keys. The baby whimpered and kicked, and I played on until she broke into crying and milk rushed into my breasts, and then I gave up on the piano and carried her up the stairs to the stroller.

Later I realized that I'd left the music books on top of the piano, but I never returned for them. Somebody would find them and wonder who'd left them, maybe an old lady piano teacher who would give them to a talented but poor girl. I was done with my Czerny, my Chopin, my Rachmaninoff, my Beethoven, certainly my Tchaikovsky. Face it: They weren't mine. Face it: Probably nobody would ever wonder at all about the pile of yellow books on top of the piano.

When we went to bed, the baby was fine. Lonnie and I were still a bit formal after the last fight. He'd stopped apologizing after he hit me, stopped crying and swearing he'd never touch me again, but he'd stay slightly aloof for two or three days, as if to let the guilt wear off. We'd spent the evening in front of the television, Lonnie with only a couple beers. In the wake of the fight, I was allowed to read. At ten I nursed the baby and then we went to bed. We were going to have to look for another apartment, I thought. I worried about the baby's hearing Lonnie on me, the squeaking that might scare her as it sped up and then with his low groan abruptly stopped.

At two the baby started crying. I took her to the rocking chair to feed her, but she only sucked for a second and then opened her mouth and cried, with milk dripping onto her face. I felt her diaper—no open pins, but she was damp. I changed her in the dark. I walked her around and around. She wouldn't stop crying.

Lonnie came into the dark kitchen with a blanket wrapped around him. "What's the matter with her?" he said. "I can't sleep with all this racket."

"I can't get her to stop crying. I tried everything."

She cried for two hours. Lonnie went back to sleep with my pillow over his head. I walked her, I rocked her, I tried water in a bottle. I called my mother at three. The phone rang and rang but nobody answered. I sat on the kitchen floor with the baby on my shoulder and a blanket over us to muffle her, and in worry and fatigue and frustration, I cried too. I tried again to wake my mother. I wanted to go to sleep. I was no kind of mother. I dragged the bassinet into the kitchen and laid the screaming baby in it. I even considered putting her in the glassed-in foyer with lots of covers, but I knew it would be too cold. A real mother would know what to do. A mother wouldn't even for an instant think about setting her baby out on a porch in March. A mother would answer the phone in the middle of the night. A real father wouldn't sleep through it. I sat beside the bassinet in the kitchen with my hand on her little heaving back. She felt like a hairless little animal, something weasely or rat-like, an opossum, furious at being stirred out of hibernation. A mother wouldn't think of her little baby girl as an opposum. It didn't matter if I held her or not. My nightgown was stiff and smelly with dried milk. I turned her onto her stomach again.

When she finally fell asleep, I was exhausted and drained, but now that she was quiet I was afraid to sleep.

"Lonnie," I said. "Wake up. I'm worried. Something's really wrong. Maybe we should take her to the hospital."

He sat up like a grumpy child himself, and then I could see him remember the baby. He went to look at her.

"She's sleeping and now you want to wake her up?" He led me to bed. "She's a baby. Babies cry. My mother said I cried all the time. I had something—colic."

"I'm afraid she'll stop breathing."

"Okay, you go to bed. I'll sit here and watch her."

I lay down and heard him pull a kitchen chair over by the bassinet.

At six, when I heard her whimper, I got up. Lonnie had his head down on the kitchen table. He sat there in his underwear with a blanket slid partway down his back. Looking at him, I thought this was the way a parent would look at a growing son, tender for the smooth back, proud of the beautiful young man. But this was Lonnie. He stretched his arms up and yawned when the baby's crying built up.

"What a night," he said. "You want me to call in to work? Take junior to the doctor?"

I laid her on a towel on our bed to change her before trying to feed her.

In the thin daylight I took off the wet diaper and pulled her legs up by the ankles to powder her. Her thighs and buttocks were scarlet and raw.

I burst into tears.

Lonnie came in to see. "Oh my God," he said. "That's the worst case of jock itch I ever hope to see."

Every couple hours I rubbed more Desitin on the poor baby and tried to reach my mother. By late afternoon, when she finally answered, I was jangly after a short nap. I'd needed my mother and she'd abandoned me. I was as worried and angry as she used to be when I'd stay out too late.

"Where were you? I've been having a terrible time. I've been trying and trying and trying to call you."

I knew my voice sounded whiny, but she only said, "How bad is it? Do you want me to come get you?"

"That wouldn't make any difference at this point. But where were you?"

"Listen, there isn't much time. I was going to call you tomorrow. But you need to do some heavy thinking now."

"Mom—what are you talking about? I was up all night with the baby."

"Just hold on a minute," she said, and then she called away from the phone, "Walter? Could you get our bags in?"

"Bags in? Where'd you go? I didn't know you were going on a trip." I was sounding aggrieved, I knew.

"There, I wanted to get your father out of the room. I'll call you again tomorrow when he's out of the house. He hates to be talked about. But he's lost his job. We were in California. He had an interview."

She talked fast, and when I interrupted—"How could he—" she said, "Listen fast, Dulcie. I'm not going to be here to help you. You can come with us to California. This is happening fast. But you have to make a decision. You think tonight. I'll call you tomorrow."

In the evening, when Lonnie took the book out of my hands and told me to watch the show with him, I hardly minded. I couldn't stop thinking about my father's losing his job. He'd worked for the company for as long as I remembered. He wasn't like Lonnie, getting fired for telling off the boss or for skipping work. What had my father done to lose his job?

When I was in high school, the president was killed. The principal announced it over the intercom. It was between classes and we heard his incredulous voice over the hallway babble and the slamming of lockers. Some girls started crying right away. I couldn't even remember the rest of the school day, just debate about whether the basketball game should still be played that evening. We couldn't believe it. Everybody kept saying, I can't believe it. The president couldn't be killed. Things didn't happen that way. That was the *government*. In high school, the only things that happened were personal, not national. Couples broke up, Becky Mead got in trouble, two guys had a fight in the hall, a girl slipped in the shower and broke her tailbone—but the adult world was separate and stable, no matter what sort of newspaper rattling our fathers did in the evening while our mothers cleaned up after dinner.

And our parents were constant, too. Nobody's mother died, nobody's father lost his job. A friend of my mother's, Jeanie Kay, had cancer and died, but her kids were already in college, and though my mother and the neighbors kept saying how tragic it was, she was so young, middle-aged was old to me. After all, she could have been a grandmother. Our grandparents died sometimes, and though we loved them, they were distant and old, and we hardly thought of them as our parents' mothers and fathers. Friends of my parents, the Newtons, got a divorce because Judy was in love with another man, and the women were all upset with her for scattering her little children and her husband and her friends as if she'd held them bundled in her fist and then opened her hand and let them fall like Pick-up Sticks. But everybody's shock and careful consolation of the husband proved it couldn't happen to my parents. My father's obstinacy proved that nothing could change.

"What's up?" Lonnie said during a commercial. "Cat got your tongue tonight?"

"I've always hated that expression," I said. It was true, I hated the way adults asked it of children, as if to establish superiority and mock children's moods, but I shouldn't have talked back to Lonnie.

"You think you're too good to go get me a beer, too?" he said.

Yes, I thought, but I went to the kitchen and fetched. At least I used to be too good for you, I thought.

"I'm sorry," I said. "I'm just tired after all night with a screaming baby."

And if my father could be fired, then maybe I had never been any better than Lonnie. Maybe Lonnie and I weren't just playing house. A baby with diaper rash was no big baby doll. This was our adult life and we were the parents. When my daughter was in high school, what would her parents be to her? I couldn't see Lonnie and me as the immutable adults, no matter how I squinted.

In the morning, as soon as Lonnie left, I bundled the baby up in her hooded snowsuit and loaded her into the stroller. If Lonnie called, he'd be angry when I didn't answer. He'd probably spend the evening silent, savagely drinking beer, until he blew up. Maybe leaving the apartment was my way of throwing stones at him, provoking him. If my mother called, she'd be worried when I didn't answer and later she'd be angry, too. She'd be thinking, *Well, Dulcie, if you don't have the nerve or the energy to get out of that bed you made, then there's nothing we can do. Just lie in it.* Maybe leaving the apartment was the way I avoided the decision.

The sky was spring blue and the air warm enough that I started sweating in my winter coat. I pushed the stroller all the way through town and when the paved road ended I pulled it backwards toward the public beach. When the dirt road ended, I left the stroller behind a dune and carried the baby across the sand to the shore.

Winter had narrowed the beach still more than last year. I walked north where dunes rose into cliffs and gray wooden stairs led up to summer cottages. I sat on the warm sand and tucked the baby inside my coat to feed her. The lake still looked like winter, gray with heavy swells. I thought I could almost hear the grains of sand against each other as the water sucked and rolled. Birches that had been high up on the shore last year were in the water now. Waves hissed around the trunks, making chalky foam.

Do some heavy thinking, my mother said. She meant for me to decide to leave Lonnie. She and my father wouldn't simply come and take me. But I hadn't ever really decided anything. I'd just gone along. The surge of the water must be making the lower trunks of the birches into driftwood, I thought. In the summer I could wade out and feel the smooth and graying trunks under water. Above the water line, white bark curled away from the trunks. I wondered if the trees could live that way. Maybe the water would recede and the lake wind would sand the trees birch again.

My mother called in the afternoon. "This has been very, very hard on your father," she said. "What with you, and now this... but he's strong. He's always been a strong man."

"What did he do, though? I mean to lose his job. Or do I even want to know?"

"Watch your tone, young lady."

I didn't say anything. She and I used to talk about him behind his back, usually to acknowledge his stubbornness and to figure out how to go around it. Now all of a sudden she'd grown loyal.

"Dulcie, Dulcie," she said and blew out her breath. "He deserves your respect, that's all. And of course he didn't do anything wrong. He wasn't fired, you know. He was terminated. It was an administrative reorganization. Your dad's not the only one to go."

It had happened six weeks ago, she said. They hadn't wanted to worry me. There had been no need to tell me. Now, though, it looked like they were going to move. The new job would be a salary cut, but nothing else had come up, and so...

"I wish you'd told me," I said. "It makes me feel like nobody. All these important things going on. I feel as if I've just disappeared from everybody's life."

"They called this morning and offered him the job. He's meeting with a Realtor right now. We're putting the house on the market. They want him to start right away. Can you stick it out for a couple days? Then your father will pick you up and you can help me box everything for the movers."

"I guess," I said.

"Okay. Your father will come for you Friday. In the morning. So you be ready."

CHAPTER 20

He had to move slowly or his clothes rubbed him practically raw. His pants and his shirt and even his underwear and socks were too rough. He felt like his insides were rubbing the inside of his skin. He felt like his brain was bumping the inside of his forehead.

He was supposed to watch the kid while Dulcie went and did laundry. He pulled up her sweater and kissed her tits. Dots of blue milk jumped out on her nipples like they had holes pricked in them.

Just let me go get these clothes washed first, she said. While the baby's asleep. She's about out of diapers. Dulcie pulled her sweater down. Her belly was flat again. She looked like she'd never even had a kid.

Are you going to be okay with her? For an hour? Dulcie said. Try her on the juice if she wakes up and cries.

He sat beside the kid and watched her sleep. Her butt was sticking up. He felt dizzy and opened up the bed and lay down. When his mother was in the hospital, Suzie and Marie had stayed with Aunt Rose. Over in Portage. But he'd got to stay home with his father. The old man came and got him every day at 5:30 from the neighbors' trailer where he went after school and looked at television with Jerry Ferguson. His father cooked fried eggs and ham for supper about half the time. He couldn't hardly remember it all. Except it was his father and him. Just the two of them alone.

Then his mother came back and stayed in bed the whole summer. She hated it if the door slammed. She sat up in bed in a pink bathrobe. He remembered that pink bathrobe that ended up gray. His father had the television on a chair at the end of the bed for her, so he still had to go over to Jerry Ferguson's. His mother kind of stared at him. She tried to be nice. He remembered that. Like she didn't really know who he was. His dad took supper into the bedroom and closed the door. He didn't want to see his dad feeding her anyway. It was scary to think about that, him holding the spoon up to her open mouth. His dad made up the couch every night with one sheet and a blanket and a pillow without a pillowcase.

The kid made a noise like she had a pain or something and he got up to check it out. But she was still zonked out. He sat down and put his head between his knees, he was so dizzy. He didn't remember when his mother got up, when she started cooking supper, or when his sisters came back or his mother started giving him a hard time or his dad went back to sleeping in bed with her. His sisters left him alone. He'd just been a kid. If Dulcie left him, she'd take the kid along. He wouldn't be anybody's dad.

He'd have to kill her. He'd find her and kill her some way. He could choke her. He could do that. There was that song by the Byrds. *For every thing there is a season.* That always made him think of sports. Football, basketball, track, baseball. *A time to be born. A time to die. A time to kill.* The story went, it was in the Bible. So there it was. A time to kill. God didn't care. God didn't give a diddly fuck. It was okay by Him. Wasn't the deal that He'd even killed his own son anyway? Which at least his dad wouldn't never do. His dad wouldn't hurt him. His mother, that was a different story. He'd never hurt any kid of his. But he used to be scared of his mother.

Dulcie was right now calling some guy from the laundrymat. Or meeting somebody in the back alley. He'd checked it out one time. There were all these soggy soap boxes, little boxes like for kids, and everything was coated with this terrible purple lint. But you could meet somebody there if you wanted to. He always checked her shoes for that lint.

He wanted to put on his Byrds album but he was afraid he'd wake up the kid. Then she started squirming anyway. Her face was mashed down on the mattress. It was getting red. He rolled her over so she could get her breath. Her hands were always in fists. She pulled up legs up. It was like she couldn't straighten out her legs. Maybe she'd been curled up inside Dulcie so long she couldn't get unkinked. The only time she made her legs straight was when he held her up like she was walking.

She was winding up now. She sounded like a chicken. Now what was he supposed to do? Dulcie said, Try juice. This was great. Dulcie was making out in the alley and he was here alone with the screaming kid. He got the bottle out of the refrigerator and himself another brew. He stuck the nipple in her mouth. He hated that word, nipple. She pushed it out with her tongue and turned her head back and forth, just wailing to beat the band. He squeezed the nipple and squirted juice into her mouth, and she started in gagging, so he picked her up on his shoulder and thumped her on the back. He poured beer into his palm and held it to her mouth until a little went in but she wouldn't shut up. She needed her mother. Dulcie had taken off and here he was with the screaming kid. It was just like his mother taking off and leaving him alone with his dad. *Turn, turn, turn,* he tried singing to the kid. He couldn't sing for shit. In sixth grade everybody had to stand up and sing *Oh beautiful* one at a time in front of everybody. He wouldn't do it and got detention for a week. The kid wouldn't shut up and he tried it louder. *A time to cast away stones. A time to gather stones together.* Whatever the fuck that meant. He dropped her back in the basket. He made himself feel the diaper. He made himself unpin it and look but there wasn't nothing there. No jock itch like the other time, either. He did her back up and put a blanket on her.

If Dulcie left him, he could give the kid to his mother. Making the kid was the only thing he'd done right in her eyes the last ten years. Although she was pissed at first. He'd never forget that. *Couldn't keep your stiff prick to yourself, could you.* And that bit about Dulcie spraddling her legs. He hated her for that. But once she saw the kid, he was a good boy again. Oh yes he was her good good little boy. He went into the bathroom and shut the door. He could still hear the kid. His head was humongous, all swelled up, like the pictures in her book of embryos. His head was killing him. Turn turn turn. A time to stick his stiff prick between her spraddled legs a time to shut up shut up. His skin was raw and everything that touched him hurt, water from the faucet and the towel and that screaming and the air, and he turn turn turn crawled into the shower stall while she was whispering on the phone to that guy that Bruce and he hit hit hit the aluminum wall and the sound killed his ears —

She was on the floor beside the shower and she put her arms around him. Oh baby, she said, oh baby, what is it? What's the matter? Tell me. She was rocking him back and forth.

I figured you left me, he said. His nose was running. I can't make it without you, he said. Don't ever leave me, Dulcie. You can't leave me.

Shhh, she said. It's okay. Shhh. I'm here.

He had Dulcie call in sick for him Thursday morning. He needed a day to get over the headache. Then he made her shut the blinds and get back in bed and sleep in with him. He needed everything to slow down but it wasn't going to. He made her keep the place dark even after they got up. She rocked the kid, and the sucking noises and the screak of the chair started driving him crazy. Then she made the turkey noodle soup so hot he burned his mouth.

The television was too loud no matter how low he turned it and it hurt him, the people jumping up and down like the brains at school, I know I know call on me, and buzzers and bells and voices, all speeded up.

He lay back down and slept for a while but then the bed started spinning and he got up again.

He thought he'd cruise around for a while. He wanted to sit in the Witch. He thought he'd get out of Dulcie's way for a while. His dad used to snap his fingers and say, Come on, Sport, let's you and me go down to the lake and give your mother some room to breathe. He wished he'd quit all the time thinking about his parents. He was on his own now.

His keys and change were on the bureau. Like always he counted the change.

Okay, where is it? he said. He held out his hand.

Where's what?

There's a dime missing, Dulcie. Don't play all innocent with me.

She picked up the kid. I didn't take any money, she said.

Then where is it? That dime didn't just get up and walk away.

Anyway, what if I did take it? What difference does it make? Isn't it my money too?

No damnit, he said. I give you all the money you need. But I don't give you extra money to call up your boyfriends.

She stood there in the middle of the front room, tears running down, holding the kid.

Is it always going to be like this, Lonnie? she said.

He hated her red face. He hated the way she hunched up her shoulders. She thought she was so mistreated.

As long as you're a whore, he said, it will be.

He gave her a shove and she hit the wall, bawling. She held the kid out in front of her. Playing it for all it was worth.

You better not hurt her, Lonnie, she said. She'd quit the bawling just like that. She set the kid in her baby seat on the couch. The kid wasn't even crying, just eyeballing him and kicking her feet.

She's not my kid anyway, he said. Is she? You were fucking Bruce the same as me. God only knows who else.

If that's what you think, then why didn't you call the doctor and find out?

We both know the truth, he said.

I can't take this. She was whining now. Do you want me to leave you? Is that it?

The kid didn't even look like any kid of his. Her hair was lighter now. He couldn't see any part of himself there.

He looked the kid right in the face. Brucie, he said. Bruce Bruce Bruce. Little fucking Brucie.

Dulcie snatched the kid away like he was going to heave her at the wall or something.

I'll kill you if you ever leave me, he said. I'm getting out of here now. I can't hardly breathe. But I'll kill you. Don't you forget.

CHAPTER 21

As soon as he left Friday morning, I took a shower and washed my hair. He'd made dents in the shower wall. It had been terrible to find him crouched in the shower, like an animal that wanted to be in a cage but still fought the confinement. It had been terrible, but it had been an odd relief, too, for now I knew he was disturbed and maybe I could figure out how to help him. Dad was coming for me, and maybe I could leave now. I stood under the water with my eyes closed. My body felt the same as always to me, as if the whole pregnancy had been a story I'd read. I thought my breasts were starting to shrink, even. Still, I felt heavy, as if I were an animal in the shower too, a water creature that was trapped on land. Maybe I was the sick one.

When he came back in time for supper the night before, I'd been ready for him. The steaks were nearly thawed, ready enough for broiling, I figured, and I had potatoes peeled and in a pan of salted water, ready to be boiled and mashed. I wasn't even going to make him eat a vegetable. When he was gone, I'd made brownies, underbaked the gooey way he liked them.

"I still can't figure out what happened to that dime," he said once.

"Look, it's easy to miscount. Or maybe it got knocked off when I was dusting. Let's not worry about ten cents, okay? When we have a feast like this?" I reached across the table and squeezed his hand.

"So you really didn't take it? you really didn't sneak a phone call?"

I bit the insides of my cheeks and looked into his eyes. "No, I really didn't," I said softly. Straight into the eyes. "I wouldn't do anything to hurt my baby."

After dinner I let him watched television while I cleaned up the kitchen. Then when the baby was sleeping again I sat right down on his lap and put my arms around him.

"Love me, Lonnie," I said and kissed him.

He shook his head to break off the kiss. "That how you came on to all those other guys?" he said.

"No, baby, you've always been the only one for me." I ran my hand down his side and over a thigh. "What's the matter? Can't you tell when your lover wants you?"

That was the way a platinum blonde in a movie I'd once seen with my high school friend Annie had done it: touching and purring. I didn't remember the man's response, but he must have believed her, no matter how affected it had sounded to Annie and me.

"I'll let you know when I want it," Lonnie said.

And he did. He drank beer and watched television in silence, while I read at the kitchen table. He waited until I'd gone to bed, and then he woke me from my shame-laced sleep. Then he let me know.

Friday morning, when Dad pulled up in the driveway at ten-thirty, my hair was damp and I was still in my bathrobe. The place smelled like shame, sour and sticky.

"Okay, come on in," I had to say. "Here, take your granddaughter." Before he could even take off his overcoat, I handed him the baby. I couldn't look at him, with the previous night's fake lewdness still on me. Lonnie hadn't fallen for it, and yet he had. He hadn't been seduced, but he'd believed I was the slut.

My father had lost his job and had his own shame. My mother had long ago lost a baby, and now he'd lost a job. That was the way we said it. Lost. The baby had died, that was the truth, and my father had been fired.

"I'm sorry about —" I began, but he waved his free arm as if to clear the air.

"Aren't you taking anything?" he said.

Lonnie had been gone for two hours already, and I'd fed the baby, but I hadn't packed my suitcase with baby clothes and my own clothes or boxed up my record player and records.

"Your mother said you were ready to come home," he said. "To make the move with us."

The baby was bowing her body and scrunching up her face. Before she began crying, I handed Dad a bottle of juice. Shame meant you knew what you'd done. Shameless didn't mean clean and pure but that you were stained and fishy-smelling and didn't care.

Years ago, a Sunday School teacher had told my young people's group that Adam and Eve were thrown out of Eden, full of shame, because of sex. Later I'd looked at Genesis myself. The teacher always wore the same gray old-lady suit with the same pink blouse every Sunday, and I couldn't decide if she was trying to scare us away from *doing* it or if she really believed the shame was sex rather than disobedience—or knowledge. The shame wasn't nakedness, but knowing you were naked.

My father knew how to handle a baby—wasn't that funny? He looked suddenly so familiar with the baby against his overcoat.

Nobody would be allowed to shame my daughter. What if I never told her she was naked? There should be a word, like "apolitical" or "amoral," but it would be "ashamed," and here we were, father, daughter, daughter, all separate, inhabited by our private knowledge and ignorance, all tied up together. I closed my eyes. I saw us bound by shiny green vines, vines or green garden snakes.

"I keep thinking Lonnie will change," I said. "I just keep thinking things will get better if I give it some time."

He nodded. "You're just like your mother, aren't you? You ask for it. Well, I guess you know what you're doing."

After he left, I rocked the baby to sleep. My father had let me stay here. Well, I wasn't a child to be protected by Daddy, was I? When I was a child, nothing really had consequences. My life just rolled along with my parents'. Maybe Adam and Eve's knowledge was that you paid for what you did. And the currency was shame.

And when you wake, I sang to the baby, *you shall have cake and all the pretty little horses, dappled and gray, pinto and bay, all the pretty little horses.*

Now that my father had given me up, I'd never be able to call for his help. He'd relinquished me the way he had the dead baby. I asked for it, he said. I rocked and rocked the sleeping baby. I'd have to figure out how to give her some sort of pretty little horses. I'd protect her forever. No matter what.

You asked for it, he said. You asked for it.

I rocked back and forth. You—asked—for—it. Then I rocked out two more syllables. You—asked—for—it—Lind—say.

One summer morning when I was a child and we were going to Lake Michigan, something was bad, more wrong than usual, or maybe I'd only for the first time noticed the something. Mom wore a muu-muu, a lime green muu-muu, over her skirted plaid bathing suit. I used to say *bay-ai-oot.* Mom usually teased me—Don't forget your bay-ai-oot, she'd said for years, until I'd wanted to kill her—but this time she'd been stiff. *Get your bathing suit.* She'd been grim. *Your father's waiting in the car. He'd decided we were going to the lake and so by damn we're going to the lake.* Mom had been giant, giant fat—or, of course, she had been pregnant. So I was five. I sat in the back seat instead of between them in the front. The beach was crowded. Dad carried the cooler and the beach towels to an unoccupied tract of sand, and Mom with her fist at her back duck-walked behind him. She stripped off her muu-muu the way I'd accidentally seen her undress in the bedroom, the gown whipped off over her head, then her flesh checked front and back in the full-length mirror. On the beach the mirror was all those other families. *For God's sake, Lindsay, lie down,* Dad said. It was as if she wanted everybody to see the big black bruises on her thighs.

We must have gone swimming. We were wet. Suddenly she was rolling on the hot sand and pawing sand over her legs and big tummy. I shrieked so everybody would see us playing. *I might as well be buried,* she said. And Daddy said, *Don't be melodramatic. You asked for it, Lindsay.*

I was still in my robe, rocking away, when Lonnie returned for lunch. "Hey, wake up, babe," he said. "How's my girls?"

"Still here," I said. I laid the baby in the bassinet and went to work on lunch.

Since I was still here, I'd never be able to go back to school. I'd have to do it on my own. What was college but reading anyway? In the afternoon I pushed the stroller through the late melting winter to the library. The ground smelled swampy, of dead things sodden and rotting. Mud spun off the stroller wheels and spattered my pants.

"Ah, the baby!" the librarian said. "I *thought* you must be staying away to have that baby."

I didn't know she'd ever noticed me. I'd been nobody in this town. I'd been a fat ghost. And I'd hardly noticed her. She was such a normal blue-haired librarian and I was so self-absorbed.

"What a sweetie," she said. I saw the face powder in the wrinkles. "What a tiny little sweetheart."

"Do you have any children?" I said. The ghost speaks.

"Oh," she said, "my children are all grown up. They're having their own babies."

I let her hold the baby. She showed me her grandsons' pictures.

"What are you calling her?" she said.

What are you calling her—not *What's her name?* Neither Lonnie nor I called her by name. She was the kid to him, the baby to me. I couldn't bring myself to say Bernadine or Bernie to her, and though Kate's suggestion—Deena—wasn't bad, it seemed made-up, it seemed unnaturally imposed on her. Besides, I suspected Lonnie would resent it, as if his mother's name wasn't good enough. What did it mean, though, that *he* didn't call the baby by his mother's name?

"I call her Katie," I said. "Katie Lee."

"Oh that's sweet," she said.

I checked out three books: an anthology of modern American poetry, *La Symphonie Pastorale*, and a textbook called *The Psychology of Learning.* I couldn't be invisible if I wanted to.

"Uh oh," the doctor said. He didn't look up from between my legs. He closed his eyes, as if his sense of touch improved in the dark.

"What? What's wrong?"

"Let's see—it's been what? three months?"

Sweat dribbled from my armpits to my elbows and soaked the paper covering the table. "What's wrong with me?" I said. "You can tell me."

"Oh, nothing's *wrong*. But let's get a urine sample before you leave. Then if we need to, we'll do a repeat, with a first-thing-in-the-morning specimen."

"You mean—a pregnancy test? No." I was not going to cry. I'd rather have a terminal illness than pregnancy.

"Well, Dulcie, we'd better find out for sure, huh?" He was using his husky, gentle voice.

"No, I mean—I just can't be pregnant."

"Let's check it out, before you panic, okay? Now be a good girl and go pee in the little cup and give it to the nurse. You can call in two days."

So I studied my books while Lonnie was at work and watched his stupid television at night. He didn't like the foam but I'd tried to use it every night before he got to me. I didn't tell him about the test. I *had* my baby. It couldn't happen again. He'd told me about spying outside my dorm last year and poking holes in the—the protection. The prophylactics. When I was in sixth grade, the class wrote reports about their fathers' jobs, and when I'd read mine aloud and said he was working on a prophylactic drug, the boys laughed. I thought it was the funny word. *That means it prevents a disease*, I said. I could still hear my prim, smug voice. Now, marriage, legitimacy, was supposed to be the prophylactic.

"Doctor wants to talk to you himself," the nurse said when I called. So then I knew.

"Positive," he said. "I'm afraid it's positive. Now, I'm going to have Alicia here make an appointment for you and we'll —"

But I couldn't talk to him or Alicia. The black receiver made a dull plastic sound when I set it down. I already had my baby. She carried rattles to her mouth. Her eyes followed my hand. She grabbed for my hair. She smiled at me. I already had my baby.

Inside me was a parasite, a slug stuck to the wall inside my womb. *Slug: a slimy gastropod related to the snail but having no shell or a rudimentary one.* I could feel its sucker-mouth sliding along, ingesting. *Mollusk.* I could feel it growing. *Class Gastropoda.*

I pounded my fists against my stomach. I wasn't pregnant but diseased. I was inhabited by a slimy foreign rudimentary body. I would begin to sicken, I'd languish, and in the end I'd die.

While I was still strong, I pounded my stomach. I pounded to start up a rush of blood to wash out the slug-cell sucking and growing inside me.

I handled the baby carefully. I didn't want to contaminate her. She was my only child and Lonnie had nothing to do with her.

But he was the cause of this parasite inside me now. It came from his orgasms. I didn't know what pleasure they gave him. *Oh baby did you come?*

he used to say. Now he just made the same noise as when he had a leg cramp and then rolled off, limp. What did it mean to come? I wanted to say, *Well, here I am. Take me in.* He entered, his cramp was eased, he came: I pictured the Great Gate of Kiev, with mosaics and grainy Ukrainian smells and enormous bronze gongs and Slavic noises. When the baby cried, milk surged up into my breasts with a prickly rush, and maybe that's all it was. It was no Great Gate, only something like a doggy door, with a brown wooden flap. And he did it every single night not for ecstasy but as the only way he could screw himself into me.

I paced the apartment, beating my fists on my stomach, stopping now and then to do the dishes and scour out the toilet and dust the living room. I wouldn't let myself go to the bathroom and check for blood.

When as a teenager I went with my parents to Lake Michigan, I left them on their towels on the sand and took long melancholy walks down the beach. One time a man coming the other way asked if he could walk along with me, and I said sure, sorry for him with his acne and baggy plaid bathing trunks. He asked me innocuous questions and commented on the August heat.

He said, "Do you like school?" He said it into the wind.

"Oh yes, a lot," I said. I was enthusiastic.

"Do you want to?" he said.

Then I heard what his question had really been: Do you like to screw?

I ran back toward my parents, keeping to the hard wet sand at the waterline. He didn't chase me. When I got to the towels, Mom and Dad were swimming out to the sandbar, and I lay down and kept my secret word, screw, to myself.

There was a slug screwed into me, a fish-belly white thing with its muscular foot screwed into me. I was sick. If I couldn't dislodge it myself, maybe Lonnie would do it for me. It was almost funny. I couldn't stop him from hitting me, but I certainly knew the right words to start him up. If *Katie* or *college* weren't sufficient, *dance* or *Bruce* would do it. This was sick. But it was funny to think of stirring him into a rage so he'd slam me against the wall hard enough to dislodge his slug.

Oh—had my father made my mother lose the baby?

I bent over to let the blood rush back to my head. That was sick. Maybe they'd had some secret fights. But all the married did that, I knew now.

At five o'clock, with supper started and Lonnie due home soon, I let myself go into the bathroom. I closed my eyes and pulled down my pants. I'd kept myself from checking all afternoon. I thought I could smell blood. Ta-da, I said, sure I'd see a bright Rorschach ink-blot.

"Well, you blew your chance," Mom said. "Listen, I'm calling from a phone booth. So when the pile of dimes is gone, we're done."

"Please don't be mad at me. I just couldn't bring myself to do it."

"So you'll have to live with it. We're leaving tomorrow."

"California," I said. I wanted them to be gone. I wanted to be unredeemable. "You'll have a real ocean. Lake Michigan will seem like a pond."

She fed coins into the phone. I could see her at the beach covering herself with sand. I saw her body like a breaded fish.

"Mom—I remember one time at Lake Michigan when Dad was mad. Before the other baby was born."

"You can't remember that. You can't even remember being in the hospital and that was two years later."

"I can't get it out of my head that Dad hurt the baby."

In the dime-laden silence, I was sorry I'd said it.

"Oh, I don't think so," she said.

I'd wanted her to say they'd just been acting silly in the sand. We'd taken turns burying each other in sand. I could remember the exciting weight of sand.

"How could you stay married all this time?" I was trying not to cry, and it came out an accusing wail.

"You're a fine one to judge me," she said. I could see her stiff wide lips. "If you want to go at it, how about if you tell—"

Coins dropped through her words.

"Tell what?"

"Oh, never mind. Let's just—"

"No, I want you to say it." I thought she wanted to know how I could stay married all this time. Before her dimes ran out, I wanted to tell her—what? That I believed it wouldn't always be so cold.

"All right. Since we're telling the truth here. Is Lonnie really the father?"

I stood up and held the receiver away, toward the sleeping baby as if to show her. Now I'd lost my mother too. Go bury yourself, I thought, and started to hang up.

"Dulcie, where are you?" she called, and I lifted the receiver back to my ear. "Our time's almost up. I'm out of change. I'm sorry I brought it up."

"Lonnie is really the father." I said it slowly, as if spreading out the words made them true.

"Okay, I'm sorry. But you did date others. I thought maybe that Bruce you dated wouldn't marry you and so you took Lonnie."

"No."

"We love her, you know. It wouldn't have made any difference. We love—"

And that was the end. Some switchboard operator must have been listening and decided to let her end with *We love.* Fill in the blank. We love the baby. We love you. We love each other. All of the above. And it was *we*, not I.

Late morning, Katie called. Josh was driving her home for spring break, and she wanted to stop by in the afternoon and say good-bye. It was only a little out of the way.

At noon Lonnie slammed in. The phone had been busy. What guy had I been talking to this time? He was everybody's slave at work and I couldn't even have his lunch ready.

In the kitchen I heated the soup. There was nothing to say. I only wanted the baby to sleep through it. I only wanted to get it over with so he could ease out of the house.

Lonnie was gone and I had my face washed and ice on my cheek and my navy cardigan over the torn blouse by the time Katie was at the door. I would have pretended not to be there if the baby hadn't been crying. I remembered my parents insisting at the door, long ago when I was still innocent, when Lonnie and I were still in bed Sunday morning. Now—what? I'd crashed into the bathroom door, I could say. Coming out of the shower half-blind. Katie was still innocent and the story might fly. I let her in and turned away to bend over the bassinet.

"I can't stay," she said. "Josh is out in the car. But I had to say happy spring to my chambrie. I had to say good-bye. Aw, the baby's sad too. Come to Auntie Katie."

She lifted the baby to her shoulder. "Oh what a big baby. Oh yes. Oh—you're bleeding."

"No, where?" I said and reached for the baby.

"You. You're bleeding."

I put my hand to my face. "It's just my lip. I just cut my lip. Lips always bleed so much."

"Dulcie. What happened?"

The baby bucked in Katie's arms and cried. "Nothing," I said. "Here, let me have her. She's hungry. I just walked into the door, that's all. Look, I'm going to have to feed her. Josh is waiting for you. I'll see you after the break, right?"

"No," she said, "he'll wait. Go on and take care of her. Josh is being terribly, terribly patient with me. He thinks I'll get over it."

"Whatever it is," I said. I unbuttoned my blouse and opened the flap on the nursing bra. "Don't look. This is the only way to shut little miss piggy up."

"I read this stupid thing over Christmas in one of my mother's stupid magazines. There's this advice column, and a lady writes in and says she got mad at her husband and started throwing dishes. And so the husband says he'll spank her if she doesn't quit and so she throws another dish and he lets her have it."

I didn't want her to watch me. I scooted down the sofa. I didn't want her to look at me. "That's a funny story," I said.

"You think it's funny? You know what the advice woman says? She's a psychologist yet. She says, and I quote, You must look inside yourself and learn why you aggravate him. Perhaps you want to be spanked. Unquote."

I could see the red car in the driveway. Josh had a book open on the steering wheel.

Katie put her hands on my cheeks and turned my head to her. The baby lost suction for a moment and then latched on again.

"Well, maybe she did want to be spanked," I said. Tears dropped pink on my blouse. They dropped coldly through the blood as if the magazine woman were crying, not me.

Katie brought a towel from the bathroom and blotted my face. The baby sucked. Katie drew my sweater off one sleeve at a time and I let her.

"Oh my Dulcie," she said. "Oh my Dulcie. I'm the one—"

Josh called in, "Parting is such sweet sorrow. But the open road calls, m'dear."

"Don't let him—" I said.

"No, wait," Katie called. "Just a minute. I'll be there."

"Sweet it isn't," I said. "But go. You have to go. It's all right."

"I'm the one who loves you," Katie said. "I wrote a letter to that stupid magazine. I'm not letting you stay here." She was crying. She was fierce. "So come on. I'm taking care of you. Don't your parents care? Where's your luggage? In here?" She pulled my big suitcase out of the closet.

"Katie, Katie. No. I can't. It won't work."

"No, won't fit in that puny car. Here—we'll take the small one."

"My parents don't really know," I said. "It isn't their fault." But I thought they did know. My mother knew and didn't know. My bruises were the same as her bruises, maybe. But at least I had my living sucking baby. All wives had bruises, maybe. They all walked into doors and fell out of beds onto metal wastebaskets. Their husbands were big-brained quiet men, and the women learned to walk around them, or they were kindled boys. Maybe everybody already knew about bruises.

A horn beeped outside.

"Okay, I'm going to stall him. Quick, grab what you need for the baby. You can wear my clothes."

I jumped up with the baby in my arms. "Oh no. You can't tell him. I mean it, Katie. No. No. No. Everybody would know."

"That's what our mothers would say. Come on. We need these diapers, right?"

The baby was crying again. I laid her in the bassinet and she cried.

"No," I said, "no, you just don't know. I can't. I cannot. Go away, Katie. Just go away. Just leave me alone. What do you think you're going to do with me and a screaming baby? This isn't storytime any more."

The horn honked. Five beats. Shave and a haircut.

"I'm not leaving you with him," Katie said. She picked up the baby. "I'm not."

"Let me have her." The baby was screaming like an animal, like nothing human.

Honk honk. Two bits.

"You get out of here," I said. "You just get the hell out of here."

"No."

"I can't stand you here," I said. I raised my hand but she held the baby. "This is his baby. I love him. Don't you understand that? I hate you, Katie Leeview. I hate you."

She carried the screaming baby to the bassinet. She turned her wet face to me. "Are you going to hit me, Dulcie?" She opened the door and in a minute the red car backed out of the driveway.

I renewed the psych text at the library and checked out *L'Etranger*. It was a random business. How much did it need teachers, gesturing and scribbling all over a blackboard and pointing? I kept reading. When I was young, I'd seen everything caught in a web—or not caught but placed—every subject and all the topics of its outline connected with soft webbing. In truth, the web was nothing but a card catalog's plan, and the discrete pieces could fall right through. Camus and the year 1456 and gastropods and Piaget were nothing to each other. My parents moved to California. Katie called long distance from Minnesota. She knew what I was doing, she said. She knew I didn't hate her. She knew I was punishing myself. For weeks I continued to read, as if I were at the lake shore, scooping out a diagram, a Petrarchan sonnet, a theory, like flotsam and jetsam. None of it was connected in the water. It didn't matter if I tossed the pieces high up on the sand or flipped them back into the lake. If a couple pieces landed on the same dune or were caught for a moment in the same wave's curl, it didn't matter. They didn't connect any more than did newt and New Testament and Newton on their separate cards in the card catalog. I had my baby, so I wouldn't throw myself in. But if I did, I probably wasn't solid enough to sink. I knew I was feeling sorry for myself, but I let the image come: I was a small sac of water in the whole lake of water, as soft and null as a dead perch. Oh poor Dulcie.

CHAPTER 22

At Barnett's it was the same thing over and over and over. Until he thought he'd go fucking nuts. One and a half inch wood screws, one two three four five blue packets, one and a quarter inch wood screws, over and over and over. Eight by two flathead screws, the wrenches, the claw hammers over and over, the wood saws, the metal saws. The saw blades hanging from the hook like saw-toothed limp dicks. Over and over and fucking over.

First thing in the morning before all the idiot customers could get in, everything hung there and it was quiet. That wasn't too bad. He counted and wrote down the counts and it was all right. All the numbers hunkered down in the little boxes.

But after hours of it he couldn't hardly stand it. He'd lose count at 37 packages of two-inch nails and fuck it start again or just write something down. 43. Some days the afternoon break could stop the way he itched half to death to do something. Use one of those hammers. Grab him a fucking ball-peen of which there was five and start in swinging. He'd go over to Housewares and give Judy something to gawk at. Judy with the fat ass. God he'd love to bust up all those dishes and glasses with a ball-peen hammer.

Some days he could wait on customers and stop counting. That was okay. That was pretty much all right for a while. Generally it was dads like his own old man and he could put exactly what they needed in their hands. Allen wrench. Hacksaw. Whatever. They all looked at the blades hanging there like dicks or tongues. There wasn't no need to mention it. Once in a while it was some broad with a folded up paper that said Liquid Wrench or 1/2-in. staples or some such. Hey, Gorgeous, he said, the old man got you fetching for him? They'd grin to beat the band. There wasn't nothing in it for him. No tips or nothing. It just helped, someway or other. He wished his mother would show up just one time. But he wouldn't have whatever she wanted. Some days he had to get out of there. He had a foul headache, he'd say to the manager. Which was true.

He couldn't look at anything without trying to count it. It was driving him nuts. Cups on the shelf at home. Green beans on his plate. Sometimes he liked knowing how many knives they had or washrags or whatever, but then he had to count again. He might have got it wrong.

Judy came over and got him lots of times for the afternoon break. She wanted to hear all about the kid. She told him about her brother the

sergeant. Blither blither. She even read stuff like Dulcie. She was going
to beauty school, nights.

I just read this real scary book, she said one time. *Fail-Safe.* Jeez. It's
giving me nightmares. I could loan it to you, you want.

You want me to have nightmares? Thank you very much. What a
good buddy.

She laughed like an idiot. No, it's real good, she said.

I don't read much, he told her. I gave it up for Lent.

She said she could give him a haircut for free sometime after work.

He cut out early. He got Judy to punch out for him. Just this one
time, he said. Dulcie wasn't home. That was the way she'd leave. Just take
his kid and run while he was doing that shit job to take care of her. He
drove the Witch through town looking for her. Laundrymat no. Grocery
store no. Library—wouldn't you know it. Wouldn't you fucking know it.
He didn't even have to go in. He could see her through the glass doors.
Talking to some old lady. Who was holding his kid. Who was probably
helping her leave him. But he'd find her. It wouldn't be hard. She couldn't
leave him.

To kill time he parked at the end of the road to the public beach. He
sat there in the Witch. The water moved back and forth. Hardly moving
at all. Like when he was a kid sliding his squeaky ass up and down in the
bathtub. He could tell Dulcie to leave. He could tell her to go stay with
her parents for a while. This lake wasn't like Chippewa Lake where him
and his dad had the boat. Now the old man had the boat up for sale. It was
all sand here and you couldn't see across the water. Could be there wasn't
nothing on the other side. Old-time people used to think that. If you tried
to sail across, you just fell off into nowhere. He knew that was the ocean
and this was Lake Michigan. But same deal.

He picked up a case and got home at the usual normal time. Dulcie
was frying hamburgers. The whole place was yellow with grease.

She came over and played the wife and kissed him. Guilty.

So what'd you do all day? he said. He could be cool.

Nothing much, she said. Cleaned up around here and made you some
cookies. Over there. Oatmeal.

Didn't get out of the house?

Oh, I talked to Linda across the alley. They're moving. Del's going to
work for her father, at his garage.

A while back he'd come home and she had steaks for supper. He'd
liked to watch her bend over and use the ice tongs to flip the meat and
shove it back under the blue flames. What's the occasion? he'd said. What
you trying to make up for?

She got her poor-me hurt look. I just thought you'd like it, she said.

He lifted his hamburger bun to salt the meat. The ketchup was soaked into the bun. But he ate it.

Don't lie to me, Dulcie, he said. I know you weren't here today.

Well, I *did* go to the library, she said. How'd you know I left?

I have ways. I know what you do. So you better not fuck around on me.

Her face was getting red. You probably tried to call, she said.

He worked on his second hamburger. The first one was greasy and this one was dry. He felt sick at his stomach. She was making him crazy. Jerry Angus had said back in eleventh grade how women could mix their blood, *that* blood, into men's food and it would drive them crazy. Come to think of it, she hadn't had that blood for a while. Seemed like a good while anyway.

He tried to get up and his thighs hit the edge of the table and dumped over the water glasses.

I can't eat any more of this crap, he said. He gave the table a shove and the plates hit the floor. He got a beer from the refrigerator and took it outside. He sat on the back step. Let her clean up and get her bawling over with.

He thought about seeing if Del across the alley wanted to sit and shoot the breeze. But Del wasn't nothing. He didn't even graduate. Now he was going to work for his wife's old man.

He couldn't shoot the breeze with Dulcie. One time he said something about Yastrzemski's RBIs. She said, what? She didn't even know what RBIs were.

He wanted to sit here with his father. Give him a beer out of his own refrigerator and shoot the breeze. His dad used to sit in his recliner and fart. One time his dad did it when Dulcie was over and he liked to died. That was way back before they got married. After that, he started noticing his dad's farts. Just *purt* into the chair and then he'd say *ah*. He kind of liked his dad's soft farts. The beany smell.

It ever happen to you, he'd say if his dad was here, you couldn't get it up?

After the steaks she sat on his lap and gave him the big come-on. But there wasn't nothing there. All those times he'd have given his left nut to have her do that. That ever happen to you, Dad? Like your pecker decided he didn't want to come out and play. Like you'd taken him swimming in April. That ever happen?

His back teeth were floating. He took a leak beside the shed and went in for another beer.

I saw that, Dulcie said. I can't believe you did that. In the back yard!

My back teeth were floating, he told her. Didn't your old man ever take a leak behind the house? Anyway, it's dark.

So then the next day the fat prick manager wanted to know where he was. He'd caught Judy punching out for him at five. The prick's skinny eyebrows went up. All concerned and patient. Like Lonnie was some jerk-off kid. But he just stared him down until the prick gave up.

What's your problem, Saxbe? he said.

No problem. No problem except every fucking body thinks they own me.

Hey now, the prick said, watch it there, buddy. He was big but he was soft.

Back in his work space under the stairs it was dark. He left the light off. He couldn't go out on the floor and work on inventory without picking up one of those hammers and smashing something. His hand wanted to do it. He could feel that smooth wood on his palm.

Eventually the prick came in and pulled the string on the ceiling light. You cooled off now, Saxbe? Everybody deserves a little leeway. But I've got to be able to count on you. You've been taking —

Lonnie jerked the string and the prick backed up and found the door in the dark.

He waited on his stool. Pretty soon he could start to see the pegboard on the wall and his worktable made out of a board on file cabinets. He'd miss that worktable.

The prick manager was back with the two security guys. Usually they just walked around trying to look like customers but all the time eyeballing everybody and trying to catch them shoplifting. If him or Judy or any of them saw anybody drop something in their pocket or purse or whatever, they were supposed to say Code Four Housewares or Code Four Hardware on the intercom. Then the security pricks would follow the person outside. They hadn't stole anything until they took it out of the store. That was the deal.

We're sorry, Lonnie, the prick manager said. But we're going to have to let you go. Now let's just let Sam and Eddie —

For an instant he thought he was going to do a Dulcie and start bawling. He clenched his fists hard. What's this 'we'? he said. You and who else? Though you got enough blubber to be speaking for three people.

Sam, Eddie. Walk Mr. Saxbe out to the parking lot. We'll put his last check in the mail.

Like he wasn't even in the fucking room.

All right, easy, the prick said. There's no need for any trouble here. Just walk on out with Sam and Eddie. Easy now.

He stopped at the liquor store. He didn't know why. He had cold Bud at home. He used the pay phone outside. The booth was like a shower stall. If Dulcie answered, he'd tool right on home. If not, he'd do something. Something else. Find her. Find her and make her stay home and take care of him and never leave. One ring. Two rings. Three rings. Four rings. Five rings. Six rings. Seven rings. Eight rings. Nine. Ten. Eleven. He couldn't put the receiver down. He couldn't stop counting. He held it until he hit twenty-five. Then he went into the store.

Give me a fifth of that, he said. Old Grand Dad.

No questions. No ID. He must be looking like an old dad himself. That was all right. Truth was, they were just out for the bucks anyway. They didn't care who they sold to. Just take the bucks and drop the flask into a paper bag and get him out of there. He liked the store, though. It was dark and warm. He wouldn't mind inventorying that stock.

You mind me asking? he said. How old you have to be to work here? I know there's some law. I got this cousin looking for work, is why I ask.

Your cousin'd have to be twenty-one to sell in a package store, the guy said. That's state law. Anyway, there aren't any openings here.

The guy was starting to eyeball him and he hefted the paper bag. I'll tell my cousin. But he's only nineteen. A kid. He'll want to know. Thank you, sir. He got out before he spilled his guts to the guy. It wasn't the guy's business how old he was or if he had a cousin looking for work or if his wife was out whoring around.

Twenty-six. Twenty-seven. God but he was tired of it. All of it. Twenty-eight.

He set the fifth between his legs and unscrewed the cap. He'd seen guys in the bleachers tipping up flasks. He took a slug. Twenty-nine. Thirty. Thirty-one. It was medicine and after three slugs it stopped the numbers in his head.

He couldn't find nothing of Dulcie's missing in the closet or the dresser. He was too tired to go find her this time. She wasn't going to be leaving without her clothes, anyway.

The phone rang and he picked it up and didn't say anything. He would find out who was calling Dulcie while he was off being everybody's slave. Big silence. Some breathing. He'd be damned if he'd say anything first.

Who's there? Dulcie? It was his mother's voice. Everything all right there?

Hi, Ma, he said. He never called her Ma. He'd heard guys calling home after practice, saying Hey Ma? come and get me? All pleased, like there wasn't nobody else in the world but their ma to watch out for them. He'd always called his old lady Mother.

Lonnie? What are you doing there? What's going on?

I had to come home, he said.

Oh no. Don't tell me it's the baby. Didn't nothing happen to my grandbaby, did it? You didn't—

Now the world turned on the baby. He said, You could maybe ask about me. Your only son? He'd never come first. It was Suzie, it was Marie, it was the old man, it was some rich lady she worked for, it was her own crazy head. He said, No, she's okay. I'm watching out for her. Like you never watched out for me.

She didn't say anything. He couldn't believe he'd actually said it. Now she was going to kill him. But he let it alone. They just breathed at each other. Finally she said, I watched out for you. If I hadn't, you'd've never made it to nineteen years. I know you, son. She shut up a minute for him to say something but he kept his trap shut. She said, Quit feeling sorry for yourself. You're old enough to know how to watch out for yourself. Jealous of that baby. Shame on you.

He didn't say anything. He didn't even know why she was calling Dulcie. He breathed at her. He hung up.

Then he called the phone company. We want to discontinue our service, he said. The lady said just cut the cord and bring the phone in to them. That's all there was to the deal. So he took out the butcher knife and bent the cord and pulled the knife through the insulation and the wires inside.

He threw the pillows off the couch and flipped it open. He drank from the fifth. He figured he'd sleep for a while. He'd take his medicine, Ma, and she'd be back. The phone cord jutting from the wall made him sick. It made him think of the kid's cut cord, how it dried up and turned black and dropped off her belly button.

He took the knife back to the kitchen and got out a cold beer to help the medicine. The wood handle fit his hand. It was a good tool. He thrust it like a sword and chipped paint off the cupboard door. He stabbed the door and pulled the blade back out. It had gone through the plywood and knocked over a glass inside. He turned the blade around and touched the middle of his chest. He pressed until it felt like it would break through his shirt and his skin.

He leaned against the pillows. His pillow and Dulcie's pillow. This was the bed they slept in together. He still couldn't hardly believe it. The marriage bed. He'd shown them. His parents hadn't taken care of him. They always thought he was dirt. Now he'd shown them. He never thought his dad knew. And he sure wasn't never going to clue him in. So he couldn't hold it against the old man. But his mother.

Suzie and Marie doing the back rubs. Come on, little boy, watch this. In the afternoon the sun ran through the green curtains. The girls all watery. Watch this. Suzie rubbing Marie's butt. The girls flopping over in the ripply green light, all bare and hairless, their hands rubbing each other's pee-pee but then he saw they didn't have pee-pees. He was crying. Lookit, the baby's crying. The baby needs his diapers changed. They took his shoes off and his pants off and, lookit, the baby's peenie, pinched him but he couldn't get breath to call Mommy Mommy, like he was underwater in the bathtub.

When the door opened he started peeing and he couldn't stop. Pee hit Suzie and Marie and they jumped off the bed.

Oh yucky. Oh ick. Mo-om, lookit what he did.

We were just going to take a bath and he took off his pants and went to the bathroom on us.

All right, girls, Mother said, go on and take your baths, and they ran away and started the water.

She wiped him on the blanket and turned him over on her and whipped him with Marie's hairbrush. She set him on the floor and shook him, Don't you ever touch those girls ever ever you're old enough to keep your little cock to yourself shame you're a dirty dirty boy shame.

Drowning again, he sat up straight in the marriage bed. It wasn't such a giant big deal. He'd lived. Nobody knew, just him and his mother, and when she was in the nuthouse she'd had her brain fried so he didn't think she remembered. He'd lived.

Then he lay back and closed his eyes, and everything disappeared. The old television set. The closet door that was open to his wife's clothes hanging on the rod. If he quit trying to hold on, it would all just go away. The alley behind the house, the trash cans, the terrible piece of phone cord protruding from the wall, it would all poof go away, his car and his mother and the pressure of all the seasick water in Lake Michigan and the kid that wasn't even his and checking accounts and bottles and knives and his Dulcie his own wife and everything including the old man. All the cars on the highway. All the little women going into stores and all the little men figures on the wives in beds. If he quit trying to hold it all together it would all go—the whole thing and everything crawling on the surface—turn black and shrivel up and drop off into black—

He made it to the toilet to puke. Then he rinsed his mouth and threw cold water on his face. He took the empties out to the trash can. It was still glaring afternoon. The sun hurt his eyes. Everything was still here. Nothing he ever did would make any difference.

He kept his crucifix in the drawer beneath his underwear. He cranked down the blinds and took the crucifix onto the bed and ran his finger over the cracks in the plaster. He kept his eyes closed to feel the body better.

The arms were out and the gut was sunk in and the legs were pinned down. He knew Dulcie was going to leave him. He didn't know how you kept somebody with you. He didn't know how you loved somebody. Did you count the kisses and the times she'd say I-love-you? Did you count the times you reached into the shower and touched her? the number of times you got inside her before she filled herself with foam? He didn't know how to abide. Could you write down the exact number of times she swore she'd never leave you? Did you count the blotches on her forehead after she'd cried? the bruises on her legs and arms and face? He couldn't breathe in the green water. He covered the dead face on the cross with his finger. *Tell me how to do it tell me tell me tell me how to abide.* Did you love by the cracks in the cross and the body? the ridges of old glue? the chips of plaster gone from those nailed ankles, the dead hand?

CHAPTER 23

I thought he was dead. He was on the floor beside the bed in only his underwear, his rump up in terrible imitation of the way the baby slept, his mouth open and leaking. His skin was the mottled yellow and gray of old bruises. The apartment smelled rank, as if he'd been dead for hours.

From her stroller parked in the foyer, the baby cried, but it was only her light Hi-I'm-awake-now cry.

Don't be dead, I thought, *oh please oh please.*

"Lonnie?" I said softly. I didn't want him to rise up suddenly like a ragged body on Judgment Day. "Will you wake up now? Are you all right?"

He rolled over and moaned, the way a corpse released to the air *would* moan.

"Are you awake?"

"Oh God," he said.

"Are you really sick? Should I call a doctor?"

He sat up. He'd been lying on his broken crucifix on the carpet. The clear, deep impression of the largest piece, the headless body and one outstretched arm, marked his skin below the ribs.

"No, Dulcie," he said. "I'm ready to do the 100-yard dash. In nine seconds. Get the stop watch."

"I don't know how you can keep skipping work like this." I folded the bed back up. It was hours until bedtime.

"I told you and told you. I don't want you tramping around town like a whore. Just yesterday I told you." He was on his feet now. "Wasn't it just yesterday? Wasn't it?"

"Look, let's not do this. You're not feeling well right now. And I need to feed the baby before I fix some supper for us." I wheeled the stroller into the kitchen.

He stood there in his yellow, dented skin. "You're a goddamn whore. I married a whore. You're a whore, aren't you? You slept with all those Bruces before. Who you sleeping with now? Tell me." He had me by the shoulders, shaking me. "Tell me tell me tell me."

I couldn't help it. "Nobody, nobody," I said, crying, trying to twist away.

"Liar. You're a goddamned liar." He slammed me against the back door and choked me. "I'm sick of this. You're going to tell me this time. This is it."

I was drowning. I could hear the faint tin cry of the baby. My hands went to his face to push his weight away. I made them claws and ripped his cheeks. I tried to grab his hair but it was too short and I had no muscle in my whole body.

"You ready to tell me? Are you?"

I tried to nod. In the surf I tried to get my head up. When he released me, I bent over to breathe again, to keep from fainting.

"So who was it? Just tell me. I'm not going to do anything. I just want the truth."

I jiggled the stroller, trying to soothe the baby. She'd kicked the blanket off. Her face was squalling red in her green knitted cap.

"When you were on the floor over there," I said, "I thought you were dead. And I didn't *want* you to be."

"Tell me, Dulcie. You said you'd tell me."

"Nobody. Nobody. Nobody."

"That's not my kid. Whose kid is that? Bruce? Is this thing little fucking Brucie?"

He kicked the stroller. At the jolt, the baby stopped crying. I went for her, she sucked in her breath in long, indrawn silence, he shoved me against the refrigerator, he raised his hand to my baby, she caught her breath and wailed—and then he looked at his outstretched arm, his ardent hand—and he pivoted his body and smashed his fist through the glass in the door.

•••

When I was young, I thought that childbirth was passive, that with both of her babies, my mother had lain there in pain until the baby was pulled out. The second baby, Derek Walter, had been dead two weeks before he was dragged out. All my life I had been passive, as if I'd had no part in my birth. I'd floated from grade to grade, through the stages my mother read about—from terrible two to typical teen, through whatever was between my father and my mother, to the college chosen almost idly. When Lonnie showed up at the dorm, I'd gone for rides with him. If he'd demanded sex or even asked, I'd have refused, I thought now, but when he simply touched me, I rode with that current. It had been sad—but easy, easy as my whole life—to let marriage be the shore that shaped me, to wait until Lonnie hit me again and then was sorry—*oh I love you baby I don't never want to hurt you*—and then got over it.

I ceased crying when he put his fist through the window.

I led him into the bathroom and ran cold water over his hand and picked out a couple shards of glass and bandaged him.

Truly, I didn't want him dead.

"Shhh, it'll be all right," I said. "Just let me take care of you here."

If he died, I'd drift along in my lassitude. I'd never find my own shape. I'd never make my own current.

And besides—he was a boy I had somehow chosen. I had, as his mother said, spraddled my legs.

And besides—he was a boy who had hunted me and taken me down, who loved me, who craved my cookies and teased me, who *was* sorry, who had needed to name the baby for his parents, a mixed-up boy whose blood now ran down the drain, who needed me to soothe and bandage, a manchild beating himself against rocks.

"Let's do something," I said. "Let's go out to eat. Or—I read the drive-in's open again, now that it's practically summer. We could go to the drive-in."

"Dulcie—I gotta tell you, I quit Barnett's, I just—the manager kept pushing me, there wasn't hardly any choice."

Of course he'd lost another job.

But my own father had lost his job.

"You'll find something else," I said. "You'll find something better."

"You aren't mad?"

"That wasn't a very good job for you, anyway."

At the drive-in we ate hot dogs and popcorn. On the screen, John Wayne helped out his old friend the sheriff who'd turned into a drunk, then at intermission hot dogs danced into buns, and then Elvis went to Ft. Lauderdale with a lot of girls. We made a nest for the baby in the back seat. The fight had exhausted us. It was safe to watch movies, even about a drunk or a wild beach. Like a suicide before the act, I was at peace.

I let him carry the baby into the apartment. She'd never remember being carried half-asleep by a father.

"Lonnie? Let me have my ring back for a little while?" He still wore the garnet ring my father had given me, as if it were a wedding ring. It was obviously a girl's ring on his little finger, but I'd almost ceased to see it.

He made a fist. "You want it, you're gonna have to take it."

I knocked him onto the bed and tried to pry his fingers up. We were laughing but I couldn't open his hand.

I was complicitous. I knew the right words to provoke him, even if I didn't know the code to stop him, though when he was in the mood, anything would set him off—a cheating song on the radio, a show about a blonde flirt, anything. I said nothing now, just let him lie on me. There was a sick pleasure in provoking him—at least it was active, at least I was churned up. And it was a strange power—I could make him hit me.

Afterwards, he said, "You'll never do this with anybody else, will you?"

"Huh uh," I said. "And you can keep the ring."

Lonnie slept in until eleven. After lunch he shaved and dressed in a good blue shirt. I pictured him once again at the front door of the big white house I'd grown up in, shaking my father's hand. Then I came downstairs in a pleated skirt and matching sweater and he smiled at my mother and said in a Peter Noone voice, "Mrs. White, you've got a lovely daughter."

They didn't know the song. "Like mother, like daughter," my father said.

Other people lived in the big white house now. And Lonnie had scratches on his face.

"Aren't you gonna ask where I'm going?" Lonnie said.

"You're going somewhere about a job?" I was surprised that he'd start looking immediately. Taking him to the drive-in had been a good idea. Now he wasn't sick from drinking beer the night before. But it wasn't a strategy I needed to remember.

"I'm going to get my money out of that prick manager. Mail it, hell. They owe me. They can just put it in my hands right now."

"Well, be careful," I said.

"They're the ones better be careful."

As soon as I heard the tires on the gravel, I packed a dozen diapers and the baby's best clothes in my small suitcase, dressed her in her blue dress and tights, and locked the door behind us.

Be careful, I'd told him. Last words, simple words. But he couldn't be careful. The rest of the world was supposed to watch out for him as he waded through it, but the water merely closed up behind him.

This was simple now. He'd cut the telephone wires, but the phone wouldn't have helped anyway. My parents were too far to come for me. Since spring break, Katie had called once a week but stayed away. They'd all tried to take me away, but I hadn't been able to go. Halfway down the block I set the suitcase down and switched the baby to the other arm. The early summer was stark, the wet trees, the branches studded with hard white buds, the telephone poles, the squares of houses, the new pale lawns tucked into edges of sidewalks, the clean black road all as keen as the hospital room just before I'd taken my baby outside. When Lonnie raised his hand in the kitchen, the ambiguities smearing the air had dropped like dust.

The side door of the church was open. I left the suitcase in the hall and followed the sound of typing.

The woman looked up at my knock and smiled at the baby.

"Could I talk with the minister?" I said.

"He's at home, but I'll just call. Or—you could go next door to the parsonage yourself."

The house would be full of other people's confusions—the minister's wife, maybe children, flowered drapes and old carpet, scattered toys, cooking smells. I didn't want to lose the simplicity of Lonnie's raised hand.

"Could I talk to him here?"

"Sure, honey. You can go on in to his office. Second door on the right. It's open." She dialed and I heard her say, "Betty? Could you send Glen on over? We need him."

The office was full of old books and dust. I waited on a stuffed loveseat, and the baby fell asleep. I waved my hand and watched the motes swirl in the brightness.

"Hello there," the minister said. He was as old as my father. "Who do we have here?"

"This is—this is my daughter."

"Pardon my dirt," he said, shaking out his pants. "Getting some bulbs in."

I heard tires screech outside. Lonnie couldn't be back yet, unless he hadn't gone to Barnett's after all, unless he'd just been waiting to see me leave.

"You don't know me," I said, "but I hope you'll help me. I've never been to church here, well, once, and I didn't know—"

"Shhh, that doesn't matter," the man said. "Can I get you something? You're shaking. A nice cup of tea?"

"I don't think there's much time. He could... I mean, my husband might figure out I'm here." Shivering but not crying, I told him about Lonnie's hitting me and then yesterday raising his hand to hit the baby. I pulled down my cotton turtleneck to show the purple marks on my neck.

"Oh my Lord," he said. It sounded like a prayer, not an exclamation.

It was still simple. All he needed to do was loan me ticket money and put me on the bus. I'd take his address and repay him as soon as I got to St. Cloud.

He wanted to keep me at the parsonage overnight and drive me at least to Chicago himself the next day—"Betty'd love to get her hands on that little one and feed you supper"—but I could not stay down the street from Lonnie. All night I'd hear him swearing that he'd kill me, I'd hear him crashing his fist through people's windows until he found me.

The minister didn't call the police. He didn't suggest marriage counseling. He put my suitcase in the back of his station wagon and drove me to the bus depot and waited with me until the southbound bus pulled up. He talked about the sermon he was working on—planting, seasons, hands in the earth. The choking finger marks on my neck were as pure to him as Lonnie's raised hand was to me.

"Now call me collect when you get there," he said. "I'll want to know you're safe. Here—in case you want a Coke or something." He handed me a ten-dollar bill.

He didn't try to hug me or pray. "You take care now," he said.

The outer screen door banged and he tried the storm door into the kitchen. He reached his bandaged hand, the hand he didn't understand was pure, through the broken glass. "Dulcie? Baby?" he said. He was scared. No cookies cooled on the kitchen counter. He looked around the front room, but my record player was still there, my Beethoven set and all my records, even the mauled piano concerto, were there with his Righteous Brothers and the Byrds. He did not count the remaining diapers. My clothes still hung in the closet. For a second he thought he saw a shape behind my winter coat. He pulled the light cord and saw only a raccoon collar on the coat and a navy blue maternity dress still hanging for no reason behind it. The large graduation gift suitcase was there. It held summer clothes and no secrets. He counted the coins on the dresser but nothing was missing. Or had there been a dime more? The closet—the closet wasn't quite right. The small blue leather suitcase was gone. "Oh Dulcie," he said. He went to the bathroom wastebasket and found among the Kleenex wads the largest pieces of the broken crucifix. He hurled them to the floor and brought his foot down on the shards of plaster. He stomped with both feet—no, he danced—*until the linoleum was powdered white.*

And—?

Nothing.

He sold the record player, the old television from my parents' basement, the dishes, the stroller, the remaining suitcase, the coat, all of it that fit into his car and that anyone would buy. Or he took the carload to a pawn shop in—where? in Chicago and traded for a gun. His right hand wasn't pure any more. Safe in his precious car he turned west.

Most of the time I couldn't see Lake Michigan, but I knew it was there, just to the west, and then from South Bend to Gary it was to the north, and finally the lake was east and I was west. The bus was nearly empty, as if it had come to collect me and my baby—no, no, that was wrong. Nothing had come for me. I had summoned the bus. In St. Cloud, I would call Katie and at the bus station amidst the smells of pine bathroom cleaner and old hot dogs rotating in a steamer, the tile floor and wooden pews, and all the half-asleep transients waiting for the buses to collect them—amidst the passive, the touched world, we'd cry and plot.

The air smelled metallic but the window wouldn't open, and I couldn't smell the wind off the lake. Nothing had come for me. Not Lonnie. Not even my father. Lonnie hit me and my father knew it. My parents hadn't saved me. I couldn't allow anyone to save me. I'd made my bed, and for almost a year I'd lain in that bed in Waterton. I'd floated in the bed of that mutating piece of furniture. And there Lonnie had impregnated me. The sickness hadn't started yet, but I wasn't stupid this time, and this time there would be a drowning—or no, nothing passive: this time I would drown it in air. I would find the right doctor in Minnesota and he'd let in that air the man in the Hemingway story promised. But it would be my doing.

Those to the east of the lake, and Lonnie, could see the oily sun bubble into the water. The water would be taffeta. In my years the water had been lit sandy blue, dark blue, gray shot with white, terrible sunset orange, winter black, gray. From the west, I knew the body of water was there, set into the dunes, but I could not see it. *To every action there is always opposed an equal reaction.* The third law of motion, oh and all the textbook laws and words, had quickened. To the colors of the water and the pull, to the year with Lonnie, would be opposed my coming life.

I nursed the baby and she slept and I watched out the tinted windows until outside was dusk and smoky orange. The baby and I were complicitous. The contractions, the pain, the amniotic fluid, the blood were ours. The hand raised before her was absolute. I could not turn it to me. One time he deflected it to a pane of glass. But it was absolute. The hand would rise and fall.

And so I made a current and I made a boat and I carried us away.

OTHER ANAPHORA LITERARY PRESS TITLES

Evidence and Judgment
By Lynn Clarke

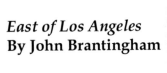

East of Los Angeles
By John Brantingham

Death Is Not the Worst Thing
By T. Anders Carson

The Seventh Messenger
By Carol Costa

Rain, Rain, Go Away...
By Mary Ann Hutchison

Truths of the Heart
By G. L. Rockey

Interviews with BFF Winners
By Anna Faktorovich, Ph.D.

Compartments
By Carol Smallwood

CPSIA information can be obtained at www.ICGtesting.com
Printed in the USA
BVOW021849190212

283171BV00003B/8/P